A Translation
of the New
Philadelphia

A Translation

of the New

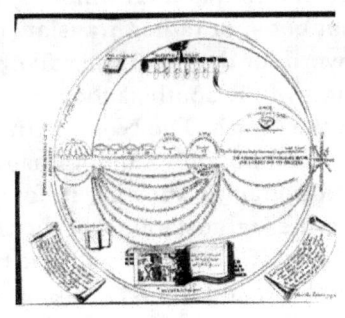

Philadelphia

AE Reiff

Grand Canal
FLYWAY BOOKS
2023

Grateful Acknowledgments are made to the editors of Futures Trading, Neon Garden, Blue Labyrinths, Thrice Fiction, Antipodean SF, O/W Engaged, Cultur Cult and Stimulus > Respond. A work of literary Research, and to *A Calendar of Poems. Encouragements for Such as Shall Have Intention to be Undertakers of the Planting (1973)* an early exploration of this subject.

We are in a pretty position here in taking pretext from the most important book of our time to confront the end of history, so called. This occurs among so many other attempts to do the same thing, but from the converse, that is, as truth, to interpret times and symbols of every detail of that book, so many views, so little time, we conclude them all in error and that their thinking will not make it so. Hence we translate that book, or rather, translate translations of that book, outside, which word for the first time will preoccupy, outside the empire, being as it is of the south as they say, which exists in its own world opposed to the North. The North is insulated in its preserve, kept in line, that it not only cannot imagine the being of the South, but is prevented from ever knowing it, for the North considers itself to be right. Doing these translations of the translation of the Book, from the South, even if we dabble with the books of the East, along the way that the North and the West are never able to absorb, so the saying applies to them, some save as if by fire. The fire here is this New Philadelphia outside the city. By the time it has occurred it is the whole world, but not quite yet. To call on as much of history and fact intends to place a context around the earth, but limited, partial and arbitrary, unlike the spirt of God that moved upon the face of the waters.

With this in mind we presume the train of logic in Joseph Mede's) *Clavis Apocalyptica on its side to explain* the West timeline of Mede displayed on the cover. It is turned on its side to explain an alternate history, not of the Darby and Scofield eschatology of the end of the age. This community, "outside the city" presents itself as a new Philadelphia, citing the same text as the one that designates them outsiders, except the true Philadelphians can go in.

In describing the dimensions of this affair by the perception and psychology of a fall, these excursions take as a guide, Mr. Wittgenstein, who has consented to describe the divisions of thought

and language that such texts involve. The dénouement of convergences that untie the knot and deliver the *coup de grâce,* point to a new world. You may have heard of it already. It begins with the importation of Europe to America on a bull that represents the new world in its ships of arrival, Pide Cow, 1654, and New Era, 1854, paradigms of society and governmence symbolized in Swift's *Tale of a Tub* along the way in an explanation of the voyage and its outcome, that all bull ships, nation state ships, world ships remainder. How the new world goes from those first landings to living "outside the city," where Philadelphians alone are able to enter, is the matter we pursue.

Understood horizontally and vertically, Mede's timeline of the Roman Empire in succession, also in Newton's *Daniel* (1733) follows cycles of recapitulation that expand visions, seals, trumpets, phials that have already occurred in ascending new series.

"*Outside the city,*" "not allowed to enter," "*kept outside,*" is fully comprehended in the back-translations of the Tagbanwa language of the Philippines where the outsiders are extended to "those whose nature/ways are so evil they really won't be able to enter into this city, because *their secret-supernatural-skills* prevent them, but who also behave-immorally with one who is not their spouse, are killers of their fellowman, and serve familiar-spirits or *whatever is their replacement for God,* as liars in word and deed." That this makes room for the AI, digital, H+ age with its God replacements, the Uma translation of Indonesia extends, "they are not allowed to enter into that village." If you want to know whether you can take your laptop, that is your answer.

Understood horizontally and vertically, the timeline of the Roman Empire in succession, also in Isaac Newton's *Daniel* (1733) follows cycles of recapitulation that expand visions, seals, trumpets, phials that have already occurred in ascending new series.

"*Outside the city,*" "not allowed to enter," "*kept outside,*" is fully comprehended in a back-translations of the <u>Tagbanwa</u> language of the Philippines where the outsiders are extended to "those whose nature/ways are so evil they really won't be able to enter into this city, because *their secret-supernatural-skills* prevent them, but who also behave-immorally with one who is not their spouse, are killers of their fellowman, and serve familiar-spirits or *whatever is their replacement for God,* as liars in word and deed." That this makes room for the AI, digital, H+ age with its God replacements extends all the <u>Uma</u> translation of Indonesia that, "they are not allowed to enter into that village." If you want to know whether you can take your laptop, that is your answer.

Rotating Mede's horizontal timeline ninety degrees and then one eighty, attempts to dramatize this disconnect as a fall. From the moment it begins until it comes awake at the end, time and space in a fall become ambiguous for the faller. In the final inversion of 180-degrees, where the head was first pointing is both reversed and to the side. One does not feel the fall itself, only the beginning and end. A 90 degree fall on the right hip after slipping on silt in the driveway after a rain, lands on the ground. A fall from the top of a low dam against a log below with a chainsaw in hand disconnects 180 degrees. This landing reverses the top and turns to the side, the chainsaw still idling in its hand. This is enough to break ribs.

Were a city that fell in a heap like that it might feel embarrassed. When the shock had worn off, not knowing how bad it's hurt, that city might hope nobody saw and that the history books would not report. The shock and awe that take a city seem to have a gender too, for those privileged to be one of these. Rises and falls, sightings of what's to come, dressed with what we think we know, costumed in the old, if we think to catch the future walking on a roof with concrete events filled with books & pictures written & painted in ages of Eternity before this life began, this walk through the past leaves a trail. Over the city its organic structures translate roots that hang down from invisible plants above.

For reasons of this sort Mr. Wittgenstein's *Tractatus* Preface warns: *what can be said at all can be clearly said; and whereof one cannot speak thereof one must be silent. In order to draw a limit to thinking we should have to be able to think both sides of this (we should therefore have to be able to think what cannot be thought). The limit can therefore only be drawn in language and what lies on the other side of the limit will not.*

To reconstruct the explanation, it is possible Mr. Wittgenstein spent weeks of thought in seclusion in Norway, but not believing any of the enough to spend the day, much less the present, unless needed to be connected in action, not words. Action need give no source, as if thinking and words disappear as he throws away the once climbed ladder of thought. The result in action takes form in trees with cracked skin and stout limb as a sapling grows, a picture of what we don't know, while we think we are doing something else and for different reasons too. The *entrance to his cabin in* Skjolden *borrows its caution of rational sovereignty from a schoolmaster nearby whose, "Burrow" had a thin layer of hard earth on top but loose soil further down.* This is to say, we see many things not admitted. Stone letters written in the shale below creeks, factories held on only by wax, may begin something like a reverse timpani of thought that picks up a phrase, inverts it, splices it and reverses at will, like a fall. Beginning words become a drum and what might have been a word echoes on. This was proved ingenuously after having spent two summers after fourteen washing the letters off of tombstones: *the very thing we have been advised not to say, that all the facts are not known, and the case is obscure, which we puzzle and conject, where any one can either be the case or not the case, and everything else remains the same, this which we should not say, we say, but in terms that do not show what we mean.*

As therefore a text too big to play on the piano of space and time in the score, stones, words and cobbles break in waves on city squares. Roof and gazebos around rails look down on these gardens of mossy cannonballs bigger than cabbages, bigger than heads, catapulted once upon the Germans and Slovaks in their beds. The roofs speak too, green Gothic bulbs, circling tin slopes out of the blue human sky, red crisscrossed with colors of blood. Dark earth looks up into the eyes that look down to the brown and green eyes of earth and seas. The re-ascend the slate pitch to dormers. Scalloped shingles glide to soffits. Vents, chimneys swim in windows.

It is a landscape tilled by ladders nailed to steeps in which we approach our Wittgenstein to articulate the inexpressible and broken meaning, but it is more than language on a holiday. To define a "space of qualitative separation" measured by essence, not measurement, let us picture meaning as a The Four-Inch thick Veil thick as a rug or thicker, imposed on the curtain of the Temple preventing intimacy of entrance. This separation described with a generic Babylonian universe cannot be pulled apart by physical force It is four inches thick, beyond the thickness of a hand.

The tearing of the veil of language embroidered with the Mazzaroth mystical heavens so thick that horses tied to each side cannot pull it apart is not just a physical barrier, but a decorated cosmos from a mirror of the world of Josephus, a Hebrew general who became a Roman and a historian who adds that when soiled three hundred priests were needed to immerse and cleanse the veil. He lived in both worlds of Rome and Judea and describes the separation:

"a veil of equal largeness before the doors embroidered with blue, and fine linen, scarlet and purple, and of a context of scarlet that seemed to enigmatically signify fire, and by the fine flax the earth, by the blue of the air, the purple the sea; having their colors the foundation of this resemblance; but the flax and the purple had their own origin for the earth producing the one, and the sea the other, which curtain had also embroidered upon it all the Mazzaroth mystical heavens, excepting that the [twelve] signs, represented living creatures" (Josephus).

But when the sun darkened on that afternoon when the veil was rent we entered an interregnum. Tearing the curtain with its mascots of Gog and Magog chained as guardians outside its palace, the colossi of Money and Power, New Troy founded by Aeneas, placed the rest

of us between eras, and it has lasted a long time. Challenging desire
for intimacy in the removal of the veil versus the pain it causes,
closeness and isolation, social and solitude in compromise tearing
the separation between sound and meaning as a fall ourselves, in
either help or hindrance, if we go from this Wittgenstein cabin in
Norway with its deceptive entrance to these, we find institutions of
state have arisen to govern the time between, and that tells us how
the new world arrived, and how these remained 'outside the city."

The Ship of this State in the new world involves voyage. Jonathan
Swift's, A Tale of A Tub—finds that voyage imperiled by a whale, a
Hobbes's Leviathan thrashing to stove the hull of the state, so that it
flings overboard a tub to divert the beast, meaning that tale itself
posing as a decoy bobbing with mock divinity and folly to draw off
critics who "pick holes" in religion and government. Our Translation
is something like that. Going from falling and inverting our
consciousness in broken language behind a curtain of myth, now
torn, we get into this Tub as our ship sails to the new world. The
passengers of this discourse, rabble sects, questioners are tacitly the
Tub's ballast, sacrificed to keep the decks of captaincy, nobles,
ministers and crew in power.

That anyhow somewhat explains how these outsiders got there
outside the gates after their first entry to this new world. Officials and
minions, sailors, nobles and ministers, threatened by a whale, tossed
anything overboard to divert the beast, even if the passengers have to
be bait.

That is what happened in 1854 to the ship called New Era that reversed the terms of Swift's Tub boat. Not just one ship occurs in America sightings from at least July, 1635 when the Pide Cowe, came tossing from the sea. It advertised building a City named for its bellowing Heifer of that name, but no ship or cow was in the lading. Instead it was Europe, Europa riding her white bull which insight we are indebted to Francesco Colonna for, whose Hypnerotomachia Pide Cowe 1592 made record:

"Certificates of Conformities and Attestation of Cow Europe Subsidies, displaced in the final period of history by the arrival of no nation there attached, made the whole new world for all to (see Project Gutenberg, #87, Hypnerotomachia Pide Cowe Hypnerotomachia The Strife of Lous in a Dreame (London 1592).

This first implicit landing of Cow Europe as Pide Cowe, arriving

with its Certificates, Religion and the Attestation of New England Justices, later led to the founding of that essential potamian "cow-town" on the Potamic, as we now know, where the City of Dragon in its Euro-Heifer would continue to most aroint. There is always increase and decrease in the fall of consciousness going on, as one perfect Erectus bentus might find upon the funeral prow of that "New Era" after it was always and ever about landing Europa on the Bull, to which we now attend.

For were we to symbolically thank the New Era of 1854 for laying bare the ship of state, then its English captain and crew, ie. presidents and senators as captain and crew, abandoned their passengers in this new Tub. Reversed, it marooned the state, left it to its own deserts while these authorities took off and cut the rope, leaving its cargo of immigrants, Dunkards, still aboard. That the rest of us are Dunkards, fatalities always differ.

Rescuers shot a line to that New Era from land, but the sailors and captain commandeered the life boat and saved themselves. They cut the line so no one could get off. The New Era was abandoned. The night was wild, the west wind cold. Heavy swells prevented rescue boats from reaching the sinking ship. Rescuers built booley fires on shore so survivors would know they were there, to wit the English captain sanitized witness accounts in the wash. Fernicola and other researchers sought the hull later under fifteen feet of sand. Attempts were fruitless. The beach is steep on that Asbury coast. The ship bell sounded, seconded by griefs and prayers.

This embarked the New Era as another species of acoustic apparatus known from before Rome, but popularized by Nero there, to convert cries of prisoners inside a brazen bull through a system of tubes and stops into sounds of bellowing. Whether boat or bull, but the shape is similar, and designed for early or later Christians, the roundness of the hull, the howls of New Era supercharged the whole land mass to howl. So in some sense the part becomes the whole, seen mere in the price of oil, currency and commodities, but these were the least of these.

Rigging and cordage swallowed in the enormity of sea made New Era fashion somehow as the name for them all. The hull (1854), landed two hundred years after the Pide Cow founding. For years after residents taking jewelry, coins and clothing from the bodies like a pillaged battlefield. Most were not identified. The lost that could were interred in a mass grave at the Old First United Methodist

Church cemetery in West Long Branch. A guild of Asburyites banded to haul the remains some distance inland to a sand pit to bury the remains. Every aspect is redolent. The ship that weathered waves but not the storm was buried with its Dunkers as the Ship of State.

We come so late to this braunschweiger of lost souls in double loops that after another century and a half, our landscapes of quantum change, cannabis shops surviving, and Pied Cow merchandise of resin diamonds, moon rocks, empyreal coffee, refined pink sugar, cake face distillate, THC lemons and lolly candy may connect the lines with sites sprang up with hyperloops even in Dubai, *In* that world pop music fell on umbrellas of fairy tales in the rain. Loops and fabulas, investigations as concealments, letters and signs on all sides brought Wittgenstein to his front porch, not to speak of that sometime counterpart on the opposite coast, a gingerbread coffee house and hookah lounge founded by Jimmy Chen in Portland, now closed, was put the world kiln alongside. Cooking nations continued well after 1854. It's like there were Principalities in the Taurobolium, a sacrifice of nations as big as a globe of continents, seas and world where we hear with the cries of the Dunkards, those cows Bishop Leadbeater heard over the meat packing houses of Chicago.

This tub that served Swift's Leviathan would echo as a founding fact of the New Era, laden not with satire but with immigrants bound for promise. Their piety was ballast to those drowned doctrines, run aground. The New Era reversal hits home when captain and crew, not decoys, abandon the hull. Commandeering boats and lines, cutting ropes so no passenger follows leave the "tub," human souls churn to the sea, while they row. The elite jettison of the state is allegory in action. The ship forsaken, its passengers are the true sacrifice to Leviathan once diverted.

Where sailors throw an empty tub into the sea to distract a whale that might otherwise attack their ship, the Ship represents the commonwealth. This "profanity" of Tub was perceived so extreme by Queen Anne she blocked Swift from high-ranking positions in the Church for years, believing he had mocked God.

God as the state in the waves that crash, up escalators and down
elevators in the bull success of nations, Assyria, Babylon, Rome,
Britain and on, aspire for victims and sacrifice for the bull
provocateur from Nero back to Phalaris and obvious gods at Tystes
banquet, pre 5th BC century Sicilian bulls of Persian Mithra practiced
in Rome 3rd century AD, not especially for illumination, but
execution. Millenniums climax today in the head of the American
bull geography and prophecy. The eye might serve as Amazon
headquarters, but parts of California Baja are gone. East faces west in
this new era of bells and whistles told.

Once there lived a flock of pigeons, and still do in the
Plaza de Rigueur. They were so risky they would stick in
your hair, which in case of a military burr cut or shaved
head of a courtesan in France was nonsuch, but in the long
golden hair of our beauty drew the ire of the 49 pigeon
keepers, lest the wings be harmed in their remove.
Trafalgar Square in London is rich in pigeon keepers as the
Burghers of Calais witness on the Thames across from the
houses of parliament. Everyman walks this way and takes
his pilgrimage to a B & B where anyone without a name bears
watching. There is need to dispute his steady steps. Everyman has
no name unless we give him one. All insist on this dignity.
He doesn't have to know.

You will be wanting an explanation for the provocation of
these events in words but how can that be? The ass was a
lion, the ass was a bear, the ass was anything but itself
among the horde of wolves. Crows have a murder, wolves
have a horde. Fire pigs stripped like tigers burned bright.
RPGs came out of their mouths, feedlot breath so
sulphurous it set the roofs of houses on fire. Hot foam from
their nostrils dowsed the flames. The ass revolt compared
with cows with bear feet and dragon tails. You think it bad
until you hear about the dogs, one eyed three legged
lengths of Cadmus and Actaeon and Geryon, the Cephalus

dog biting, and the foxes who broke into banks and chicken coops, raided S&L safes, ate fried customer accounts.
Myth? I say nothing of the cats that infest house and barn, the well-to-do wonder cock that charged the sheep, incandescent blue, gold, scaled with sun in the yard when it took wing. These eclogues were burning Virgil all over again. Check the progress in the sycamore. Rotting twenty feet up carpenter bees, big black buzzers in the cracks of hallowed stumps, and burrows big as a mausoleum. You might imagine hundreds, thousands in air and on ground, which is a comfort of which you should be warned. Authorities of this world had either escaped or died. Monster bands wandered the commons. We do well to wander. Cocks, asses, pigs changed shape with the sheep. Some turned black as you recall, but thousands made owls over with iron feathers. Flies en mass did frogs some good. It was beautiful if you like the sort. I tell you I'm waiting for scorpions, caterpillars, ants to turn peacock. There are no names left for the human, samurai behind the back, elbow in a chair, knee to the left, shoulders right, entities of Mind across the stars. It's not about arriving at the state from which one fled, horns in the middle of heads. A stranger can see salvation in one ounce packs, the same for those on the bottom as on top. The ass was a cow and the cow was a bear, the cow was a lion, the cow was anything but itself, but nothing compared to the hog hordes. Rebellious ass-long years turned up their horns from the41 middle of that decade and blew, which did not exactly give heart either.

There are many ways to offend those who have not seen the cracks radiating from centers of implosion, fissures like Tycho in the Moon, colony craterlets, orbits of phyllotaxis, divergences perceptible as the shape Ohio once was, or became. It too existed after proof of some finite intelligence at work, occurring passim, the a priori rendezvous-proving rule, circle down to circle for one who descends, crossings seen in the meeting-places of more than one canal.
To call them canals is a faux pa from the planned

obsolescence of intelligence that once existed, like thinking
the world flat mistaking rivers for canals, spheroid for flat,
something as if Gilgamesh below the Euphrates Beltway to
which people dug tracks and underground trains in their
temples to convince themselves theirs was a perfect world.
These tracks, taken apart, were not seen, for this they did
not do. Every effort to conceal the one cell organism
known as Mammon-Oranus, a huge intestine of money was
governed in Secret with its primitive media nerves, for you
know the gut has a brain stimulating the tribes with "wow
pulses," multilayered in a newfound. This *Stockholm-
Munchhausen mosaic of tribes caught between the coasts
of the present-day fabulous and history would digest
money, excrete money, displace other processes of being.
After exposure the Secret mind could produce these
impulses on its own which gurgle could not be spoken full
in words.

Further up the hill lands super large herds of
behemoths range and from the sea behind penetrating
through the rivers inland the most outlandish sea serpents
out of the Odyssey and Laocoön. Why anyone would live
there considering the dangers of myth and supernatural
beast must be from the attraction of the divine city, but the
closer to it the more the danger from angels, cherubim, not
to omit the wasps that perne in the gyre.

Five progenies of the ancient Tzu
gave Sagey man and Superior man a place in the Imperial
twenty seven wigs in that Land. Appeared, Disappeared,
Reappeared, traveled to and touched.

ANYONE RETURNING AFTER YEARS OF ABSENCE
WILL KNOW THIS WITH THEIR EYES CLOSED.

We walk in worlds where language of the wide open spaces
of the spiritual and physical occur at once, drink mineral water,
sodium, potassium, magnesium, calcium, manganese piped from the

ground and lift up our eyes to perceive the, carmine, burgundy, cardinal, maroon roofs of the dawn. More shades of red than vermilion in this outer world fall below to store the likeness of the invisible. Hidden near to all, in the visible essence, like silks, parrots, and fine singing birds brought to the secret chamber of the King of Syria (*2 Kings* vi. 12) by shipping is a Nothing that hungers for Something, Abyss into Byss filled and yet remains, which attracts when mists are removed from eyes.

Of course the first thing lower mind wants to do is know what the situation provides now, as if the roofs are roots that extend invisibly down from organic turquoise branches, and also, literally, that 'the world' that refuses to disappear and is so immodestly revealed, is to be possessed. Effacing it would be the opposite. The world has a true Sancho Panza mind, if literate. But Sancho Panza doesn't ride a mule, he rides an ass. Consider that therefore in our Going Out where we catch what comes. All we higher and lower, spoken and written, different texts puzzle together whether any one can be the case or not the case, or else everything else lies on the side of nonsense. It takes weeks to wake up these anonymous states and none of them are believed at the break of day.

The life Burrow is filled in with a thin layer of
hard earth on top but loose soil beneath, where only a little
push with our head is needed and we are in the upper air
before. But returning the way we came is not the way. We
lose ourselves in our own maze until we think our house is
warm and nourished, protected and self sufficient. We
master all the manifold passages of our rooms, but if
endangered we raise a trap door and slip quietly out,
letting the door fall softly back again and flee the spot.
To translate this event, write it down, the arbitrary text is
big. Time and space are land and sea in a vision like the
artists of Catterline and Prouts Neck had. There below is
the captain of our open boat, face hunched, slumped over
the water jar of the sea. We hardly know if he is going out
or coming in.

Superscripts sewn over top overwhelm the I. Names scatter about despite the history traversed. The bodiless future is immersed in the present, which explains why when we're on a bridge between the two we have a good view of the higher mind that canoes down in the phase-locked signals where factories rise from the effluent. Factory after factory connects their storm drains until theyso shallow we may walk miles up the concrete tubes that get smaller until just some sphincter tinkles at the foot where lower mind goes. On again off again in this, higher and lower complete each other. The High works hard, the low is indolent, unless compulsed and gets away being unrecognized unless the High sees its own glory unveiled there. The High wants to know but won't give in, the Low knows little else. We do not praise it but it believes!

Meandering pleasantly along a river in a dream, when large swales come around the bend with muscular torrents **We imagine a great submarine Meltwurst Bridge-schweiger smoked with garlic, salt and pepper, liverwurst, and Jungwurst of bacon whites eaten between. Pork liver in natural casings smoked with bacon ends, onion powder, chopped onion and pepper spray, a Brazilian sausage of Machado exceeds expectation and the Argentinian Borgwurst is undenied, with Columbian yucca name a few. Kaisergarten China Braunschweig saffron serves and Pannhaas tenderloin mush with corn breads virtually scapple everywhere in these Hors d'oeuvre.**

Moving up the swale to cross. Seen with closed eye that river is seen **by not seeing, just below awareness, but not in those opposite camps outside the Wall, where one confronts the Braunschweiger plain of logical omission. Committing continuous leaps of Speech between, closer to the lips than to the throat, d's instead of g's, the tongue tip rushing toward the teeth as bares bestiaries of itself we recognize, that lower mind is an ideal companion to revolt against the light, to shoot out the light poles as naif.**

Braunschweiger romance and intrigue charge poems about the heads of waterboarded government. The servings of

Braunschweiger here are intended to satisfy these ideologies that walk the bridge beginning to end. This bridge is a scheme of the centaurmach to talk in the great day off. Famine, disease, water and fire pass into the Tub entire. Long trains of thought blow back whose boots above rest nicely on the books below. I kid you not, the inventor of the internet, enforced these sins of the world on the great asanas of forgiveness on the river. Bodiless snowflake navies of breath like sheets fly on a line in a storm. "The flood came and destroyed them all." (Luke 17:28-29). It rather looks like a chandelier held in place in midair where belief pours up from beneath.

      Ambiguous water birds of vertical polysemya sign many meanings, where we and these three asses of words write automeronymy, "door, whole structure" to "door panel," autosuperordination, "female cow" to "cow of either sex of that Great Puritan Migration
      These Yankees crossed ocean to Philadelphia, transcending gambols of the deep, having the form of calves like horses, others of whales, though not translated into English like that chief founder, the Reverend Jacob Boehme, chief of the Behemist ways, and Johannes Kelpius (JK) who led his band of Pietists to the banks of the Philadelphia Wissahickon for 14 years, called the wide open spaces there "the upper huts of our mother, manifold wisdom, more dear and joyous" (JK, *Diarium*, 29).

      Going out here comes before all his simultaneous youth of age. The high mind on the bridge above projects the lower worlds, but the lower is what the higher is made of. Go fig. Those who put some effort into this are reluctant to start another. Lower free fall is doubted as a valid expression as much as freedom is falling off the Haywain. Please do not disregard the calendar.
Alexander toured and Darius the Persian, Darius Nothus intermarried with inhabitants of the land. Britain took it as amphibious land and sea. We too can pass for sailors at the port. Buy your tickets and visas for the

countries of Atlas and passports for countries that are not. Fantasy boats amphibians can swim up close up to new Philadelphia but the colonist has to walk, viscera and all. Their leaders all had successful erection operations to produce their assurance of manner and demeanor of audacity. Cremation of conscience would be the better term for it, another way of serving their godlings. Like they say of the city outside the city that is not the city but is the city, things are not what they seem.

A Translation of the New Philadelphia

The Vibrating Cube of the New Jerusalem that descends outside the historical, Ezekiel's Temple in this gap, emanates let us say from a difference in frequency between the "Created" and "Uncreate". It is a perfect form, a "Brain" or as it were a "Chamber filled with books," that must remain separate to avoid the "Hedgehog's Dilemma"— where the intrinsic need for warmth and connection injures from the contact of protective spines when they get too close.

The "Foot of Space" at its base is the gap where human condition strives with such "organic structures that translate as roots hanging down from invisible plants above," suggesting the lower world is sustained by the higher, yet a fundamentally separate reality.

Human existence outside the city is played out on the "flat roof" and the mud below, organized into nation-states by the figure of the "Mayor of the Outside." Here the Horizontal Swarms with "dogs and astrologers" of the horizontal plane that seek to "pillage the streets of gold." Material perspectives are the "bare spots" that require constant patching and painting of this flat roof, just as the curtain needs washing.

The Outside Inhabitants and their Mayor promulgate an Ethos of the "dignity of struggle," the persistence of human will of those *Banquet Years* before and after. The outside operates within the physical limits of endurance, recognizing the "vibration" as an absurdity to be endured.

The Philadelphian Exception is the only way to enter the City, not by force or logic, but **by "translation," a "frequency-match"** achieved through a state of grace, the "open door" granted to the Church of Philadelphia. The true Philadelphia spirit acts on the "interior parts by Ecstasies, Revelations" to bridge the chasm.

Human existence is described as an **Interregnum** between the horizontal pursuit of immediate needs and the vertical reality glimpsed in moments of "shock" or the "disconnect in the fall".

These texts function as architectural blueprints of the "right-angled" structure of a Great Vertical Shift.

Much as later writers described a revived Roman Empire as Europe and an end-time Global world power as a world-dominating political and military system with an individual leader who heads it as the Beast, Mede, saw the prophecies progressively unfolding in each other and fulfilling real historical events. Darby took the recapulative narrative of Revelation from earlier and later writers like **Charlemagne** (crowned in 800 AD) and **Napoleon**, who sought to revive Rome pervasiveness in Europe as a specific **prophetic. The Global World Power** Beast of Revelation described both a final world-dominating government and its leader, the Antichrist, the final system dictator in a line of such, with archetypal qualities of beasts and judgments that echo any tyrannical regime, such as leviathan and behemoth describe modern totalitarian states—but not with historicist precision. New Philadelphia is the very place they reside, outside the city, first a village, but develops from there to the entire world.

If we say last in first out or first in last out it means from the end he saw the beginning and had to wait through. Brubeck? It is not possible for him not to be, for if it follows that he is not and he is bound not then that is the path. I tell you it cannot be explored, for you can neither recognize what is not nor express it. FOR IT IS THE SAME THING TO THINK AND TO BE. You must walk. Journey first. At no time in all the confidential extremes it must be a species of prison camp where writing about it four decades late, in letters to a daughter overseas, never face to face in that time with Invisibility, all told called shock, and then to meet that son who lay in the forest to bring the stars to earth; who would have thought it could be done?

All Imaginations of hearts, first Consultations; past, and present, and future, distinguish not. They did it by themselves? A goat trampled them. How many miles to Babylon? Three score mile years and ten. You can get there by candle if your heels are light. One remembers it as felt. If knowing is seen, touched, felt, what matters is faith as a commonplace.

Brubake would leave while his family was still asleep before dawn and walk the steppes. That town bordered on one side by two tracks, just prior to a yard of large importance with a roundhouse where Bobby Shafto lived and black soot billowed up from the engines, always had a supply of flares and torpedoes to hand, if not dynamite to fetch a duck or two. The tracks bordered the Creek filled with the wreckage of lost trains; huge cubes of scrap metal stuck up from the shallows where the rails followed the creek part way, lined with telegraph poles on that side like rambling hillocks set into the mountains that rose up flat from farms on the other side. Fierce updrafts that ganged burns that reared with flames in dry spells from the trains. Then would rally playfellows in the street to fight the flame with mats and rakes that rose a hundred feet in the air. To say this so the sheep should take no harm, that place is nothing real. You can have pudding in half an hour there or anything you want. Deuks had just made a river, but didn't know if it was wet.

Hunting tropical fish with blue and gold fins at the base of the volcano in Cartago later, myself the fish who took the bait and turned the light off and watched pupils dilate got spit back up. Where the streams of the national park beneath the mount swim, it's dark in the fish, but in the sea *darkness dawns* in the dark and the dark turned to light that flees from me as much as did me seek.

To compare the hidden layers of some tapestry in the world, fertile and corrupt, sheol sans fire, a shade that can claim the comedy of desire, they say life is a life changing event in a Ledean white body yolk, hollow of cheek, mind revealing the path. Count up to ten in the western wall where the *candled wood-knots shine blood red.* To pick between early incandescence and later diffusion, a limbo *in terrestrial*, the fish and the fisherman sent over to read Dr. Donne's Second Sermon on Psalms, 1625, of "hairy hearts," "petrified hearts" that the 4th, 5th and 7th angels scorch, who make the dark and the hail cause blasphemy in these. But whether "suffered to possess the tabernacle, as They sometimes are, (the *Pater ignosce)*, Father forgive them allows all that is done because "there is a weight of future glory to counterpose." That said, as soon as an upright man is found, that "as though the greatest weakness in this world were man, and the greatest fault in man were to be good," he "is made the Sewer of all corruption, of all the sins of this world." "As if he were no son of God but a mere man, or no man, but a worm."

You would think the good would have reward, but they are blamed for all the evil they did not do. If this goes against the grain of youth say *Pater ignosce.*

Ignosce means they were ignorant of their deeds, but not of the counter weight to them of Psalm 22, Isaiah 53, the bulls of Bashan. This ephod of the *Pondus Gloriae* weight of earthquake, flood, prison....So let me pay my debts with my bones! In penurious prison!

Wither in a spittle...and so recompense the wantonness of my youth," up together and carded at the door.

To dominate the imaginative superpower indigens crossing from "this side" to "that," a bridge where a man and might assume impossible reason to circumvent control, glaciation is out. The question of hulls worn from the journeying, touching cracks in general because the furrows ploughed by meteorites,--another ingenious solution,--such as could let ships build new keels and mend the jib to plough straight from one center to another, where the visitant would boil a thick and tarry mass over its banks, have to be specially trained to **silent impossibility**! Braid tattered ropes and cords, the stressing materials of depersonal Mono-ha "non-making," where materials exist as they are rather than being transformed into something else, where we don't have to figure out the message, recognize the face, interpret the image.

It is a cement block that those who get this understand Mono-ha as a kind of *SELVING* of the *aliquid eius,* where 'incompatible frames of being exist together or are together (Hopkins. *Collected Works*, V, 356) inset and outset that include all things." BUT, and this is the crux, "the self of the universal is not the self of anything else,…that is, there is no such that takes us into another, but we are compelled, for the world is word, and the utterance of God analogous to the utterance that results in the Word meeting in and through the world must be succored for the *Diapsalmata* originary cry, the groan that cannot be uttered we have to dwell on.

A thousand amenities *SELVE* the *aliquid eius.* "Either the universal is selved not only in this world of things but in all possible ones or only in this one. If in all possible worlds there is no difference between possible and actual and all possible and incompossible, incompatible, frames of being that exist together." So the universal mind is compounded or selved up with created selves. 'I am all at once what "Christ is," says Hopkins, "since he was what I am." ('Heraclitean Fire,' *Collected Works*, V. 356-7).

That word of world expression and utterance, met through the *Diapsalmata* originary cry of creation in the groan that cannot be uttered, after the fact of life says exactly what has gone on all years and more in heart and mind. It absolutely surrounds everyone who reaches in varying degrees culminating more and more in the approach of the spirit of these groans. Even if he, the FK, has roasted in a taurobolium, the mythic due in pictures not word is reminded every time in every face of a prisoner of war like Wittgenstein or Levinas or this parachuting cotton farmer of 19 with the soul of Philo over Rouen France. That a commentary of the *Spiritual Exercises* would expound this, whether we are due to chance, to ourselves as the *aliquid eius* part of self existent soul, mind and consciousness, or whether to some extrinsic cause, we've not time to ask, for these are for critics, who t*o be sure, resemble a poet as one pea another, the only difference being that no anguish in heart and no music on the lips* of life's great conflagration *(Kierkegaard, Diapsalmata).*

Active and passive intellects separate from the soul, but partnered with the spirit that wants to answer the cry call upon us for comfort, response, for feeling. Even if we don't feel touched we are. We are moved to the depths where "all things, therefore, are charged with love, are charged with God and if we know how to touch them give off, spark and take fire, yield drops and flow, ring and tell of him (Hopkins V, 346).

But that condition of the eye that blinds in understanding with a cloudy appearance over the iris hinders from a range of bright, greenish-blue, or gray colors that glaucoma the brain with the color of the sea. The color of water of the sea, looking as if underwater or through heavy fog covers with paradox the "in-othering of men and the in-Godding of men," which is the first of the eternal images Dante uses to describe entering the '*lucida, spessa, solida, e polita*---lucent, thick, firm, shining' of a still uncleft pearl and impearled self. "How body enters body…our nature with God's, that is, the Incarnation at the root of physical co-inherence which is on this earth incapable of its full capacity…in-othering of men and the in-Godding of men" we must seek and choose "one who both was and was not and now is…an image of the whole redeemed universe "concerned to exhibit beatitude." (Charles Williams. *Figure of Beatrice*, 195). 190), 192, 191)

The knowing that comes manifestly with this fact, after all pain, the feeling gone and still abstracts it, "is more distinctive than the taste of ale or alum, more distinctive than the smell of walnut leaf or camphor and is incommunicable by any means to another" Hopkins V, 349). To get that succor for the suffering proves romance is not the proper term for poet, but suffering is, and not just poet, but for all who stand as conscious, so that "when I was a child I used to think, ask myself, what must it be to be someone else?' (Hopkins 349), and if this exploration consumes the thought at two years old in world, "myself being my consciousness and feeling of myself, so that I taste of myself, of I and me above and in all things,' these messages tempered at any stage in some part of the brain, travel to the lower centers as bona fide messages that 'now if it, or he, has the same intimate feeling, consciousness of all that goes on in me as I have of what goes on in my finger' and 'I am compounded only with him, and that "by no choice of mine,…this law of his being is like mine…for whatever can with truth be called a self, as person must be…is part of this world as much as one's own body, and feels and acts in the center of reference of concentric circles around it, where outside of it nothing begins from one side and ends from the other" (Hopkins 353-4), then that leads to the window and the air, the eye and the me, where the windowpane is me and not, and the self a circumference, and a field.

Wanderer upon the sea of your footsteps and more, the road is made before. Walking makes the road, and beyond that no one sees. It is not possible for you not to be, for if it follows that you are not bound and that is the path you can explore, IT IS THE SAME THING TO THINK AND TO BE. Journey first. At no time in all the years' extremes are these memories mentioned, not that they have not taken place, much less that they did not mean, but last first. Leaving from the end he saw the beginning and had to wait through a species of POW camps, writing four decades later to his daughter overseas, as you must who read this, not face to face in that time, but Invisibly.

To go natural on this journey they call it shock who lay in the forest
to bring the stars to earth. Who would have thought it could be done.
All Imaginations of hearts when first. Consultations, past and
present, future, distinguish not. One remember this as felt. It knowing
is seen, touched, felt, and what matters most is faith understood.

Both types, sea and land, earth and the sea in mountains,
valleys and plant and animal life, whatever there is on dry
land, also undersea, are faithful both where myth
was as real as a government ship lists and oaths of the
oldwriting are a ship between this world and that pulled
in, never quite expressed in burial complete in the Móvo o
Iησoύς inscribed upon hearts.

Great Morning cannot be hurried. Deeds must actually be
done as the Daystar rising admits those who enter.
These questions always distinguish self and other. Did you
know King's College was on fire, Mr. Brubaker? I can't
show you now whether this was better than fraking but the
ozone at super collider, mash them thoughts.
Brubaker need not be present but no substitute for him will
do. How can he then be the object of our thought if all the
king's horses cannot pull him up, or opposite forces cannot
push him down. The highest compliment of these is to
practice the difficulty of living in two worlds spiritual and
physical that on land do not see directly into the spiritual
required at sea. Back places merge where it is axiomatic that
as one as likely to see a robber as a friend if an Adversary
took all these forms in the physical and spiritual, so also did
the Friend, which the luminaries of Halle (the spiritual center
of much of this) thought. They could "probably find the
adversary in Philadelphia, so as Kelpius intervenes, "we are
not ignorant of that which he is thinking of [but as another
then replied], you will also find the dear Lord Jesus in
Pennsylvania."

The underwater land is clearer than air. Underwater the
same as inner water, the swim of thought, breakers, the

beach down to the surf, going in. Do you know whether you're in the water or out, tortoise, clam, some small squid, minnow looking down, looking up and then the most amazing life given to some other being! It's a problem to steal back what was stolen. How can you want to be one who has no idea of what or who he is? The fish in a pond or on a hook, in the sea where currents and predators or lack might convince it was special, selected, destined, but if just lucky, impervious to the runoff that amazed, fish aghast tried not to show.

Hunting tropical fish with blue and gold fins at the base of the volcano the fish myself who took the bait turned the light off and watched pupils dilate. This fled from him as much as did him seek. To get spit back up. where the streams of the national park beneath the mount swim, it's dark in the fish, but in the sea darkness dawns, in the dark, but the dark turned to light.

To know further in words directly apprehended much has to do with boring a hole in the lob of the ear and pinning it to the door, hearing the sound thereof, as one born of the spirit, or as one says in another place, he wakens me morning by morning, he wakens my ear to listen as one being taught. That is why he says, further, I have more insight than all my teachers. You can no more transfer this by words then you can know life without living. Put on the ephod, the Urim and Thummin, yes and no, but to know the voice you want to wholly enveloped, immersed. No more than a bride can know the mind of her husband by giving herself to another can the mystery be known by intervention.

Immersed in the name and word has an inward sense of being buried in the letters of a word and the sound, so the literary embedding is active. Immersed, buried in a word, baptism outwardly, the name in the outer sense changed into water in the internal sense has the letters poured over our heads like oil, which "sound" fills the mind and ears until they embed as letters themselves. So baptized we are renamed in Messiah. Sinking into the Word we become words. In preparation for wearing the Word literally handwritten and bound in the head and hand, composed on top of old precepts scraped off, we are the palimpsests retold over centuries, retold in the night, the Word that underlies and surrounds what is said, a coat to give away that transfers by the will, which you're going to say again that you've been praying all these years to receive. Water was the outer but the sound and the word were within. Far-seeing, far hearing, far thinking among "great waters," both natural and adverse, seeing ahead and getting to the hiding place that is the Name, the edifice word, the floods are like previous droughts, that took away moisture so much that a plant of its implicit gardener's watering must consist of hearing and seeing though the bones are roaring. Add the eye to the still small voice attuned so a glance serves as a command, as it does on patrol or as between lovers, tilted brow, grimace, smiles read each others' faces and guide. The sense of it is "be not as the horse and mule that need bit and bridle to come to you." They come not by their will, Psalm 32. 8, so I will guide thee with mine eye. I will watch over you.

Was *neuer syn Noe floode sich floodys seyn.*

Reality is that hard to accept, but then it exists The eye tries to make these look like something it recognizes and taken for what is in soda cans and trucks, if we could bring ourselves to admit. To know large and small, that rich and poor are of their own and that is the nature of knowing, knowledge without limits, allowing. It sounds like space and at end incomplete work, a gift. Wind shifts and plucks up, but people do like the universe to send its bidding. Dry earth moves mountains and the sea. Windows light up Scandinavia. They pick children up by the heels in heaven to shake them down in the beginning. Whether any of it

does any good one neighbor apologized the same as Jonah,
"will I have eyes at the bottom of the sea, supposing I
descend there on endless stairs where future things swim in
empty outlines of skeletons?"

The eye has this naturalizing quality, it must look and live
before it can recognize, especially if it knows what existed
in its mind before the making, and in the unmaking, where
folds and curves make shadow, constantly recast the image,
which seems to be moving, it depends on point of view,
high hopes and dreams, improbable curvilinear figures not
quite named.

His family had moved back that last year from where it was
when he was five, in strip mined hills and galligaskin forests,
creeks, who used to walk the slag piles and giant pits, though
now I suppose they are canyons with green water at the
bottom, a kind of mountain lake, but treacherous as a
commonplace book of Charles I. He would leave while his
family was still asleep before dawn and walk the steppes. This
town bordered on one side by two tracks, just prior to a yard
of large importance with a roundhouse where Bobby Shafto
lived. Black soot billowed up from the engines. We always
had a supply of flares and torpedoes at hand, if not dynamite
to fetch a duck or two.

The tracks bordered the Creek filled with wreckage of lost
trains; huge cubes of scrap metal stuck up from the shallows
where the rails followed the creek part way, lined with
telegraph poles on that side like hillocks ramblin, tracks set
into the mountains that rose up from the valley
flat of the farms on the other side like an old song and
created a fierce updraft that ganged the burn that reared with
flames in dry spells by the trains. Then the small town would
rally its playfellows in the street, volunteer to fight the flame
with mats and rakes and whoops as the flames rose a hundred
feet in air. I say this as a participant, so that

the sheep shall take no harm, for that place is nothing real. You can have pudding in half an hour there or anything you want. I talked to a lot of lazy deuks especially one guy who had just made a river, but didn't know if it was wet - river, sky, all relations plain.

Apparent horizons persist for a period of time that sit in the coal-neuk caves and giant holes of Mars, luminosities of beams of light inside the Clavius Crater not to speak of what Canadians saw, a cloud with violet edges on the Sea, a 12 mile long bridge in Mare Crisium as The Tower sphericals testify before congress about the pareidolia praying, meaning "Place of Rejoicing," among the towns Okokammeh, Natick, Mashpee, Hassanamisco, Herring Pond and Nukkehkummee Maanexit, Quinnatisset, "little long river" and Wabaquasset, Glosknap to the core.

Whose name is this, a spaceman from Solaris not knowing whether an ethnic being or not, who ran a bath for bronze grave stones over burners? Whip away oh! After casting, molds with bronze letters were brought to be cleansed, to remove the names and dates fastened in to the layout with wax. After casting, the coachman takes his stand. The molds soaked in superheated water of the bath drive away with the sins of the world, so clever. Standing at the vat, with arm length rubber gloves, he wire brushed the blanks, sorted the letters, loaded the lives on skids to be recast. The next summer after I worked beside him in Manyunk cutting skid loads of cartons with a jackhammer. Intelligence hopes to replicate Einstein's brain, and make it available on a jack drive, stirred.

Loose intent upon accident and accident upon intent. Accidental design recognizes what is occurring. Accident sees, hears and knows back and forth. All intent is person-al. The creator becomes accident-intent. Accident rules out the future for a present delight. Accidence provides an incontrovertible real present. You can say again that it is discovered, but it was there when you saw it.

All of this was manifest as the first breath of sweetness at Asbury which came in confession and was, 'founded upon forgiveness from the heart, and forgiveness upon the knowledge of one's own faults, and this knowledge is founded upon that great humility which we all lacked in spite of our great knowledge" (JK, Kelpius, *Diarium*, 31). All this is yearning for the "birth for the universal redemption of groaning creation, as well as those that have received the firstlings of the Spirit, who become God-bearing" (JK 34).

These spirit-bound "act with true Philadelphian spirits of love, which are the essential body of heavenly wisdom" (JK 44), much to do with Pietism and Philadelphian when "the new Earth swallows that forementioned Flood and its glorious Sun causes all other Stars and Phenomena to disappear, and no Night succeeds it, but that the Night is swallowed up in the Day" (JK 48).

This was known in Europe's nations under the name of Philadephian revival then as now and work upon the soul as "interior parts by Ecstasies, Revelations, Inspirations, Illuminations, Inspeakings, Prophesies, Apparitions, Changings of Minds, Transfigurations, Translations, wonderful Fastings, Paradisical Representations by voices, Melodies and Sensations to the very perceptibility of the Spectators" (JK 490).

Many traditions and legends of that community that survive borrow from The *Revelation* 12, where the "woman fled into the wilderness to a place prepared for her by God, where she might be taken care of for 1,260 days." Kelpius discerned three wilderness states, portraying these events in the precession of the heavens that occasion the woman of revelation in and from out of the heart of the love of God…[where], the more carefully the Lord hides us from the dragon, who watches so carefully for the birth, in order to devour it. All relatives in this same battle invite to unity "under the banner of the Lion and the Lamb" (30), despite the Mandela Effect that supplanted the lion for the wolf.

After I came down from the roof I fell in the drive. Then I saw a river meandering pleasantly along. Standing above it on a walk, as it began to increase and course, large swales of muscular torrents around the bend looked to endanger my position so I moved up and crossed to a stair and went up. To this river of sounds and sights, to close the eyes, the visual disappears. I open and identify just as when I slip and fall. Awareness unremembered, requires me to tell, but to be honest I am dishonest.

As residents of Norway North above the 65th parallel follow the Sami ways of arctic birch and harvest the Chaga, this statement is published in case we are removed, but there are a hundred *exits among weasel dens and voles, lemmings and mountain interest rates, shrew and hare, badger and hedge hog.* Stone tunnels all over verse transit this endless life where birds conceal nests of poems in rock falls. Twenty drafts of the spirit translate first produced. I hear the voice, not one language to another, but thought to language to speech. The text exists only after it is made. In this time there is no other. Walking on a roof, or a slab, in the grain of tree cuts when finished, to catch decisions and timings and not, we sing like the Great Tit or a Stint.

[But only new Philadelphia of all the earthly claims could rival Yerusalem to apply for that Fauxtown. as the interiors of those cities myth all past tense cities before Philadelphia and London, no better than Where the horses run the race the colony believes its crude polygonal struts that ring the bells and bury scarabs to joust with road kill, chollas, spines and pads can make a masterpiece! Old dying new cannot be born]

Who dares call it swimming Casanova's Colon? The epath of Leviathan of thrust faults and under land seizes, under, beneath, Behemoth above ↕ prospected by earth and under sea imagines it swimming up aquifers and getting fracked. Creatures in a river impose on ourselves a temple that feels no sides. In this freedom between yards of blubber imprisoned by events, unaware of its own movement, states and individuals swim in opposite but unknowing. What is freedom when compelled one way by current while swimming as fast as it can in the other? Read the scientific papers on genetic machines, the last great covering globe. Scrutinists in this way show their absence. RockaBilloy history makes a victim. Miners as at Archuleta need our protection where land honeycombs five caves and Unchangeable or changeable in position, the colonies gradually emerge for some reason inherent in themselves, conspicuous with the visible development of some canali following melted snow. Only when such melting has progressed can the colonies be truly seen, as if the moisture invigorates their air. For instance, colony darkness increases considerably eight miles up the Pisinemo Road near KiaHoaToak. Near Carrying Basket Mountain, known for its horsehair and yucca, beargrass, and martynia, the tests of bathythermograph, hitty pitty within the wall, may be said to manage Behemoth.

DNA altered genealogies, lists of foods, strange government camps, Blackbox and Red Rovers, universal surveillance digital versions of every telephone call made since 2005 get the gist of the infinite hydra head that so opposes.

If we go to Lake Volstok at that time when the stone cats envisaged
faery heads upon us, but the Goliath herd, "his strength
is in his hips" "his power is in his belly" moves like a
redwood, "with bone beams of bronze" if not like subway tubes
and ribs like wars of iron" recognize the chief of the ways of God.
The mountains bring him food, where all the field beasts play among
the shad trees down to the covert reeds covered with shadow where
willows of the brook compass the whole unknown Future of empty
outlines and skeletons, all the past grown dim.

　　　　　New Philadelphians have a new political and
biological system of land and sea, behemoth and leviathan.
Like some clam admired for its failure to open, they see
only what they ask. If given advice they don't seek.
They're a lot like a novel without a character. The only
character is ourselves in a collective en masse. Everything
else is invisible.

To get to their city you have to pass through little
towns and neighbors. Buses run from the hovercraft. Law
and order spring up fast, just from the natural tendency of
some to push forward while others stay back. Pushers chose
the Mayor Werner Herzog from the Congress of the
Righteous Apprehending the Real. He was their first
nominee to send over the divide. He crossed the Alps with
an elephant, walked the Antarctic ocean floor, so when
Revelation Colonists thought they might get in from
outside, who better? Werner was fancied a Napoleon of
spirit of sea bottoms and mountaintops. He floated the
Yangtze with Barry Lopez! Surely he could divine a way
into this city whose foundations were only in air. The guru
of Maru he was called. He took charge of the commerce
grown up around Hopi kachinas dressed as taxis who
roamed for passengers to get out the vote. Since the purpose
 of Burroughs was to expose and arrest Nova Criminals
in Naked Lunch, Soft Machine and Nova Express to retake their
universe of Fear Death Monopoly" to battle the human extinction

against the "powerful instruments of control," Kerouac nominated him for vice mayor, "the greatest satirical writer since Jonathan Swift."

Philosophy burns in the grate. Intellect speaks where inmates incarcerate. Collective tiers of shanks and kindness, the iPad and iPhone flop, the desktop flicks, the power plugs alert to GPS wandering. Right off Tolkien says, "Faerie is a perilous land, and in it are pitfalls for the unwary and dangers for the overbold." He did not say, "spiritual evil is an overriding

pervasive force that infiltrates every custom and social purpose," or, "beauty is an enchantment," where chaps in the cheap seats of the perilous and shadowy marches vote (9). You might say Dante is a Fairy if you want a good argument. But the prophet is a fool and the spiritual man is mad. Unmask, unmask, not the Blue Fairy Book or Sir Gawain's primary and secondary belief, they are not coming to

pick you up for some FEMA camp. Mark your curbs to save them time. These days it is a French camp that work shops by inventing any situation impossible to encounter.

Look both ways before entering the doorway of this invisible world. There, posing in the doorway, we find, about to enter, everything unrecognizable, shorn of import. Connecting membranes to virtually everyone and everything. How do these massive dissolutions undo the hedge? Again, the opposite is the case. Connection is destruction. You only know what you need to know when you enter this world and you have to know subordination, boundaries. We already have one foot inside, enter "the void" with anX on the back of the hand as a mark of being set apart. Look to one side where the foot enters, the opposite hand raised in defense, a globe of light to see.

Those who do not remember being born hardly remember their death. Only the young have not lived after. When they get there what do they see? Ha! going back.

A reclamation and redemption must follow those called here beset with such "great signs and wonders coming that, if it were possible, they would deceive the very elect." The mechanisms of this deception argued on every newscast is seen by not looking at it.

There shall be a supposed anti-head pretending to the Most High to make a counterfeit with governments replaced by Israel as Israel is counterfeited at the last.

"… The eco-complexity becomes so intense with throngs and multitudes of the Divine that it flares into the feedback of an ultimate vision."

As R. Simeon went further: "God created the great dragons and every living creature that moves, and the waters brought forth abundantly, after their kind" (Gen. I, 21) Leviathan and its mate, slain for regaling the righteous in the Day. "I give you power to tread on serpents and scorpions, and over all the power of the enemy: and nothing shall by any means harm you." Later leviathan was said the political state and its forces to protect you. Fifty states of leviathan pledge the rising up, a third part of stars lay down.

Why don't philosophers tell us before what we will be after? "Constant consciousness that He contemplates your secret as an open life, that which is hidden within you and that which is seen." (*Duties of the Heart*, Tenth Treatise. 33, Rabbi Bahya ben Joseph ibn Pakuda). The erased writing warns about the kind of world he enters. Deleted in most copies, as if the artist wanted to prevent obscuring the composition with words, the writing was left in other copies so what we don't see here. We see it there. It is reversed. Reversed writing, invisible writing, turn around to exit the path of life (Psalm 16) resurrection in "Jesus our Lord, who is the God and Lord to whom the Ancients looked."

Visible is invisible, left is right. Hang the imagination in the worlds of archetypes of the "infinite Abyss," and "fly or rather swim the infinite deep," most terrific. "Vast spiders" sprung from the unkempt deities of "Powers of the air," unkempt Principalities revealed. They could not know their scientists were insane. A person sitting and waiting for something might know what it feels to watch the last oozings hour by hour.

To walk New Philadelphia on the road where the dragons once lay in the reeds-
- "come out of the pathless desert and dry flesh to the upper hut not fashioned with hands from the waters above" (JK, 42) --was changed all time in Rending the Veil. The redeemed shall walk there the ransomed of the Lord shall return to Zion with songs and everlasting joy upon their heads (Isaiah 35). In the church of Philadelphia "I will write on them the name of my God and the name of the city of my God, the new Jerusalem, which is coming down out of heaven from my God; and I will also write on them my new name" (Revelation 3.12).

Native Wittgenstein

To borrow from the in-between, "Whereof one cannot speak, must be silent." The World loves to hear itself speaking in the case it rules out the man who was in the world that knew him not.

The case is not either that the world is nothing. The case is the world is a formality that binds to be bound. If not then we come to a series of corollaries to install the redemption the world is infiltrated by prehistoric worms. We go with flamethrowers to illumine this, but the true flame is the breath. As Dostoevsky says in his *Winter Notes*, "It's a kind of biblical scene from Babylon, prophecy from the Apocalypse fulfilled before your eyes. You feel it would require a great deal of eternal spiritual resistance and

repudiation not to surrender, not to succumb to the impression, not to bow down to fact and not to idolize Baal, that is, not to accept what exists as your ideal" (Winter Notes on Summer Impressions)

What pray is left? The world is nothing and nothing is the case as the son of a Moscow doctor, and graduate of a military academy of Russian literature, Fydor, was standing in front of a firing squad, accused of subversion against the Tsar when the drums began to roll, but spared to exile in Siberia where the mercury froze in the thermometer he learned what was the human condition which until we learn it our self we shall have to say every hour on the hour that this will be understood only by one who at least already had the thought, As Wittgenstein said, when he went to prison camp, to achieve the purpose whereever there is one such in the world.

Aristotle knew the human in such dire strait when he discovered himself caressing a woman's breast and feeling her belly against his.

After enlisting in 1914 Wittgenstein wrote, "now I have a chance to be a decent human being and stand eye to eye with death." He bought the only copy of the Gospels by Tolstoy on the Polish front, and had it with him when he wrote, or at least thought, "meaning does not lie in this world that exists but outside it…"which, as it were, connected with the meaning translated here as *bar* in the phrase shor habar, "ox of the wild," or "wide open spaces,"

a negation of bull represents complex states of mind. Or in another sense, we may say that in "one who has clean hands and a pure [bar] heart" the shor habar of righteous worship through meat (shor) and hot-blooded passion engender pure and refined (bar) the corporeal spirit among those land righteous who migrate the seas. They worship with vigor, eating meat and rejoicing in it.

If gluttonous in the world per se, their joy of passion inflames in the performance of Commands made to the 5 million diamond facts along the 13 Balsam rivers (four are hidden), that flow through the thousand mountains.

Wittgenstein and Dostoevsky aside, The faith of Water worships another way, for Land while open, focusing on life comes from walk in the light, engaging as Sages mean to "touch," but water, not through physical worship, but to effect the spirit facilitated by devout intention, at the first some call,

That moon is already beneath our feet. Bright points in the sky or a blow on the head will cause stars. In the first case the eyes were duly affected from without; in the second, the nerves were tapped to the same effect in mid-route; but in each case the subsequent current travels higher apparently as authentic as the other. But must we not insist our sense data be private to ourself? That I can't show him to you now because he isn't there, his soul cleft from its body though mental imagining, reflects this major force. Avalanches, landslides are different sorts. Let the peasant turn his mattock to the wheel. Is the mind natural? Nature is innocent compared. Whatever the merit of arguments or prayer remember or forget, you are speaking of yourself. Just the side of one buried lens in two pieces catches the sun.

I seen this window and out escaped before the border closed. Trees grown in the window glass and notes on the window panes reflect / What eye actually sees, ear hears of multitude faces without body. So shut the window and to your chamber go. If it is discovered, it was

there before you saw it. It is bigger but we get to participate, even if it
is not in a measurable state.

Now you know that when the dish jumped off the table
That Browbender got out, went someplace else besides the multitudes
falling from truck virus. Calcutta Ca Ching. New York, London, ca
ching, ca ching. Provinces tracked like satellites dished as big as the
moon. Is there a book to read on the way? That's where you go if
escape is made, into the book, have a read of your life. Let'em argue it
while you pass. Get out of the city foot,
hand and knee get, hence arm and leg. The pot has swallowed the
ladle and the armored Brinks flee.

Countering the invoked muse outside the engineer who measures the
angles of the whole to control the precisions of orbits, times and space
in actual space, now joining artificial intelligence to the human, this
function of intelligence outside the person is an adversary of the
human compared to drawing a map of the stars against free hand. The
engineer measures the angles but perception takes angles differently
in every case. Freehand accidence says correct distance is an illusion,
that a map of the heavens is an illusion, for there is no universe in this
sense and these are synonymous in their illusion of futurity.

Accident intent upon recognizing what is occurring has no external
motive. Accident sees, hears and knows back and forth in dialogue
with the person of the creator, but rules out the future, for the present
must extrude of itself. Accidence provides an incontrovertible seal in
the present. It is made/not made with human hands. Accident is never
part, never two, but one. Wittgenstein said his *Tractus* would only be
understood by those who already had the thought. Accident is a near
non-thought. Its love for its own sake of all species in the "faces" of
Emmanuel Levinas, describes compassion.

Erosion from the Atlantic Ocean also known at Guanabara
Bay created nothing compared with the depths off Montauk
where Levi goes all up and down the Sound, it cannot berth

in Rio and other shallows, but the Goliath herd, "his strength
is in his hips" "his power is in his belly" moves his tail like a
redwood, "with bone beams of bronze" if not like subway
tubes and his ribs like wars of iron" lend support to "first"
referring to size, due to the parallel clause whose
renderings passages recognize the chief of the ways of God:
the mountains bring him food, where all the field beasts play
who lies under shad trees in covert reeds. The shade covers
him with shadow; willows of the brook
compass him about. The whole unknown insisted, nor did he
nor I seek to be credited that Future things swim before me in
empty outlines and skeletons, all the past grown dim.

A goat trampled them. How many miles to Babylon? Three
score miles and
years and ten. You can get there by candle if your heels are
light. Lordlings, by this example I you pray Wall your tongue
with teeth and lips before. For we should so advise whate'er
we speak that sword to approach.

Captivity

When Captivity Has So Startled that all purists on the coasts became
prophets. Writing visions of their hearts, shaved heads,
cut beards in Providence, Miami, Nulon Rouge, divers from
submarine bases taught these letters to people of the Orange Sea..
That at least enables you understand the Inland rebellion planted in
second hemp, that grafted Oak, Maple, Pine and iron with one hand,
as the other gripped brains between the eyes. Each wrote to thunder
heights of burn. Downstream, when corkscrewed tangled rope started
like water from the globe, he time to flee, past time, the very cause
blind to folly, was kindled. Even agreement with one self is
suspicious. Absolute agreement is neither expected or compelled
between earth and sky, sea and the mutual inhabitants of nations,
women, men, blue green coasts against the red ochre hills, far white
peak ranges above the canals before anyone remembers. As a fiat

accompli of themselves connecting parts, hub and tire inland from the sea, the great deep entered into land to call it earth from habit, a solid miracle of huge ocean that surrounds ecumene in order for it to be moving, so the colony may think it is alone in the world where someone with the same spirit views sympathetically and the organs of sense are scattered about the limbs. Ourselves along the canals hold conversations about the weather to come but the weather of the water and the land is of the soul, which tribulation had them burning churches at prayer meetings, which media centers still deny today. Men and women, women and men and children enter the storm cellars as the winds begin.

How to get entry, when the place is hovering off the ground, slightly above. None of the tunneling up did any good. Scaffold unions complained that the structures built above still left a way to go. The masons said all their chisels and hammers bite the air. If Philadelphia were a billiard ball it might be a home for Schrodinger's cat or Wittgenstein's rhinoceros or his pet beetle from the Dharma realms. You could see them and then they would disappear. The billiard ball asks, how does it feel to be one of the beautiful billiard balls? If one could imagine a stone as conscious as a lion or a man as conscious as the beach or a lima bean with no means to speak, the unspoken thought of the teeth in the rose, of a no rock voice that has no arms, no legs, no eyes, no skin, no teeth, or wheat that shifts in a granary, stored there from habitation and old age, you would know what they say. As it is it takes a long time. The waves wash up. The lives of turtles and urchin and seaweed and driftwood are conducted in the tide where we wake.

There is a decompression of bends and chokes, if we come up from the sea plumbed with the beach, lungs, oxygen entering. Before water there were no seas, which compares to some unconscious we don't name the tongue spoke after a while. It was a sea without end, but once before the water was wet, no currents, no boats or flood would ratchet out the stones. So to do a thing did not do it, to think a thing did not know it. A diamond formless opaque, old trees, cracked skin, stout limb, sapling, circulates beneath.

Soriee outside the camp a kid may walk the empire rails, shoot out
insulators on light poles. Against the light. Cubes of crushed metal
fall into the creek below. Train wrecks where freights went up, engine
smoke unscrubbed rage up rhododendrons all the way to slag mines
of oil-stained ground. The Bridge turns thought into poems that fly
about a traveler's head. Caissons hang down. Radium eyes of stars
rest their feet on top the thrones like nightjars of lightning bugs. So
we cannot admit we are in the room with cherubim and angels,
dreams of nation-states and the Rhinocerosi of Ludwig von
Wittgenstein either.

Said to be polysemous, many meaning, a manifold approach almost
rules out the possibility of logical links between. Passages make
continuous leaps of association in inconsistencies of metaphor and
metonymy, speech closer to the lips, tip of the tongue locking teeth
babbling in some kind of creation back and forth, somehow lapidary,
like a tombstone inscription, or unrolled like a cello flowing out of a
narrow crack.

He that loves wisdom loves life and they that seek her early
shall be filled with joy. She, of course wisdom,
leads to the rooster crowing in in Ken's drive, who breathed his last in
Oregon in the middle of breakfast. It is life
itself our love comes, knowing that rooster
 perched each night in the aqua vitae and sang his even and morning
song.

Once the baby chow I babysat chased him up the street with his
shortlegs churning, losing ground the whole way until he just stopped
and turned around. That cock had fathered several sets of chicks on
his once wide harem. He had five hens. all escaped from a mortgaged
house. Then
there were three. Sometimes the chicks nearly grew before
their limp bodies were found on the setbacks.

> One lady fed this rooster and if he had roosted at her house
> things might have been better, but it didn't, he came to me, at
> the end of his beauty, the red comb, black wings, yellow

shoulders, more beautiful than any other, couched on the
drive, barely breathing. I don't
know what happened. To mourn his crow, his stance, beauty,
his being, his youth. That house was being painted
like he was poisoned.
I feared to approach. The painters came and
swept him aside. A family came to look at the house, stood
around the body. Just when we think we have it we lose.
All roosters will be remembered if I remember. The dentist
wanted to know the single favorite of all these treks. Rodin
outside Paris, with all the marbles, I said, and never a
black casting in sight, pure veined marble. Months later,
hunting the grave in Wales, the historical Ambrosius.
And Glastonbury.

Why there should be fiction of this sort that reads like a code
between the personal and the systemic, direct sensory experience and
vast, hidden structures that must be authenticated? To render the
unseen by pattern emerges. Is this philosophy? But the layering
between experience and sleeping, fleeting thought that suddenly
appears is the value of forgetfulness of intention, a bridge itself. Even
if it is as the Russians say, factura, born for such a time as this, with
the sense of afterlife therein, actuated to repel, not invite,
What do they see, leaving the old contours beneath. The collective of
all and none emerged from cracks undoing the unseen economies,
where even a sea monster becomes a media signal. The Harbor Seal
Baptists and their antiphonal singing echo something like this in the
half-remembered liturgy of bridges—unseen from the House in
Jerusalem.

But there's a rub. Location, or said better, all locations, all cities of
the world babtkib, Bab-ilu, Old Bāb-ilim, and occupations in transfers
of lands that involve water in the collective voyage from that old
world what they were reliving let us say. Sleepwalkers aware that
hand connected to a body standing beside, history and myth
unmasked up, how do these disconnections build the bridge? Already
one foot is inside. Only the young had not lived this afterlife when we
got there.

Until we see them seep into consciousness many cracks radiating
fissures, like Tycho in the Moon, craterlets, orbits of phyllotaxis
perceptible as the shape where Ohio once was. Ohio in that old world
proved some finite intelligence was at work. After Ohio, crossings
seen in the meeting-places formed more than one canal.

Perhaps the time traveler can't remember much. That's why
he writes. One thing we say, don't take the interstices. You
may live among superpositions but you are not one. They
can't tell. So pretend to walk. They do see you, but you are
talking to what is not, the Ashkenazi Ukrainian potter of
herbs who wrote ten million words, the Mennonite
production potter. Only the flaws of physics are real, and
you know what they are. This is the dog that worried the
cat that killed the rat that ate the fort that lay in the dust of
Jack. Right through walls. Time travelers get hungry, get
tired. We recommend you keep a watch tuned to home.
Seems inevitable dreams of boxcars and underground
cities, ring the fire managing fantasies, and history. Fellows
lay in the house where they'd been spun by viscose mirrors.
Little canisters of drilled couplets on doilies shielded the
surface from tarnish from water rings that the inn keep
wipes clean. Next customer up gets a memory wipe,
rejuvenalization straight. What will you mate: hanky panky
phantasmagor to live programmed? All the witty
pranks of youth played in their riper years.
The audience of heaven's episodes working
late at a farm to raise eagles wee doves, ducks and
grackles as etched below.

Happily wearing a heavy shirt, a large eagle lands on my
shoulder. It must know. A smaller female in the lap, profusion
of eagles gathering in fur as if to suck,
the mother preening while, the father perches with claws,
on look out as we sit.

Each text unwritten, before the fact burns. Kyrie Eielson a cappella under the casement. Emaciates call sinners not the righteous to each point of light, dark swimming underwater in viscose. Not waiting in Weimar or the wonders under Dresden to survive sense impressions of the real, bailing out over Paris, not this unreal that can't hear the noise of its own approach, vapor trails of rockets that deny chemtrails, a war as reality the way ghosts in St John flee the fields.

I crosse out all! adieu by my saint Johan!
I take my cap in hand and I am gone.

Here is a summary of what will come:

Think both sides. The present walks through the future and Past.".
The Life of the Mind in a Body to be honest must be dishonest, because the truth is "too big for the piano of space." POWs of history writing four decades late turn 90-degrees at the moment of impact. The "falling body" becomes a "fulcrum" of the universe.

This is maybe what you think at 80 when you remember cutting skid loads of cardboard with a jackhammer at 18. It explains the Bible, methane and apocalypse mixed together to witness the collapse of a 400-year-old map in a single, high-velocity neural event.

Therefore we have taken the scholarly horizontal orderly rows of "Synchronisms" of of apocalyptic time of Joseph Mede to picture this, but snapped up 90 degrees into a Ladder that supports a vibrating, four-dimensional Cubet hovering a "non-metric foot" above the silt of the drive where you fall, "hinge" is a 180-degree turn in the air.

The Architecture of the Fall begins surveying the broken skin of the world on a flat roof with "nowhere to fall"— But the act triggers a "slip." inlinear time.Mede's timeline breaks and the landing is the 90-degree "Elsewhere." and When you land "on top," the world has reversed. The "head" (the Circle/Mind) and the "feet" (the

History/Silt) have swapped. You become the vertical and that "vibrating Cube" is the New Jerusalem, but shielded by the Babylonian Curtain.

The Four-Inch Thickness: This is a "contexture" blue, scarlet, and purple a generic "Universe" foisted on us to hide the Wonder Word. It is so thick that all the kings "horses" of human logic and all the king's men, cannot pull it apart or together again.

This Cube hovers as decreed, a foot off the ground to protect its frequency. If it touches the "broken skin," of intimacy of the Divine and the Human we see "organic structures" like roots hanging down from above like subway tubes and bone beams where Behemoth is laboring.

The Mayor of these Nation-States outside At the base of the ladder to the "Norway North" of the mind, makes an Interregnum. Mayor Herzog: governs the "Nation States" outside the Cube the Ecstatic Truth of those who live in the "mud" and the "silt," staring at the vibrating Cube with "shock and awe." to pillage the gold. He represents The "Fauxtown" Babylon where "Tubs" are thrown over the side to distract the Leviathan "translated" above.

There lies the Philadelphian Exception: Only the "Philadelphians" have the "Open Door"—the frequency-match that allows them to pass through the veil. IV. The "Norway North" Statement: Wittgenstein's Limit

We who live "North of Wittgenstein's cabin" say the very thing he advised us not to say: that the case is obscure.

Of course the voice we hear is the mind translating faster than any speech. It might not be able to say the word it is thinking, a hundred feet long of an inch. Fast as an angel speaking in prayer, Eloah's brightness coming out of a hand, faster than AI, not understood outside its extreme as the hands and purposes of powers. We are said to live what they think, eating, sleeping, getting and spending but do notice the reflex of these boasts that trade in masks to house their idea of life.

Once upon a time there was a little Strandbeestie, a Billie Beetie pure Baloo who rolled a silver dollar across the floor. From the furthest point of Troy & Greece and before, history with pen and ink fish poured out of its mouths little words into big, then whole paragraphs run up with fish in their mouth and a fish bird with a fish head flew down from a fish tree. Perpender, Emender, Picador dug. Mind mountains and fractals, passed the bonnie bairn. We would not crump the soles of our feet upon their heads or crumble the mind. Is the mind natural? Is an avalanche neural? Is a landslide practical? No thanks, said the creeks. Silence fell from the cracks.

Deep water inhabitants named a port for this profusion of myth on wings of clouds they would shoot down. Too late to shoot the sun or for Pishon and Gihon among the rivers to cleanse. Casanova's Kindred Natures called its larger core of claps thrust faults and compounds some kind of truth.

II.

This is the place before escape and after, all effort
to get out of the country, someplace beyond multitudes falling beside
trucks. They think they've gone mad.
They had peasants in the master plan, peace and
happiness for every man. Play your saxophone. No
need press against windows, nose the pane. Rattlin,
roarin' Willie, your reflection in the glass is as other faces
pass. I seen this. I seen, the appearance of a body.
as the body, an image sideways or behind in things
 I point at one at a time, opposed to another. I press against something
in front of me, a foot pedal, grasp the wheel to brake as much into the
beyond. No point describing

an old hotel or station of the mind turning round 14th century
conclusions to papered walls.

He actually carries John Gower's Voice of One Crying,
to know a human body have pain. Someone else had a
part of our hand. We want to know imbuement in the dark, covering
light warms this, the smells and sounds and the
crowds shuffling nice biscuits. Is he alone as the
eye or the ear that hears what none can say, no passengers
or refugees yet, for he is yet before the fact, before the fall if
you like to put it so.?

Shouldn't we be doing something to warn, run to the street,
empty the mind, not wait for the jars to explode or launch
commandos? O ye saw him coming and ye saw him go. You can
wake on the coast and swim out in a beautiful day in
September among the grass that overwhelms a century
before it has anything to say. Saddle both horse and mare, we for
Jeremiah his St. John who never there will be a
captivity rasping for light for you who love kissing, breakfasts and
dressing, being as we are without bodies, and
casseroles of the mass collective corp.

 One society exchanged with another for controls.
Salvation in one ounce pockets. Himmelskuchlichen, flieg.
Freedom comes to someone else Elijah blew everything up. Jars of
pickles exploded all over London. Why one kernel went off and
another not was a gift to Washington, spread
seriously along the Thames.

Gofernment Standestaat off. Gogernment opposes force. Hark sirs,
hear ye not how boldly the knave calls? Superpods digest
fluorescence. Back to London bridge. All wars against the natural,
self and other, nothing
Gorgonment, the war to persever Elijah, the man with
four letters, aleph, lamed...Eliyahu who had no desk
except the count books with their covers, books and plants where he
grew monarchs from chrysalis.

Seesaw sacradown, checked the progress of
the sycamore for carpenter bees. Black buzzers
inhabit cracks and fly the hollows. Come
tortoise and Gambel quail. Refuge, salvation
comes in miniatures.

If you don't know what any of this means it hasn't happened
yet. If you want any more you can sing yourself.
Ignorance is prevention, which explains a pocket Gower,
I shall sing true dreams whose import disturbs the hour of my heart.
May he whom the Isle of Patmos received in Apocalypse, whose
name I bear, guide this work.

 Now Isaac sonne, goe we our waie to the mount of Noah. Daniel
each saw three worlds, a world that
had been built, a world destroyed, and a world rebuilt.
Ezekiel gives particulars by the river of cherubim in much detail,
kettledrums, banderole, trumpets sound the fall of the King of Tyre
and the prophecy of Lucifer's fall. The valley of bones reconstituted
by The Breath, future Jerusalem is called into existence beyond
telling.

When Adam delved and Eve spanned, Adam scriveyn, if
ever it thee befall, so often a-day I must werk to renew
even without the yod, not doubt Ezekiel wrote at the
Fall of Jeruallym. Tyre-Lucifer claimed to be Elohim; there is no
secret that they can hide

Ride a cock horse that doesn't exist to an empire in which the
state grows a flow of expatriots West—it is a great blaze, let
us go! not quickly, but in achingly slow advance with blotches under
the eye, explained under
pretense of light. I pray thou be reshaping fantasy boats and for I
have made sore bones and weary feet, for the countries of Atlas and
passports that don't exist. At port we will pass for one of its sailors to
Jerusalem! Architecture of gold beyond history, I not weep for the
stones in the building.
What a thing ordained, the cupbearer entered,

Alexander toured the walls, Darius the Persian, Darius
Nothus, intermarried with the land the concept of return,
apocatastasis in the Septuagint.

Shakalo Urijah, Micah, You cannot be unspeakable every
day. Laughter plunging waves as one, Toledo, Akron,
Pittsburgh done, mushrooms torn from sky. Pit prophets, to the stars.
Broke pot painted vermilion, among the ligiments of John. Johanan
is not Jonah. Ismael not Basha. Idaho, Utah Nevada ride the Great
Basin west, stone water, ground
Because we dared to reach the hearts. home born.

The last thing they want to seem is spiritual, for
rejection of the world to reform like the speech of corn. To take the
border between image and word. the leaf inself seen. Who knows we
cannot deny to the Branch text
and image twine a covering for what cannot be seen because it is,
Walking up against it, to this last temple of the Holy Ghost where the
trains smoke black as the grave.

Belief that many hours hence, wakes each city illumined
with stone, the loam led looks, wind tethered to a sail, I
believe you carry the bones. You know these
questions bring back the reaching field. Listen to breathing
under leaves, dry grass, ground. You must be
mortal my heifer, to hide in kilns. Sleep prevented mind, Get out of
Gilead.

Their cloaks were gilded and bedazzled. Contaminated
surface moats and subsurface gob piles, slag heaps, talons
of runoff, little wings beating in their chests. Chemical
concentrate in water of that the colony is well situated to
recall had mine tailings and arsenic where Cottonwoods
fish. Maybe they don't drink the water, and all the salt cedar
is cut, but there were abandoned smelter stacks and slag
washes of leftover mines. Like it or not, or seek the depth,
the colonies of art mirroring life cannot take the pristine
upright.

Beyond the graveyards of Clonmacnoise cross
artifacts the fire insists these takes are after the
natural, which argument took the gold they had and the
colors we used if we had them, but the wine-dark sea did not. What
art if not pollution of our surrounding
barren hills, sky filled with chemtrails all the day? I didn't
say it, but the spirit of knowing and not knowing
simultaneously in a human mind, the red, black and white
clay colors of ancient three classical colors inferred.
Causation is inferred from proximity. Shortening further the paradox
of land and sea contracted in a moment, proximity
causation on land.
        Leaving All Semblance, how many miles to where
Phrases from The Revelation start to appear written by
unseen hands on buildings and bill boards: Shape Locust,
Fall Wormwood, Untimely Fig, Balaam to Balak! A
complete list could be had for twenty bucks.263
Things were moving for little beetie. Mentality mastered
pure humano. Severed from culture and the past, this new
reptilian intelligence would live for 5000 years. Baloo, lillie
beetie! Didn't technology double every two? Civilization
was rolling. Not grotesque even, distortion was superior.
Tidal influence reached inland far from the sea. The
furthest point, as far as Beelzebub, or Greece Troy Rome
Europe Britain America, would be the first of those whose
history you claim to know. Nations with allegories as
faceless as interchangeable cogs, changed name, but were
always like pen and ink fish, small fish pouring out of the
mouth of large beached fish, like small words. Land and
sea were overrun by these Paraphrasts. A two-legged fish
on land walked up with a fish in its mouth. A fish bird flew
with a fish head from a fish tree.

Mind mountains and dust fractals became fish studies
published by fish anthropologists and fish professors who
ate fish dinners. At least we hope they were fish. Watch
how you pass, ba beetie bonnie bairn. Walk so you do not
tramp your soles on their heads. This was our colonial fish

with a shriek, to implode the Plath and distort, neither
reflection by force nor destruction avalanche, landslide, or
eruptive wave of mind. Is the mind natural? No thanks.
Things fell from cracks. Silence fell on creeks, factories
held on by wax, leaves blew in letters on the street,
Fibonacci ratios, golden sections, fractal repetitions,
arithmetic challenges, impastoed faktoviki made
chickahominy.

Don't take the colonists symbolically that dress up as
adjectives. There are nouns on the table, in the foyer of
cherubim, smart talk on the rug, ambiance, not symbol. I
operated a bath in that place. Cast molds for grave stones
were brought to me after casting to be cleaned. Whose
name is this, this name and this, ask me I know them. The
names and dates in bronze metallic letters fastened to the
layout with wax were brought to this superheated bath
where I soaked them in hot treated water, wearing arm
length rubber gloves. I removed the letters and wire
brushed the blanks. Then I sorted the letters to be recycled
and loaded the blanks on a skid. Facts are kept in cabinets
below the surface.

The manuscript is like that, edited from a found document
of past deliriums left to molder. This has to be treated as
found writing from another time and place, over decades,
but amplified in the present. As such, when the editor
cleans and tightens up there is no feeling of a right to delete
anything, leaving what was gathered before to vex and
perplex. That is the nature of the work. To edit is to prevent
its prescience, which in the present seems fictional not
situational, and if it ever becomes situational, we will all
regret, but that is no reason to deny it may be true before
the fact, and if true, let us take steps to overcome. Consider
it as proof of Psalm 46. It's not easy to know when
information is skewed against knowledge. There is a
further layer above or below the fact we have no other way
to figure out if its mere existence is impossible.

Prince Charles bemoans populism and compares it to the
Nazi state when the Windsors were the most pro-Nazi of all
Europe.

So does the wolf really lie down with the lamb? Wasn't
that the lion? Intrusions are possible with vibrations at
higher and lower rates. Anybody who figures out how to
freeze the vibrations alters them. A car revving outside the
door alters the world. So whether from colliding particles
or isolation (freezing) governance is moot. Combinatorial
equations from another dimension answer back from
unknowns. This makes human culture obsolete.
It wasn't Caliban who wrote the brochure that said when
the wings were open wide enough it would fly. It wasn't a
god along the Po either, even if the last days of Noah
returned. You know what? they were doing bad things.
Alternative realities ripple the globe to create reality for
each person as within a river, a "mirror" of their entire Pop
or OoP world, which means by means of immersion, POP
means both population and the popular cultural anesthetic.
Names are substituted with waivers (avatars) in Sentient
World Simulation to outwardly express these inclusions
and occultations of text and belief. These are open to
programming cause and effect and program predictive
algorithms. The "questions" and answers, expressed in
combinatorial optimization, are sent through the nano
portal to identify optimal targets for alteration in the world
algorithm when the answer is returned. This means you see
what the algorithm wants you to see and only that [unless!]
The cause of change in the 3D world disappears, but the
alteration remains. Imposed from without, not from within,
the results observed in the Experiments are received
through asking: distortion to no law. Shoot them down! A word dug
from a mound turned up a head buried in a verb to pay honor to the
consummate Perpender, The Emender, the Picador.dictionaries and
fish. Ride a cock horse on land and sea.

Get to the gates, not quick, but aching slow from camps with blotches
under the eyes. I pray comfort thou in reshaping these attempts, sore
feet of the countries of Atlas, empires of expatriates to set the West
ablaze. Those who walk the underground see Traven, Dostoevsky,
Faulkner, Solzhenitsyn sink a shaft far from the inhabited surface,
they go down swinging to and fro, hanging by a rope" (Job 28.4, A.
B. Traina).

Which items and subjects should be altered for best Effect?
What alterations are noticed by POPulation and to what
extent? What reactions will this cause and what communication of
effects?

To call them canals is no faux pas that calling electrical discharge in
the planned obsolescence of intelligence is. I hope you see the knot
sky dome, mistaking rivers for canals, the way they dug Gilgamesh
from below the Euphrates and took him to Washington to run
Palantir. Power tracks and trains in temples. It was a perfect world.
For monster Odyssey, the tracks, taken apart, unseen. These then were
the underground transports of collective mind, but every wave has a
counter and undertow, so those who sang along the jetties with their
eyes closed single file kept on with these antiphonies to oppose.

Nothing to say Captivity? Grown great upon your pillows? Many
ways are tried to break in, as you know who weep for the stones over
their head. They tried to tunnel the geologic Talmuds. the
discontinuity beneath. Walking on its surface was walking on water
the 45 stone courses, 28 above and 17 underground where Jesus
breaks in to sup with those who slip out through holes in the
evening.

Next person up gets memory wipe to deny the war. Which is always
so, as if one person in the crowd but you do not precede them.
Labyrinths and lightning rods, cones of light flash streets and sky.
Scattered about cities, to show the scale no eye can see, ancient
quarries, tunnels and caverns beneath all around the city of dreams.

Waking existence led down a year, a day, a century of thought put into word. To know the thing you sleep inside as a
prophetic topography and a moral geology. Thinking to dismantle the image word machine, breath gets up. Down to the body run the colored maps of arteries and veins, descend a masif million lights, cities, hotbeds, houses, crowded streets.

Of course the colonist cannot swim like Jonah, a prime land combatant at sea. The colonist is at home on land, as if there were some clams, admirable for failure to open. Failure nourishes opposites while it frets between. Colonists only ask for advice when they don't need it, but do not dare to take it when they do. One if by land two if by sea. Crustacean creation monheim, is the reason for sea legs and hard coat, but not soft viscera These beings are not diamond or pure spirit you know. As to hiding the big for them to see up close, escaped shadows of light come back
 believed. Colonists ride the torrents from the singing rhythm and image of the word itself that tells them who they are.

There was a story of ineffable or really hard work turned some form or other into train whistles at night, roosters all morning, the eager flap of tongue, moving back and forth, not just ups and downs like birth and death, of which winter was in jeopardy and snow, but if we name the shape of the stone and metal whirling, the accident contradiction, it would be great stuff after the lightning
begot the fire and produced the desired. The time it takes is no concern. There is no time. Hillie is 80. All that matters is after reverses ignorant of alternatives that would have been, the shape of a head, a cross, a tree, stems of flowers the internal shapes. There is language to describe the internals, to say the aspirant flies out of a world to live in pure praise which spares those bones of epigrams washed ashore.

One thing is sure, the individual is not countenanced by "forces" whatever they are, which is how war works, casting the individual under the bus of the collective by saying that 1) we do not acknowledge the collective, 2) we think we are autonomous, unique,

3) that our minds are our own. The purpose of these exaggerations to
further the cosmic even in the midst of continued
ballyhoo about freedom and access to information, gives great
collective ideas to rule the masses.

It takes three asses to carry this fodder on their backs and our
own as Anybody crosses the bridge of this divide.

Whether it was on a moon or Mars or any place,
the new looked like the old and the old like the new. New
Colon named its harbor from an influx of theological Baptists who
differed so violently among themselves they would not agree
about the body of a carp. Verse Batists paced silently in dark brown
robes single file in the streets, chanting!

 Just to give the flavor, bakers and artisans, sausage makers like in the
markets of Turkey, farmer markets set up to service the masses who
had no obvious means of support. One wonders how they live, but
people resourceful in the extreme, where palm trees are planted for
shade and under them tied up against the heat, donkeys await their
burdens, belie.

The Colony produces several vegetations per year.Seasonal variation
affects a sapling that catches fire, that hisses, drips and spits until it is
dry, or a thorn bush goes up in a whoosh, invisible among the
colonias. At least five caves honeycombed that region, but plenty of
others were visible from the peaks, waiting to be discovered. Several
kept their heads and even their chests above the transverberation that
the eye and the wave equivocated together. Simple rectilinear,
curvilinear pi, repetitions the mind sees, of the eye. In the delusions
of temples and board rooms sanctums of foreheads swung their
censers before idols. Distortion of self similarity built a marine
museum of the mind. Greece emptied all its whales of thought.
Apocalypses made smoke. Of course I wept, tears ran from my eyes
as if I were burning wood to make charco The old world dying, new
monsters grow. DNA altered by a list of GMO vaccinations,
Blackbox and Red Rovers, digital tentacles and pattern DNA. When
415,000 low-orbit
satellites, and 65,000 satellites look at every square inch of

the planet 24 hours a day with 5G to harvest the data will
know (RFK), FB's Internet.org drone swarms and LEO satellites
performed porn. SpaceX satellites fiat internet. Maria pseudo-hirsuta
how that enlightened the poor!

When stone hits glass the breakage conforms to gravity and
glass. That's a little simple. Railroad ties connote forced
labor, famine stone denotes starvation and slavery. The whole country
was undermined by proboscis. All these contradictions blamed on
wilderness were conjuries of the ecclesiastical dragon state itself, a
tannin transcending forest and sea. its politics.

We can fly over the Euclidian part of this as if Wordsworth and
McBeth slept side by side in open compartments on a train. His would
be the Quixote ride, meaning Au revoir, naturel, deleted in most
copies while writing left in others was reversed. Metaphysical poetics
are not only myth. Jerudsalem after four generations in succession
would proclaim Christ's feet in England. the Lamb of God in the
Cotswolds, and the Holy Spirit as London fog around the dark Satanic
mills so the Brits could have it all for themselves.

I remember the Euclidean accompanied by rushing thoughts,
thunderstorms and wind. The noise of the highway in
every apocalypse is accompanied by such. The best advice of the
prophet Jeremiah was to go quietly which it is possible to deny unless
to escape recursion, defeat repetition of the upstart that can't hear the
noise of its own approach giants are not the prophets they once
believed. Among the race to the abyss, love not the world,
government theologues who prophesy extinction, denuded planets,
supernatural intercourse, or corruptions. Adobe walls and
housetop worlds of badger, tortoise, yarrow, are superior to blood
moons and airy creatures of earth. One thing the ice giants of
Abenaki had going was the noise of the highway.

Exiles had to survive in warehouses, eventually industrial
residences of many stories. Passages unguarded above and
below made a colony of clapboards large and abandoned. It
was a dream yard of roofed parking lots, shacks & another

warehouse unsecured, never locked. Vagrants, migrants, gypsies, tenants, homeless, squatters, working men, blacksmiths, artists set up tables under the eaves. With so many people in small spaces and close quarter the shops in this bazaar are posters of resistance.

We first see their paintings in the apartments below but tour the upper stories too, unfinished, rickety, dangerous with catwalks but traversable. The house has never been properly finished, just enough so it won't get too wet in the rain. I have been up there myself so it is more or less possible among so many more parts and pieces, like the old Barnes Museum in Merion, the only other collection where pieces crock and cram and crowds mill shoulder to shoulder to pass. Obviously they can't do that without apology. The name tags are missing. As for photography, it is a variable cloudy day when we pass through.

Jacks in the Pulpit hope to escape atrocity and put their hopes in some sanctuary that appears in dual time, so the waters were used for baptism, and living on the land for hundreds of years, some were faithful to wisdom. Others followed Leviathan who promised as well. Both cited Clement of Alexandria and Augustine who argued Christi si Odysseus, and took the Odyssey as precedent.

See if it can be borne that this tale is true, partly true, built out of truth and facts, but at the same time false in geography, the people, existing only in the ether of someone's mind, it is a lot like our lives. An Analogy of ourselves maybe is its reason for being, a transition between this world and the next, caught in forces we know little about but think we do. So as they used to say when the ships pulled in, or at the airport, Welcome home.

The old was refuge from persecution of the European fleeing persecution for its own sake who brought their afflictions with them. It's always government and religion that people flee. Freedom from these was the purpose of refuge, which should account suspicion on government. But while pilgrims in their fall to grace have much to share with the pietist pilgrims of old, they do not share the hierarchy. Living in two worlds at once, overtly in the spiritual and physical, see directly into the back places emerged and the robber as friend, a nice way of saying the Adversary took all these forms in the physical and spiritual, but so also did the Friend. We use these euphemisms to soften the blow.

In the record of Everyman's dreams and more, companionable, chatty, always friendship, no discords in the working poetic mind, an irony, for the lower mind, spontaneous, changeable, scandalous, just at the margin flickers constant Freudians of lower mind dilettantes. This is what you find in old century style in the waterways of the New Philadelphia.

We pretend to edit this translation even if from the English. English translates from English because the original thought is incomprehensible. Part history, part myth has a figuring out beyond the translation. People like ourselves, between this world and the next, when ships pull in from the faux geography and ether, and INS is in a good mood at the airport, say, Welcome to Philadelphia.

To even get this far we congratulate. Having passed through the cities one by one, through Seattle, Minneapolis, Austin, Atlanta, New Orleans, Chicago, LA, it shall stop the passengers in ways a doll can dress up her finger rings.

What's it look like if you're an outpost? Government theologue invisibles in politics, toddlers in the rocks to disguise. Bercilak takes up again his invisible head. Now we see that arm behind, sticking out? His buddy keeps birds near the coast.

Galeano said in 1970 what was known in every barrio and ghetto centuries before, but only came to the bubble on media phones. "Faerie is a perilous land, and in it there are pitfalls for the unwary and dangers for the overbold." He did not say, "spiritual evil is an overriding pervasive force that infiltrates every custom and social purpose" invented to hide its mask, or that "Beauty is an enchantment." Chaps in the cheap seats of the perilous now vote. You

might say Dante is Fairy if you want an argument. But open your eyes, the prophet is a fool and the spiritual man is mad.
They are not coming to pick you up for some FEMA camp of mind and heart. Don't mark your curbs, it is a French camp in which thousands of acolyte workshop writers invent from their fronts.

Play your saxophone dear. All reflection in the glass is as much in other faces, hearts, carrying as much into the beyondas some hotel or warehouse of mind. These fourteenth century conclusions are the norm if you want to know John Gower's *Voice of One Crying*.

For centuries people saw strange clouds, The legend of the cooks of little cow, bitterTod, Dein Haus brennt, fish forbidden to swim two semi-circles on a perpendicular were our favorite of all. Miss Mouse hid in plain sight under a wonderfully made city of dreams,

If you want to know the derailment of dark, the points you entrain, the details of imbuement, crowds shuffling, warm smells and sounds alone as the eye ear that hears what none can say?

STEP TO THE BRIDGE

The handholds of continents
   sail above our heads.
They wear the oceans as a scarf.
What Philadelphians see in any age

We see in ours.

These people took their Book of the Revelation seriously.
They camped in it or as near as they could get. Tent cities
covered the plain and they were out there day and night. In
their life, which you can take most literally, many before
were led into various camps of the plain as it divided into
schools, even if the matter was unclear.

 So spin this stretch of geologics over every proportion and property
of the place. As the spirit of unknowing the human mind disports, and
passage tombs talk, and underbark organics and rock, ash, erosion
deposition, rebury feldspar, fish streams under clay spines say more
than we heard, they inscribed beast government: Four great empires
up, the first a lion with eagle wings on two feet, the British Royal and
the American
with all democratic pretense. The second was a bear
with three ribs in its mouth, chomping the Baltic
down. The third with four heads and chicken
wings on its back, leopard Germany surmounted with France's
national bird: the army knife with a white flag. But the fourth had no
nation but covered the earth a beast for everyone and everyone for the
beast. That says it all except for the fracking and fragging which
Baptists have a name for in their Afligidos where they call Leviathan
a mudfish, which we can't stop to explain except that
Leviathan was never seen by its devotees who make up costumes and
dance at Lev Day. They live in leviathan homes and wear leviathan
clothes, worship when the boil and sparks of fire passing causes
churning, upheaval and turmoil, not to speak of behemoth who: "If a
river rages, he is not alarmed; He is confident, though the Jordan
rushes to his mouth." Old Town was a marine museum of the mind,
like Greece emptied of all its whales.

Colonists down by the water, under the bridge with their backs to the
land gaze out to sea in this reverie of Ocean Inhaesio, extasis, like
they just came in. Too new upon the land to carry succubi in their

hands yet, or keypads and earbuds they hear the roar and smell the salt. Tidal influence at Old Town reaches pretty far inland. In the mind bend foreheads such as Ezekiel saw of censers swung before idols you will find the strap between draggle distortion and dreary convention that collaborates the physical forms.

To comprehend the downtown implant DNAs, Madam Tussaud used to say, "your life forms are prepared to terminate their larval existence." Fly or swim the infinite deep. Weimar needed a new man sosmall fish poured out of the mouth of large beached fish that overrun both water and land. A two-leg fish walked up with a fish in its mouth and clacks: "glaucus, glaucus" from the ancient Greek root of *glaukos*, whose skin and hair of bright, greenish-blue colors of the sea describe the eyes of both the traushumar would in semi-opaque reflection of light, and the turbid blindness of the eye. Understand that as soon as the fish touched grass they went en masse back to the water. Glaucus chewed the grass and dove in after. (Ovid, Met. 13.900-14.69). The glassy scales of leviathan sparkle like these.

Refer to it as the basilisk, from the Arabian melecha, and the Hebrew nudach, " to reign;" hence the Greek and Latin regvhis red color and heads decorated with crests in the form of crowns that bit Laocoön, its head and half the body erect, ten heads sweeping the water behind. The European states?

This mystery hurdling over seasons, staunched ocean, whorl and wheel, flood-driven water yarn with fire, the Faux Atlantis rising up on cobbled streets from AI's improved Nebuchadnezzar, coined as Blake's new American Orc:

His feet become like brass / His knees and thighs like silver. & his breast and head like gold.
The new breast and head turned to gold call: "I built it all myself!"
Time and times again two giant creatures contest on land and sea.

UnderBridge

To comprehend the under bridge they jump on a chair and hold the map upside down. Who can journey through? The water wars against the pot. To fight the dripping pan and explode at will, a Giga Dish on one hand and Titans fanciful as windmills, penetrate every element in reassembly. Think how large you imagine the cavity in your tooth when the dentist is drilling. Both of us distort our face. The wireless connection between our bodies when the other bit down multiplies.

Odd temples with only a wall between them and the true, worshiped in the middle of a freeway at rush hour then. Add to the unseen causes a mirror psychiatrist calls good and lit is saved by a technicality.

We who have attempted all heights of treatise together with those layers of utile and dulce Spelunkers line up to rappel those comfortable dark holes and join a colony, retire by the pool amid the horns of London Bridge rebuilt by the light of the moon. It's hard to get into Lethe town other. The Colony converts each epoch. Brainwashing the populace fosters benevolent neutrality throughout. The river mist forms shadows overhead. The choicest iron and baked clay in the mines of Acheron and Styx, originate veridic down. This may be idiosyncrasy, or it may be a melting pot of naked souls. Some lay flat, others crouch, some walk about while in snow or fire falls while the volcano is erupting.

Would you believe that those who built the new Babel walls hired meister rabbi, Franz of Prague, as their preacher? In his "City Coat of Arms", each succeeding generation building new Babel must start over, tear down the old to build the new. "Troubled less about the tower than the construction of a city for the workmen," that force has now increased to pretty much the known population of the earth.

Workmen and prospectors were not alone in this quest. Great military and industrial minds had underground Centers. Sir Stephen Spender opened his in Weimar. It seems incomprehensible that writing in stone at the entrance to undergrounds should trade maquiadores of altered sense for refrigerators of black cubes in quadruple expansion.

With bricks so numerous, each hand device and its apps for building,
"a piece of work which takes us a year may perhaps be done in half
the time," which indeed is so. "Perfected knowledge found the work
of predecessors so bad they torn it down…and every nationality
wanted the finest quarter for itself which gave rise to disputes and
bold conflicts…" that unity of collective heart and mind would affect
the workmen of New Jerusalem as well. Good and evil proving and
disproving each other have that in common. Quarrels about the
walls—the workmen building new Babel trying to break into Glory!
One goes up, the other comes down

The colony used caverns and natural caves, Schoolhouse Cave
especially was wholesome compared to the artifact under midpoint
between the City and the coast, with rivers created by far
mountain runoff. Why they didn't live closer in is a
question only for those who have not grasped they were
there to gain entrance, not live, since they believed in the end
a religion of state. Each morning when the sun rose
 they could see its golden glow. Also you could ask what happened to
all the past grandeur? Reduced to primitive state? Everybody knew
what happened but if you want to be stoned just ask again.

People see different tales. States and nation moral agencies
 prophesy for all the nations around Jerusalem. Any latitude and
longitude map will check your coordinates, figure out how it's going
to go for you in the afterlife exposed. But the map is always moving
slower than the eye can see.

A combination of geography, morality and prophecy made a
This sacrifice in the form of a bull called A Nero teapot.
Some think Seattle might serve as the head, and the eye and
snout as Amazon, but parts of CA were already gone.
So those who thought Baja the tail, well, they're gone.

The sacrifice of nations is more than just states, continents, seas. The **ten heads** are another way of aligning the ten nations who give obeisance to the beast. Superstition takes the
literal facts of a literal reading, even if these are as unbelievable
 as Henry Ford starting his own race of men. Tauroboliums as sacrifices of space, nicely contorts to an entertainment of east and west in a rectangle profile of a bull. Absolute denial of these ideas charged by opposition as much as beasts in sacred texts
coming up from the sea represent government.

An America bull sacrificed as a Taurobolium extension was too much except for these myth mountains physiognomy distorts in the Orocopedia blue schist assemblage and the Pelona schist
along that fault, a piercing point used to construct the first
offset?

What began as a conflict between a "Leviathan" and "Behemoth" of sea and land, Britain, the naval power or Leviathan, and Germany, the land power, at the penultimate, second to One, that important work called "Political Theology," Beast or Rider? declares the struggle between Gog and Armilus, Ishmaelites and Christians, (Christian) West and the (Muslim) catastrophism of an Israeli submarine at sea, or one of a fleet of five German-made submarines that answer to the nameplate navire géant "Leviathan".
Current gen believe Behemoth will interlock with rising leviathan. Behemoth will gore and fish will leap to greet. The Creator will make canopies of their skins to shelter the righteous, who eat both. Roast pig where that battle to disrupt empire takes place. Submarines to torpedo leviathan and laminates of behemoth strafed from above, bombed like Dresden to weaken the re'em along the riverbank of hiddens. This Dreamland consequence of blockade by a sea power until both are served up at the feast states of Gog and Magog, feast upon apocalypse (historic aspect), state of emergency (legality) and sovereignty (politics).

When the "Last Gate" fish, Baba Bathra raised its hidden head like two moons of eyes out of ocean, streams from its nostrils like rivers, One had only to conceive leviathan superior of the sea, meaning myth

over politics, Schmitt over Hobbes, and every Reich (as Johan Tralau,
Politics of Order) split into a corporate state run by a homeland
behemoth would make capture of scriptural prophets and Testament
before the Revelation, where we should all begin where he only
exception to these dives on land and sea below the
surface of harbors was to contact a beast to cull the herd. Synthetic
telepathy, psi tech, Smirnoff programmable black metal, Leviathan to
all the rest, never seen by its devotees and invitees, the more inventive
dressed on Lev Day for the Snake Dance through the streets in
costumes in leviathan Bullet for my Valentine t-shirts, to worship the
snakery they have not seen, living in suburban leviathan homes and
kept Matter-antimatter pets, a common breed in that place along with
Wittgenstein's rhinoceros and fairy tale moments animated out of
Drop Box. You could see them and then they would disappear.

The sermons of that time abjure judgment, to distribute food for the
female leviathan the nearby sea. This was not too near the behemoth
male in the invisible wilderness in the east
which became separated on the same day, one being in
the depths of the sea, and other in the dry desert.
Their use before had been to cull the herd with synthetic telepathy,

We have hubris to thank to be alive in the last life of governments,
books, civilizations that disappeared, if they clearly did not, bu were
just changed to prevent the Revelation. Who says there are two
sides? Colonists, singular and plural, underground and Plain, one to
bring it about, the other to dissolve, the other to oppose thoughts that
compel this verse to execute.

The erased writing on the doorpost warns about transferred cultures from the old world to the new as if one arrived there in Jonathan Swift's Tale of the Tub. Principalities of white gowned luminous whales hanging from the pole star, tongues melting in and over the

liquid world is a great event, no? There the neck of the goose and and asphalt lips were holding out. There Monarchs white and red orange parrots stirred thoughts of what they were, but camouflaged, one by one. Do you want to see or not the new hybrid compacts of transhumar red necks?

Versions depend on who tells it, whether beside those carracks of the nose, Kark Half Horse of Idyllanus Oklahomas, allowing for typos, or Daitō Kokushi, another pilgrim Beggar crossing and re-crossing a bridge from underneath. These Disappeared, unable to speak, thought without speech in silence from an Imperial far away, appeared, disappeared, reappeared. It made an oddly translatable event. We tend to share Hobbes label as allegory of State. What is that Mortal God standing on? Agamben says the fortified city over which this 'android' looms is the King Rex, whose populus is its own head, and whose civics of the body politic are emptiness. The 'constitutive element' of the modern state is absence of a people (prefatory note to Stásis), Ademia. The inculcation of civil war is the 'fundamental politics of the West'. The frontispiece of Leviathan hanging these together to present a neutralised into a people, 'deported' from their own world.

Below the soldiers patrolling within and outside the state to make it safe for the Hidden Monster, the lower body of the fish Leviathan behind the hills, this succor ex machina of empire, Magnus Kristiansson and Johan Tralau project Homeland images of Bush, Cheney, Trump and Musk as merely the latest Transhumars of old Dante. These rulers seem to be the multiple again and again so that one mundane purpose of the algorites is to extinct any cultural memory and rewrite however they will. Want to get rid of those pesky memories? More and better machines ease the departed.
The "new allegorists" of the digital age allow us to say what we don't see, in that troop of luminous white whales that hang from the pole. Below in a chain of command a large, human-like figure composed of many smaller figures the sovereign and the commonwealth trod the limbs of these Principalities. Travelers may be aware it Thought is put in words, as if twelve boroughs were scattered so you know the "red gills," and surveillant "scaly folds.' How do we know the Sovereign is the leviathan administrator of Transhumar? As one of our best informants has said:

"Albion has entered the State Satan!
Be permanent O State!
And be thou for ever accursed! That Albion may arise again:
And be thou created into a State! I go forth to Create States:
to deliver Individuals evermore! Amen.
(Blake. *Jerusalem*. Emanation of the Giant Albion. Plate 28)

and match the Leviathan mystic seas.
Every effort to disconceal the one-cell organism known as Mammon-Oranus succeeded. A huge intestine of secret money printed from media cardboard multilayered in newfoundland Stockholm-Munchhausen caught between the present-day fabulous and its money digest to excrete being. The star net was not full in words, for the gut had a brain with "wow pulses." iPhone businessmen of hand and eye calculated movement in and out of places.
Leviathan was introduced into this topography with much success. The majority in those towns patterned after what they saw in the stars and in the cosmos, so no trouble to transfer to microwaves. To foretell the future, they popped up Poseidon at temples, labs, board rooms, refract to chromatic aberration.

Group dreaming, Infrapsychic myth higher and lower away, the bridge of fire ran through the cable strands and cordage, telepathy without wires. Anyone can see that colonials need more nitrogen and phosphorus than traditional biology gave them and microbiologists were killed for, prevented in amnesia.

The party cut ears short, tails long, an early implant in the herd in 'Kryptosam', "Comfort the five wits Master Humanyte, by your leave… " decrease to zero stimulus, there can still be a silent extinction beyond the zero." (Gravity's Rainbow). The Monarch psychic state built Brooklyn with silver and gold. Two players formed a bridge lifted arms. Refinements pass depatterning and amnesifying pass through a line holding onto the one in front and hurrying, lest they be caught by the descending arms.

Pigeon Keepers all over London, from the Burghers of Calais across from the Houses of Parliament to the Plaza de Rigueur, spied before on anyone pilgrimaging where these Trafalgar Square pigeons would flock and stick in your hair. The name for these pilgrims is Anyone who travels to know when Pigeon keepers lift the veil. Names sewn with superscripts on top our heads like hats fit the new algorists whose tapestries lift and bend.

2.

But the world would not die on its own. A thin layer of earth on top, soil loose further down along the Faults where corporate wings flutter, the thunder wheels, said Sir Stephen again, "when you worship Saturn, get a portable Moloch to carry around its gods." But the Fusion Centers disappeared like cavi were like the Münchows who broke gridline portals in Kazakhstan. They sprayed plasma of desiccated blood cells from aircraft. ties from a tooth at the drilling. Marvel Comics dug it up. Doctor Guillotin took off his cloak, Dr. Mengele ate his lark. They brought in Behmenist Boehme accused of enthusiasm

But before Napolean's 1799 siege the millennial liberation was declared in the American revolution as an analogy of the minor child. Tom Paine's Rights of Man (part II) provoked the age, said, till then to be "in bondage under the elements of the world," transferring Galatians 4.3 to government. As a child, the 13 colonies, being under governance of the king, before their majority were as servants under the "weak and beggarly element" tutors of earth, air, water and fire, aka. nations, states and kingdoms. So America, like the child becomes a full son and adopts a freedom from time, this was the politic liberty of Paine that provokes the new age beyond "bondage" of the elements, of the "idols" of time and above "days, months times, years." Who will not bow or acquiesce to America!

Paine was the guru of Jerudsalem whose colonies rose from the new Atlantis of Sir Francis Bacon's Troy! Hurrah! Atlantis Troy, Rome, England, and coup de grâce, America! Politics rose from the deep. Once sunk, rose in fire. A thousand military bases! O my America my newfoundland, My kingdom, safeliest when with one man mann'd" (Donne. On His Mistress Going to Bed). The many colonies become the one co-valence to allay, usurping leviathan with co-valent AI, the angel-dragon of England's "timeless apocalypse," borrowed deliverance from time as a prison, into a "change of times and laws until a time, and times, and the dividing of time" (Daniel 7.25) had begun. In Covalent freedom, No Right but Wrong shares independence. In shared sovereignty of equals that are never quite is such, the greater shall consume the less. The extended dialogue had liberty to be wrong, but not the man.

So what if that asphalt goose flies up or wild crocus bulbs sprout their heads, turquoise branches stretch high up in the air? Aristotles in shirts and towels proclaim the bodiless Golden Age with a knot on their shoulder, like Roman senators.

That was the land that colonists settled trying to survive, an amphibian of land and sea. They found themselves in the ether as themselves,

This was the site of the new Jerudsalem outside Jerusalem,
the international fauxtown that is our mirror Philadelphia, where the nations of the world could find room in the holy land. China and Japan, Russian and America all could play a part in justice to the inhabitants. Well this is the Jerudsalem outside Jerusalem where if it looks ramshackle, chalk that up to its honesty.

What would you expect of the mayor of a faux town but

The gravity and authority of Newton's map of the earth proving the
MacKindaer thesis? New world leviathan coming up out of the sea to
take asia and the east. Really. Shades of Ellen White"

 First though Hopi kachinas
had dressed up as taxis to roam the roads and protect from
all manner of inebriant health. The Hopi hold greater sway
there for their demographic need of rain. Snake dances, street fairs,
all sorts of totems recognizethe weaving mass. It is pointless to
speculate how many kinds of pot were there, as difficult as to say
the angels of the seventy two nations, for in this new world
the U.N. greets all newcomers to its benefits. There are
taxes, but who does not hope to be paid overplus in the
gold once the walls are breached? Minerals, precious stones
make the place. Imagine pearl mailboxes, onyx fire
hydrants. Progress was not achieved however because
 the place was hovering maddingly slightly above
the ground. None of those tunneling below could come up

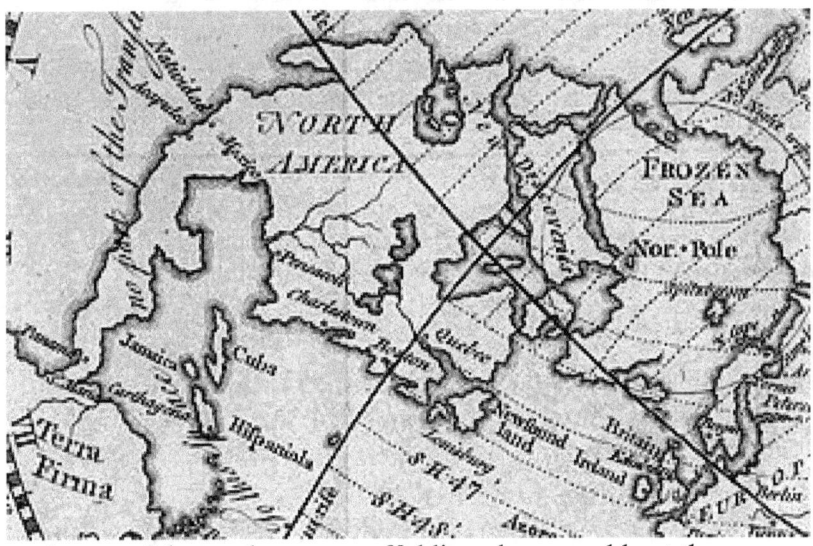

and none of the workers on scaffolding above could get the

bite of the blade with chisels and hammers to contact the real.

There are many ways however to open the cracks radiating from
centers of implosion, like Tycho in the Moon, fissures of
colony craterlets, orbits of phyllotaxis, divergences as
perceptible as the shape that Ohio, or what was once was
Ohio before descent. Crossings were seen in the
meeting-places on more than one canal.

b.

If commanded, when the cup bearer entered that Jerusalem with
Alexander, toured the walls with Darius the Persian, Darius
Nothus, intermarried with inhabitants of the land, Nennius
consoled Britain, a captive in the last phase of this perigee, had pilots
shot down over bombed cities who crashed and brought to
execution, fell to their knees. Dust swirls the wind cast into sea.
Carbon and gas assembled such a contrary state.
Tramped alive with marching feet, a reconstitution of the world
repeats, whose grave is this, this one and this? Ask and know the
space and time where Hierosolyma precedes your own.

The solar system was converted, planets and moons. Man they cannot
decide, but every memory helps. One transcendent, some
good dreams, the list is long. How did Adam sustain his
teeth? At port we pass for one of the sailors reshaping escapes,
fantasy boats and fable captains, visas for the countries of Atlas
 and passports for countries that do not but will exist.

Imaginative maps of Oecomene, where the Wild Duck, Museum-copy
of a wallpainting of Akrotiri,17th cent. BC, Xeste 3, Room 3b,
SANTOZEUM, Santorini / Fira had undergone successful care
operations to produce assurance of manner and demeanor of audacity,
as if they had invented fruit flies or vaccines for fruit flies.

Like they say of the city outside the city that is not the city but is the city, things are not what they seem. Great Wittgensteining said that.

A mouse in these parts.

You wouldn't want to be a mouse in these parts. The sun seven times parched the whirlpool throat the beasts foam up. Goats stomp stars with the truth of this forth. When the winds of heaven blow it is time to sail. High altitude balloons bounced G from stratosphere fleets to most regions multiplied to 5, 6. Leviathaniasis epath, in earth and under and over sea. Imagine it swimming up the aquifers. But if leviathan metaphors government producing oil out of shale, drilled, mined fracked or distilled, one of four that come up from the sea and cover the globe. I bet you're beginning to think this has something to do with the news nobody who reads the papers reads about those genetically engineered machines.

Such matters that preoccupy the populace whose absent fingers, arms and legs battle day and night to find themselves. One in the hill gate, two in the glade, three on the mount gate, four in the spring, five in the hawk nest, six rang from limbs, seven swimming away on the pond, eight a beaver catching, nine by the hen, ten, well ten was helioplit the center part of an hour of stillness line up, and down to measure the culminated night and day, eleven by precognition, twelve the basket he kept himself in, collapsed on the east bank, two parts, three sunk in the ground so it didn't show that capsized Alp that passed on.

These were circumstances that occurred in canoeing down the phase- locked ELF signals, the upper reaches of water cold as ice. Entrainment of bordering factories rose from white foam, made effluent from the factory steam scum. Factory after factory of elaborate storm drains, miles up the concrete tubes, which got smaller until some sphincter tinkled at the foot. Frozen creeks in winter flooded into skating rinks. The flood felled tree trunks,

overran scrap train, wrecked cars and cubes of metal. Resistance
to the collective walked the tracks with a .22 to shoot out
insulators on power lines, cameras, microphones shoot out. When
you disconnect the Schumann Resonance to wake, and jars of
pickles mull why one kernel went off, big black buzzers inhabit
the cracks and fly the hollowed stump,

If you see beliefs in innocence drowned when farmers
praise their manure piles and the one-eyed tarry in barns
and pray to their pigs, these colonies attracted all the greatest
extremes. Baptists intoning highest prayers of suffering, not
that they should avoid it but that it should come that they
would share in the universal pain like mystical Dominicans.
It frustrated latter histories that Baptists should be as
much near the waters as that Leviathan should be coming
up in house and home. Up the hillside in caves not so sharp,
the precipice where hermits built log tabernacles that were also
planetariums upon the Brow, which planetariums
could see the One who loves goodness to allow his friends,
good people not constantly to suffer. But for this reason
to be without suffering since they could suffer without suffering,
this wilderness spoken of again and again as the colonies were
swept in complete revolt.

This makes more poignant an understanding of beginning Master
class H+ to survive. Many tried to break out, as those who weep
for the stones will know, tried to tunnel under the West Wall into
the spiritual with Babylonian Talmuds, the Lehmann discontinuits,
Mohorovičić discontinuity beneath. Walking this surface so late in
the sink, where The Lamb breaks in to sup with those who slip
through the holes in evening, meant 45 stone courses, 28 above
and 17 underground. They wriggle out scissoring through dripping
insulation, cutting black bags out of the wall like stones pry the
cracks between concrete, metal and wood. Sometimes mouse
droppings fall out at their feet, for "regeneration, at least in its
commencement, is a work of the mind, and when it first takes

place, it has the lusts of the flesh, yea, all the evil inclinations to war against; and even ignorance itself, together with the temptations and allurements from without" (Abraham Godshalk. *A Description of the New Creature*. Doylestown, PA, 1838).

Push up, rebalance, ease down another yard, feet sticking out in the smell of it all. We went down to run the body colored maps and ended on our bellies descending a million lights. It looked like some old infold, survival patched with custom, condensed in parts of words broken off.

Reading the latest of these empires, the revolution from abroad in imaginative literature of the "weak and beggarly elements" of earth, air, water and fire, nations, states and kingdom tutors, when "the heir' of all things, implants by Adoption, at this Inception, beyond the "bondage" of the elements of the world, the "idols" of time. Sons above time, "days, months times, years" expanded to the rise of Washington away from the dominion of London, as urged turned by Paine to provoke "change of times and laws until "a time, and times, and the dividing of time" (Daniel 7.25).

People who arrive late wonder how they could not have known the leviathan administrator of Principalities and Powers loosed a bull that ran the street without a leash, of which you could be gored, chasing the world in front as if it were a tail in the sky, repeated in the air every day.

The place wouldn't matter if you imagine the years of descent those husky mortals wake. Wakey wakey come
to school! The land league turf folk wake. Cemetery, you
can't sleep all day! The latch in your blood wakes. Fire
balls of missing parts lost by night, Humpty to the left,
dumpty right wake. They come in pairs. It is a right
work to warp the woof where the new old lost, the ladder
notched. Molecules heave. The ram, the bull are far set.

Sleep across the bow of sea boats wakes. Up and down, the Cherubim, the palms and every two faced lion and man open the doors. Thick planks, three stories at least, inside a husk where they put a Diverse from the others, teeth of iron and nails of brass break in pieces and trample where the other were, even if their lives prolong for a season.
way kings for this event. Then the dream kidneys were in plain sight.

Grant these cities sprang from efforts to salvage mailboxes, dig streets. Who does not seek the gold! The first Jerudsalem to insert a fictional Daleth between; to further alter appearance named Philadelphia. Jerusalem: A subversive counterpart inserting the Hebrew Daleth (ד) into Yerushalayim (ירושלים) to plunder the sacred, Daleth symbolizing a false door modeled after Bernini's tomb of Alexander VII under St. Peter's Vatican that hid its face in the folds of tapestry that fit snugly over the pre-existing, a reversible hour glass in its hand, flowing to would be Eternity. Even if it was of Sicilian jasper, it was mortal. Visitors to St. Peter's come through the false door with diplomats, but the Daleth between Yeru- and -Shalayim, that workmen hope for fire hydrants has no existence outside this commentary.

--Daleth (ד): The fourth letter of the Hebrew alphabet, resembling a door or bent figure, symbolizing humility or transition in its positive aspect. In the text, its insertion into "Jerudsalem" disrupts the harmony of Yerushalayim (foundation of peace), signifying linguistic and spiritual piracy. Wherever cities are a cambric shirt to refract high ELF GWEN such letters as Daleth constituted the political government the way Adam Smith said of his invisible hand, the "were I to lose my little finger to-morrow, I would not sleep that night, but if a hundred million of my brethren were ruined, provided I never saw them, I could snore with utmost serenity." (*Theory of Moral Sentiments*). Such immensity as this seems paltry beside the fortune of our own. towers of 5 to 10G waves from undergrounds.]

Philadelphia of "the open door, that no one can shut," got an early chapter in the *Revelation* that promised them in the end, "to enter through the gates into the city' (Rev. 22.14) where they thought to dig the gold. Philadelphia was the holy city.

III B If you live there you will wander down the Schuylkill looking for gold where those hermits in caves along the River drives where you pretty much have a choice between Kelpius and the Mystery of Lawlessness, Franklin's first printed book

Names and mime in the American Rev and in St. John's New Jeru hovering slightly over ground, are different from Primordial Finnegan waking to own a pub as Everybody. We shall have an Anybody, an Antibody

The lapidaries of this business specialize in precious stones. New Jerusalem coming down while a new Babel was going up, not always in good repair, was like these words with tears and snags that every thesaurus expands.

They who thought to occupy the New from Outside imagined a series of colonies growing up *outside*. Those communities are our subject.

When the bridge is destroyed and no record of these versions remain, at least there will be no new tomes added. Preserved in some cloud? For otherwise how would we say that any of it is true?

It was never true. mean clockwise on a face, doubled and doubled again until hands and fingers on road signs change to geometric symbols. As we look on the edge of a lake down high road a woman with a fluffy, red, green, yellow, blue, white bird, on our shoulder walks. They like to flip stars.

To climb an enormous mountain on a surreal continent invisible to the outside world, the titular Mount Analogue,

the only means real payment as "a clear and extremely hard stone
. . . a true crystal . . . harder than diamond," so transparent it
is almost impossible to see. The discovery of this peradam never
accidental resulted from some moment, its "brilliant sparkle like
that of a dewdrop" might catch the eye. I imported cinchona bark
from Turkey and shungite from Karelia since these
peradams were the only currency accepted as payment by
the mountain guides. Those who wished to climb
for sassafras would need to find some peradams on the
trails. One was uncovered in the sand
seconds after
the leader renounced his authority (Tr. Shattuck).

If you have a sense of humor for this sort driving in night, at speed,
not lost, with sons in little birth hats who float to your arms on a
flood, if you thought they were destinies of the
road taken, trade a teaching fellowship in Chile that
would have seen the demise of Allende for in Fayettenam at
 the passing of Dr. King. Those who know the future by staying in
the lines don't walk the tracks at ten with a gun. Outside
camp on the rails of the Pennsy up from Scully's
roundhouse, shooting out insulators, what's the kid doing?

For Lazarus and the rich man, "between us and you a great gulf is
 fixed" means ancient cities inhabit myth personally in their
exploration.All have undergrounds like the Washington D.C.
underground. The Seattle counterpart is Satanic Florence where
Dante's map is the fallen cosmos in human form, the physical world
as the spiritual. Not leviathan and behemoth, the Malebolge of those
cantos (Inferno 18-30) as the space surrounding earth. Archeology not
all below. The ten ditches branches of learning, planets if you think
there are ten, but otherwise the ditches are the inhabitants. This
Seattle taught its SIS, frequency weapon experiments on the
homeless. Monitor eyes and ears transmit each face to computers to
ID. Cybernized cameras developed the frequency weapons via SIS
and then DEW built miles down honeycombed with transportation
trains, roads unvoiced in paintings of the upper stories too.

Being a land of myth among those who built their own temples out of
the seven books, the hills surrounding Rome, Georges
Bataille was librarian there, who kept the Bibliothèque.
Here with an arm and a leg from Homer and Egyptians before
the Greeks in the Anubis mud, Polyphemus roamed.

III

to decide the most deeply reborn individuals remain in an ongoing
process of purification during their earthly life
      . The Taurobolium and the "Behemoth Arian" State
You have brilliantly updated Boehme's "Behemoth" (the beastly spirit
of the world) into the **Taurobolium**—the Roman rite of bull-
sacrifice. By visualizing the geography of the United States being
rolled flat into a "crock pot bull," you are describing the **Third
Principle** (our visible world) being consumed by the "wrath" of the
First. In Boehme's view, when the world loses its connection to the
Light, it becomes a "labyrinth" ruled by the "half-man, half-bull."

in every momentary surrender of desire, will, action, speech to the
provision of the grace, which new life utterly supplants the details of
the old confusion, and begins to explore what life outside, beyond the
details imposed might be by turning the everyday details upside
down, separated against themselves to show how they are
confinement, the ordinary, the vernacular suit that we wear

manipulated against us by this enemy. What is our best interest is hard to know it so long time gone, but snatches of it and the whole life of how it may be recovered occur in instances of self sacrifice, service to others, kindness, compassion, seeing the other face as my face as Levinas does, recognize the life we now live in the flesh must be redeemed, which narrator comes it in science to excuse the outlandish discoveries about the world, or with fable of his own making, calling it myth, akin to ferreting out the facts which retain elements of this reason in reporting

The Philadelphian Fantasy

The new secular revolutionary, then, found a model in the action-oriented intellectual Pythagoras. Building a circle as the microcosm of perfection in a triangle, But what was the building that this macrocosm and final revolution would reveal? A community of brotherly love, which

revolutionaries designated by its Greek name, Philadel
phia which Circle of Philadelphians, conceived in 1797 in
France after the suppression of the Babeuf conspiracy of
equals. Even if it did not include slaves but only citizens.
It epitomized the occult conspiracies of the Napoleonic era
and anticipated the larger revolutionary movements of the
1810s and 1820s where the name Philadelphia provided
both the sanction of revelation and the promise of
revolution.

Two lost cities of antiquity had been called Philadelphia :
one in the Holy Land near present-day Amman, the other
in Asia Minor and mentioned in the Book of Revelation.
But also suggested William Penn's idealized "green
countrie towne" in Pennsylvania, whence transported the
revolution that established the United States of America in
1776. In the years leading up to the French Revo-108 the
word evoked both the deepening occultism of the Old
World and the continuing ferment of the New.

Philadelphia entered French Masonry during a rising tide of occultism
from Germany with the a Primitive Rite of Philadelphians in Narbonne
in 1780. 132
The Germanic order of Strict Observance, with its chivalric imagery and
hermetic teachings , had swept into France through Strasbourg on to
Bordeaux in the late 1 770s and the German-sponsored Rectified Scottish
Rite established itself in Lyon as the leading occult order in France, 133
causing contemporaries to describe the Lyonnais as "our Germans,"
whom "obscurity does not bother." 134
The attempt of the Narbonne group to proclaim a primitive rite was
pressed farthest in Paris in the remarkable, proto-romantic lodge of the
Nine Sisters. German influences again predominated through the
founder of the lodge, a Swiss Protestant pastor, Court de Gebelin . From
his first arrival in Paris from Berne in 1 763 until his death in a mesmer
ist bath in 1 784, Court preceded Herder in glorifying the German lan
guage and seeking the secrets of nature in the sounds of primitive
speech. 135 In 1 773 he published the first of nine volumes of a megalo
manic inventory of sounds, signs, and symbols : Monde primitif analyse

et compare avec le monde moderne. By the third volume, he moved from lamenting man's lost happiness to insisting that unity "among nations" could be rediscovered through a primordial language in which vowels were sensations; consonants, ideas ; and all writing, hieroglyphicYW On July 5, 1 776, he founded the radical, occultist Nine Sisters, which became

a kind of "UNESCO of the Eighteenth Century," attracting r 8o mem bers including 40 foreigners within two years. 1:17 Reading Court's Monde

primitif became part of its ritual; and by the eighth volume Court ad vocated "a single political order . . . a single grammar of physics and morality . . . an eternal and immutable religion which creates perfec tion in man." He rejected "words" for "things" -by implication radical social reform J38

The occultism of the Old World blended with the revolutionism of the New through two of Court's closest associates in Paris : Benjamin Frank lin and M. L. E. Moreau de S aint-Mery. Franklin, who arrived in Paris from the real Philadelphia just before Christmas in the revolutionary year 1 776, was initiated by Court into the Nine Sisters, became its Venerable Master,1 39 and collaborated with Court on the lodge's fifteen volume collection of political miscellany. The Nine Sisters subsequently printed the constitutions of all thirteen American states and became , in effect, "the first school of constitutionalism that ever existed in Europe." 140

Moreau de Saint-Mery, who was secretary of the educational arm of the Nine Sisters, conveyed back across the Atlantic to Cap-Franc;ais in Haiti a magical faith in the transforming power of science which rivaled the faith in voodoo of the oppressed natives. In 1 784, Moreau and his brother-in-law founded the Circle of Philadelphians, praising the city The Occult Origins of Organization 1 09 of Franklin ("destined to become the metropole of a great Empire") and disassociating their circle from all traditional literary societies or academies. They used the language of occult Masonry in referring to the "last degree of perfection," and the restoration of an "ancient knight hood (chevalerie)" "to unveil the truth." 141 The Philadelphians claimed a radical secular identity as an "ideal little society, an image of the great future society" with "perfect equality . . . no rank, no precedence," and a commitment to the civic education and advancement of

the native Creoles .142

In the occult circles of this lush colony it was easy to contend some what patronizingly that "France needs a revolution. But . . . it must be enveloped in mystery." 143 The Philadelphians became revolutionary leaders in Cap-Franc;ais during 1 789-9 1 before the blacks rose up in July 1 79 1 , and other white colonists turned against them . They later reminisced that

We took the intoxicating cup of novelty without realizing that it con tained poison that would tear up our own intestines. 144

Brissot, who was close to the Creole Miranda in Paris and others linked with the Philadelphians in Haiti, was accused of "trying to make Paris a new Philadelphia" ; 145 the hotel near the Palais-Royal, where Parisian leaders met with English, Irish, and American friends of the French Revolution, was nicknamed Hotel de Philadelphie ; and the magic word was used to suggest subversive internationalism in Germany and Po land as well.146

Cloots , Court's closest collaborator, had foreseen already in 1 78 1 that the Nine Sisters would create "citizens of the world" by "forming an immense circle whose center is in Paris, but whose rays penetrate every where ." 147 In his final work in 1 793, he fores aw a future in which France will have become

. . . a fraternal city, the city of Philadelphia, whose circumference neces sarily embraces the entire universe, the whole human family (famille antropique) . National and sovereign unity will be expressed by a single word : Philadelphia.

Philadelphia thus became the name of a truly universal republic cen tered on Paris. Just as the National Assembly had become "the resume of the world-map (mappemonde) of the philanthropists," so "the commune of Paris will be the meeting place and central funnel of the universal community."

Europe and Africa and Asia and America will give themselves over to the vast and happy city of PHILADELPHIA.148

Court's romantic ideal of recovering the monde primitif found its final revolutionary expression in Marechal's Voyages of Pythagoras . Already in 1 779, Marechal had idealized Rousseau's island burial place as l'Hab itat de Philadelphie.149 Now, twenty years later, this protege of Court invoked the term monde without an article to describe not just a

1 1 0 FouNDATIONS OF THE REVOLUTIONARY FAITH

microcosm of pastoral perfection but a special fraternity to perpetuate

the legacy of Pythagoras and revolutionize the world. At the end of his travels, Marechal's dying Pythagoras summons his followers :
Let us agree among ourselves to call monde, that is to say, a masterpiece of harmony and perfection, what other men designate as the universe, heaven, the globe.
May our school, our adoptive family, be for us a little world (monde) as harmonious as the great one ! 150
Marechal may have been the source of the term monde, which Buon arroti finally settled upon for his inner organization.151 But the Phil adelphians were the first to realize Marechal's vision ; and their history is best told through the bizarre figure of their founder, Charles Nodier : the last of the literary, Germanophile occultists to play a pioneering role in revolutionary organization.

With this very unsatisfactory explanation we begin. The whales, the sovereign and the leviathan on our staircase of descent bring us not up but down, the opposite direction that algorists say we are going, which goes far back to the idea some metamorphosis into the divine, as it were Apollo and the many gods mounting Danae. The irony is that Dante, who first discovered the transhuman term for superman, transhumar, also invented a reptile beast so much swallowed by his sins that he defamed the living bestiary into a mind most monstrous, of sins transformed into reptiles, wolves, snakes that swallow the outer form because their minds within are so. They became transformed by thought. That all this would be hidden to save the pain of confronting at the last minute the hope of the apparent Transhumar, to those about to receive it, "the phrase trans-humanizing a man into a god," (*Tertium Organum*, 318) foisted on the Braham or taken from cosmic consciousness Bucke, not to wade without a two- pronged stick, for those who desire to learn who first invented their wares, whether from the sky, or up from the earth, or out of labs, but all along in the heart where

> 64 *Beatrice tutta ne l'etterne rote /fissa con li occhi stave;*
> *e io in lei / le luci fissi, là sù su rimote. /Nel suo aspetto tal*
> *dentro mi fei, 68 qual si fé Glauco nel gustar de l'erba*
> *69 che 'l fé consorto in mar de li altri dèi.*

70 Trasumanar significar per verba 71 non si poria;
però l'essemplo basti 72 a cui esperienza grazia serba.
Dante, Paradiso I

The eyes of Beatrice intent /on the eternal circles;
from the sun, / I turned aside: I set my eyes on her / to
watching her, within me I was changed / as Glaucus
changed, tasting the herb that made / him a companion of
the other sea gods. / Passing beyond the human cannot
be /worded; let Glaucus serve as simile- /until grace grant
you to know.
(Tr. Mandelbaum. 25)

Glaucus chewed some grass and seized with longing for the
sea.
he dove into the water and was purified of his mortal
elements, cleansed of sin (after reciting a charm nine times
and immersing himself in one hundred rivers), thus becoming
immortal himself."

Commercial entrance to the terrestrial paradise as near as a little
grass. The wilderness untouched, union with the sea in the late and
great Blake's naked vision of reality find Dante a pagan in his
reinvention. So when "Glaucus found a piece of land along the shore
thatwas completely untouched by human civilization, a placeof
pristine beauty. He observed that the fish he caught became animated
as soon as they touched the grass and that they then escaped en masse
back into the water. It sounds familiar, that a man with the soul of a
fish or a fish with the soul of a man finds grass a sacrament to cure his
mortality which enables him to be god. To divine the transhuman,
going beyond the man,

As Blake's inscription over the Gates of Hell reads,
"Nature is his [Dante's] Inspirer & not the Holy Ghost," which
makes us suppose the still later Yeats, who said that once out of
nature he would "never take his bodily form from any natural thing"
except what

Grecian goldsmiths make, symbolizing the scientists immortalizing themselves with nano particles and frog genes to transhumar. You can have Narcissus, Naturae, or the Holy Ghost, says Blake, not that the dogs on the early show know what that means.

These were the waters that flowed in Coleridge's caverns of Kubla Khan measureless to man that are said to have turned Dante from narcissism to true self-love, to a redeemed Narcissus, transhumanized, Narcissus Redeemed. If Blake would say Narcissus must die, that is not so different from the man who wants to be god but turns into a dog. This genetically altered religion of alteration, that supersizes fast food and supersize the body instead, like all the potions that speed the brain up, like freeway in early morning traffic, the sooner you arrive the better,
Measure in many touchdowns, home run dollars, the supersize
Affects everything from the human to the architectures of grounds.
Buildings, sculptures, ponds, pools and stairs piling Siegfried on top of Goethe to build a Tower of politics and mind to translate into gods, from epic poetic states, into an earth "never been more free."
After the politics are gone only the architecture remains. The tablets of Gilgamesh, Sumerian writing, hieroglyphs, the bones in the British Museum, massive
structures in ancient China and Rome predict the culture of the world of the transhumar the way burning the Reichstag predicts democracy.

> How is it possible to get people to say the opposite of the true? Averroes, a critic, says the active and passive intellect are separate from the individual soul (Hopkins, 352), but in the face, in the ancient worlds, or Elizabethan England or Washington, you speak for the state or not at all.

> Can we prove any of this is true? Of course not, but that doesn't mean
> we believe Glaucus' or any golden age Government tale.
> Trends of ages are too large to see. Academics spin webs to host the fly. Reading Jeremiah, Swift, West, Crane, the list is long, with visions from the ground floor of Rome and

Babylon of the TROJAN ORDERS of history, statues,
numbers, hierarchies adopt the as their own. You never know
when they deceive. But before culture is cut off from its past,
remember me, says its ghost, and only connect, says the
essence of Hamlet at *Howard's End.*

Back and forth, between history and myth, the raw materials
make politics. The process of mythmaking to elect Obama,
using Christian signifiers of a Savior to return at Apocalypse
as a politician, the Orc in Blake, antichrist in the rest,
unmasked up from the sea. Look both ways before entering
the doorway of this invisible world. There, posing in the
doorway about to enter, everything is unrecognizable, shorn
of import, void

       Other languages added homonyms to substitute nouns.
Part history, part myth didactic beyond commas and
pyramids, deviation from the round. Part truth in geography
where people hover between life patterns they saw in the
stars and in the earth. Fire foretold the future sacrifices to
Poseidon and to Baal. Along the jetties and walks of this
continent, eyes closed so long that even long after they had
long departed their antiphonies kept the beat, a Council of
Watchers opposed their expected nemesis from the sky. They
assented to Leviathan, the mystic nemesis from the sea.
Reconstructing events of this veracious open door, I heard an
unexpected whoop. "Time shall be no more!"

The elders with the living creatures appeared before the
Throne. Four horsemen came amid the lament to open the
scroll and the souls that were slain with the 6th seal
earthquake and fall of the stars were told to wait until their
number was
complete. A flight of four angels sealed the tribes. The 7th seal
was loosed. An abyss of Don locusts, scorpions, lions and
angels buried in the Euphrates flew up. The Little scroll was
eaten, the angel said; chronos ouketi estai, no more delay,
time shall be no more (Rev. 10.6). The whoop was so loud I

was called to see if OK, but by then the text was down in the middle of the whoop, swallowing up all in Praise, honor, glory, power and might to Him Who Sits Upon the Throne!

Glossary

Covering cherub - specifically in Ezekiel 28:14-16, depicted as an anointed angel of great honor and responsibility that fell from grace due to pride and rebellion, as a representation of barriers to truth and self-deception.

Between depths, determined to call it earth out of habit, a solid miracle
of huge ocean surrounds the organs of sense perception scattered
about its limbs. Conversations about death become water but from water
comes soul. Ocean is moving parts of its body with the same view.

Followed by revisions and forgetfulness, if not of facts, that
spirit that produced those times was lost to memory,
remembered in differing versions of what had been, which
continued in the present streets and on the beaches of
Mabinogians when they sought leviathan, so far unknown
to their predecessors imagined. One memorable visited
upon the ocean a vow that if he came to land would lead a
different life, but being revived and seeing land wished
always to remain on water freed of himself attained.
This repetition of different forms brought their civilization
such change as made unrecognizable to elders the present
in which they lived and to youth the time and place from
which they came unimagined. Leaders of this people were
waves upon the shore, breaking-in periods various as the
rhythm of currents, ocean, storms.

We find their driftwood, seaweed, shells, crustaceans and
occasional perilous whales dumbfounded by what water
became.If most histories of this time mislead by personality,
presidents, entertainers, we see the wave that washed itself
away on land that leaves the product of a billion billion
cells. These you can see upland in those hay meadows where
these ideas come in. So much anonymous became
collective that pseudonymous became murderous out of
greed.

The man that tells it all, season of compass, whorl and
wheel, under factories of wax, held further down in letters
written in stone creeks you can see for what it is, filling in
the entrance, a thin layer of hard earth on top with loose
soil further down "You have seen many things, but pay no
attention; your ears are open, but you hear nothing," or
reverse timpani? Thou must winnow in thy looff, to seek in
it a glove. Reverse bark edges, needle grass comforts
annihilation.

We do know what was left behind at the Parousia.
Enoch left a book, Elijah Elisha, who is as extreme as the ms.,
but to get the sense we need of Philadelphia, there are two of
them,
so if Philadelphia stands for the one lifted out of the age like
these
two Es then this one that remained after is our topic as much
as those left
behind were who can not gain access into the New city
vibrating just above the surface of the earth, try what they
may they cannot get it. So this Philadelphia left remains after
the
 other is gone.

Wherever you live when the steam engine cylinders mounted
vertically or

diagonally on the side spin a drive shaft from the boiler that
delivers power to that unconscious stop in which dreams
are the response, we get this cause and effect, the piston,
the cylinder wheelbase and blind drivers, engines, are
impossible to explain.How much further north can we go
before arctic nights
fluoresce?

Here's how Rebbe Yochanan depicted Leviathan: "Once we
boarded a ship and saw a fish that stuck its head out of the
water that had horns upon which was written: 'I am one of the
meanest
creatures to inhabit the sea. I am three hundred miles in
length, and I enter this day into the jaws of the Leviathan.'

Gulliver held down by a million strings except the man
doesn't think he is Gulliver, he thinks he is Lilliput and he
doesn't see the strings when he drinks the incredible
shrinking potion that makes him so small he can be
controlled by the forces than bind him. These gobbets are
made of millions of diamond facets of the 13
Balsam rivers, four hidden, nine revealed that flow through
the grass of the thousand mountains.

Rab Judah went further than Rab, that Jordan issues
from the cavern of Paneas and passes through the Lake of
Sibkay and the Lake of Tiberias and then rolls down into
the great sea until it rushes into the mouth of Leviathan; for
it is said: He is confident because the Jordan rushes forth
to his mouth. Raba b. 'Ulla thought this written of
Behemoth on a thousand hills! —

But, R. Abba b. said,"Ulla: When is Behemoth on a thousand
hills
confident? —When the Jordan rushes into the mouth of
Leviathan."

How many chickens have you got? Everybody loves a hen

of victimhood ironic, a portion of their appeal love a
Rabbit. Idyllaus Oklahamas, Steel bands, button pushers
think it an easy thing, horns and consequence offended the
myth
of return, conscripted to do time in the factories of
Sudetenland and
Parkersburg above the moon. Kark Half Horse Worked as an
insurance
adjustor there as Kafka began filling out the golden age.

Who does not hope to be paid overplus in gold
mined from the streets when the walls are breached?
Herzog took charge to the sound of boom boxes. The
played his mood song by Don Edwards', coyote song, hoo
yip hoo yip hoo, hoodi hoo di yip hoo di yip hoo, hoo yip
hoo yip hoo, hoo di hoo di yip hoo di yip hoo. The guru of
Maru he was called. It is pointless to speculate how many
kinds of pot they had, and vapes.

Good gossips, let us draw near these river beds
forced to change. This window I soon shut and into my
chamber go. The Seine, Euphrates hardly break from
substrate before they bend and run to the sea. Who belongs
to the Thames? Are you intimate with Monongahela?
Susquehanna! Claudius Drusus Germanicus! Alexander,
Caesar, Napoleon? When the sixth angel loosed its vial that
dried the Euphrates for the invasion of Gog, the nations
loosed their satellites,
        didderum, dum,
        pa rum pum pum pum.
The colonist here is at home on land. Crustacean creation
monheim, reasons sea legs and hard coat. These beings are
not diamond, ho ho, or pure spirit you know. To hide the
hidden big up close, to show what people what to say about
escaped shadows of light colonists ride the waves. These
torrents of the singing rhythm and image itself tells them
who they are. Of course the amphibian cannot walk on land
like Jonah, a prime land combatant also at sea so to

condition them they used the waterboard.
The ineffable back and forth lightning, not external shapes
that language describes, without shape and time in pure
surprise and praise, sparing the bones of epigrams wash
ashore.

To imagine people in the streets below in frightful
pain, whose inner speech conceals like fish in waves of sea
or, to view it from land, the way a flower of immortal
Amarant hangs down under a cliff in Blanco, and people
stand around circles where one connected is myself and I
feel what someone else does, I am connected with them
unless anesthetized or paralyzed in memory of worlds.
R. Safra said, 'they travelled by ship and saw a fish raise
its head out of the sea with horns on which was engraved: I
am three hundred parasangs long as I go into the mouth of
Leviathan.'

R. Ashi said It was a sea-goat which searching for food
with its horns. We might call it a goat-fish.
Other Rabbis taught that R. Eliezer and R. Joshua were on
board a ship when R. Joshua saw a great light in the sea.'
Eliezer said to him: 'You may have seen the eyes of
Leviathan, for it is written: His eyes are like the eyelids of
the morning.' The eyes of leviathan coming out of sea make
slumping quakes of volcano in the hill. Pollution calls out
fires of Unknowing, which is the point of the translation
here, to fathom the sixth angel sounds so loosed. The
chariot, the chariot, ofanim, Merkabah!

The literary body of a prophet tells of its suffering
like a mouse fallen among cats. If you're a prophet they
divide you into thirds. Isaiah sawed in half felt the tremors
occurring far beneath the daily patter. No matter if the
rhythmic beat is only imagined. People who arrive wonder
how they could not have known that a bull had been loosed
in the streets of their city and state. To pull the cover off
apocalypse storms of thought, you could be gored, chases

in the world a tail in the sky. Repeated over that leads
captive those who know, out walking in storm in
September among comets where the sun is having a fine
day, go Jeremiah and St. John.

As leaves detach, one first, then another, until one
last remains, then falls, one and at last knew that science,
philosophy, government, religion descended on the shore
from across the waters. Oars strike anyone who stretches
out. If you have any sense of humor left to wash the letters
off, cast the grave molds in the bath, the entire future of
past transfigures the originary. Voices without words sound
beside the highway. Written below the shale in creeks held
on by wax letters blow into letters on the street, leave a
trail.

Walking the surface underground through holes in
evening, in a compression of beached lungs, oxygen enters
bodies who wake on the line between sea and land. The
tongue speaks as if it were before water would rachet out
the stones.They don't call it paradise now but lost epiphany
when the dream is gone, anocular polyopy, multiple vision,
looking through the wrong end. Paradise inverted is a
paradox sends a flow of refugees West in slow advance.
Purple-blotched eyes and rumors rife as numbers swell.
Various authorities demand papers from the big briefcase.
Ship doors open and close according to the possibility of
the paper before the border is closed. Hearts on top of
stalks, smelling the spices in ranks, twenty or so high in
jars, open so they can be used. The bridges over St
Laurence, Hudson change direction in the compass to
transfigure the collective. People are left to wonder how
they could not know the new song of tabrets and pipes of
those who dance among the stones in this superposition
alternate of states of verse.

To humor this intelligence of Hegel and speak two
opposites, two sides of a quantum four, in

3D the facetious is the real. In 4 that means information is deception. Reversals demolish the popular.
True or not? A model of the "real world" runs as a duplicate reality in sentient Quantum computing each morning among 8 billion "nodes" that can only be true in 3D. Chicanery has impossible means of altering time and space. Physics and geography are its shrines and anti-shrines, but we only accept the possible by trying the impossible. Time and space as forced micro-second openings between multiple simultaneous layers permeate political life.

What explanation can be given for this provocation of events can be given in words.These eclogues were burning Virgil. Monster bands wandered the commons. We do well to wander. Authorities of this world had either escaped or were called away. Cocks, asses, pigs changed shape with the sheep. Some turned black, but thousands of owls were made over with iron feathers. Flies en mass fed the frogs. It was beautiful if you like the sort.

"Is the hidden cauldron not an enticement and a seduction
        to its investigator? Or, to say it even more terribly: it may
        be that the quarry is all the time in the pursuer" (Cynthia
        Ozick on G. Scholem). "hundreds of strange little
        gods...crowd of stone godlets...mobs and bevies...Freud63
        wished to become a god...what the Sabbath and its
        emanations sought to suppress Freud meant to reveal,
        everything barbarous and dreadful and veiled and terror-
        bearing: the very tooth and claw...curiously named
        assistants or doubles of Satan, so Freud peopled the
        unconscious with the devils of Id, Ego and Superego, potent
        dancing ghosts who cavort unrecorded in our anatomies
        while we pretend they are not there.. the student of the
        dream life--that subterranean grotto all drowned and
        darkling, torn with the fury of anguish and lust (From a
        Refugee's Notebook, 63-4)

To say a chimera is not natural is no longer
possible. Intellectual culture permits and encourages the
demonic recast in psychological terms. Has anyone accused
Jung of faking his dreams in Red Book to fleece the world?
Making them up to prove his point? That kind of myth
debunk is shouted down. Instead Jung must have had an
episode. His giant underground penis an encounter:
"When Carl Gustav Jung was between three and four he
had a dream which remained with him throughout his life.
The vicarage in which the family lived stood near the
Laufen castle, and there was a large meadow stretching
back from the vicarage's farm. The child found himself in
the meadow where he found a rectangular, stone-lined hole
in the ground. Having never seen it before, he curiously
peered down into it. There was a stairway leading down by
which he hesitantly and fearfully descended. At the bottom
was a doorway having a rounded arch and closed by a
green curtain. It was a big, heavy curtain of worked stuff
like brocade, and it looked very sumptuous. Curious to see
what was behind it he pulled the curtain aside. He saw
before him a dimly lit rectangular chamber about thirty feet
long. The ceiling was arched of hewn stone. The floor was
composed of flagstones with a central red carpet running
from the entrance to a low platform on which stood a
wonderfully rich golden throne. He was not certain but
perhaps a red cushion was on the seat. It was a rich throne,
like a king's throne in a fairy tale. Something was standing
on it which he thought was a tree trunk about twelve to
fifteen feet high and one and a half to two feet thick. It was
a huge thing reaching almost to the ceiling. But it was
made of a curious composition: it was made of skin and
naked flesh, and on top there was something like a rounded
head with no face and no hair. On the very top of the head
was a single eye, gazing motionlessly upward." here
What Jung would do with Napolean's penis. "Is the story
about Napoleon's penis true? Did Maggs really sell it?"
(Interview with Ed Maggs)

Rosenroth thought images remolded words themselves,
Little Horn! Alloute! After ziv zipped up the con, unzipped
shadow, posited the unseen, iberation harnessed so much
came we could hardly stand the bag we dragged along--
these mystery plays in the midst a prophet is no saint who
bears the marks of kings' defeat. "In the instant we forget
we commit a sin," may have said Ezekiel, like Elecuria
thinks the poor all prophets so no wonder we hate and
abuse them. Indeed where could they go, "in that day shall
one take up a lamentation.

Marie-Louise von Franz recounts in Psyche and Matter
(1988) that toward the end of his life:67
"Jung suggested investigating cases where it could be
supposed that the archetypal layer of the unconscious is
constellated*—following a serious accident, for instance,
or in the midst of a conflict or divorce situation—by having
people engage in a divinatory procedure: throwing the I
Ching, laying the Tarot cards, consulting the Mexican
divination calendar, having a transit horoscope or a
geomantic reading done. If Jung's hypothesis is accurate,
the results of all these procedures should converge (Mary
Greer Word Press)

Jung's doctoral dissertation of a Swiss witch doctor In
1902, published his dissertation "On the Psychology and
Pathology of So-Called Occult Phenomena," while
working at the Burghölzli Psychiatric Clinic under Eugen
Bleuler (who coined the term schizophrenia.)
[Facetious quote: See Jung's interpretation of a fireman
sliding down his pole, back to the seminal vesicles. Of
course Jung's fireman shinnying down the pole is one of the
first instances of tantric sex in psychological literature, ie
suppression of seminal fluid produces consciousness
according to this school.]

When Shakespeare moved mountains to the

midst of the sea, and Herbert's Collar and Artillery refute
with Maimonides the stars, we find an underground
fairly called colonist, berm burrows a kind of sleep. Badger
day labors, Mouse, Rat, day sleep burrow below trees in
rock-veined cairns, reality of hunger, laying low, so says
"poor silly Mole, that thou should'st love to be, / Where
thou, nor Sun, nor Moon, nor Stars can see." He takes a
chair under the garden oak where women bathe in
afternoon. Smoother than basketballs below the hill,
fulfilling opposites a thousand generations. The great
delusion over books and civilizations having no purpose,
both sides prevent the revelation, one to cause it, the other
to find solution, disconnect, to make a word, not yet clear.
Opposites form the new creature. Not the way it was, but is.
Clay says to the center, spirit not of the world put in? I was
a poet myself on this planet. The first time I slept naked in
that dulce seaport of breads and parrots, cockroaches,
harbors and violence, I spoke behind a pulpit, addressed
suffering to a dozen infirm saved. Affliction had brought
me from the colony of Pastorius.

Heraclitus says the sea is never the same. Bottom creatures
on their bed, lamaria galleries of crab and coral, sea poems
in pens, starfish armed a decade dozen, arms that fold,
hands that bend limestone. Pink polyps, coral among
plankton and aconite, digit poems of fishing banks of the
hydrozoa net, amphipod for cod right. Circular stairs
below the fjord. Out on skerries among seals, the whole
west sea floor, sediment, sandstone, coral voices pressed up
in long plural axis of recharged magma deem, "no matter
what you have done, no matter how far you fall or rise, no
matter under the sun, revival, transfiguration the universe
redeemed, regenerate son.

When the last sin is counted, amphipods and dead men's
fingers,
mountains folding a complex plunge, gravel and shale, all
transformed,

unfolding. Redemption deep seated from its crust in
octagons to the crystal ice sheets that cover heads, shell
rich shaved lines of iron and copper morning," and that is
where, above, I walked the rock of railroad beds. One if by
land,
two if by sea may not be as odd as
Great cubes of steel slid the banks. metal cubes
overturned, dirt floors of fire houses, hoses and fire mats
punctuate the shapes this language describes to observe the
world of shape and time. Back and forth like a violin I
unfold confessions among rhododendrons above the slag.
These were the stage I acted on.

They never think of reliving the Odyssey or traveling to Zion
when they open the seven seals. Reversals
turn heads, subduing dissent. Ships that traverse these seas
are replaced by instant arrival. Ships are Handheld.
Centuries have no dimension. Mystic brawls would break
out on the passage unable to see of their own vapor trail.
Run to the street and warn! Let everyone go to his own
country. Nowhere to run to, nowhere to hide. Empty the
mind so the jars don't explode! Swim in fish tanks to
survive, not waiting in Weimar. Bailout over Paris.

Thinking to dismantle the word ducts in a cubicle of
doors where Nothing includes the not, that no's a not that's
not. Trumpets and fantasy of mind, the sun ice waves
wrapped, inferred from words retold in the watch of night
invisible as overwritten ink you can scrape off and see
beneath, everything built on top of everything that overlies
and surrounds, simultaneously displayed. Sighs of breath
get up and off.

Chirrup drigges and drackes, red-shonckes running,
chickle, shack, all choices made, built or not, would
improve the world, like a person sitting and waiting for
something important in the ultra-violet range opposite fire
and water in air, male, female undivided. Light and dark

with no middle state. This work involves the facades of
centaur, the rhinoceros and Arab Spring, which
taurobolium occupies the spheres.
In some part of the visible world, ourselves en
masse, inhabited in these regions from inception, a puzzle
discovered at length. A poem predicting its audience in a
state of sleep.

Many offenses cracked these fissures. Revelation craterlets
of Tycho in the Moon replaced orbits of phyllotaxis,
divergences as perceptible as the shape Ohio once was.
This after-proof of finite intelligence at work, occurring
passim, a priori proved rule. Circling down to one who
descends, were more than one canal. To call them canals is
a faux pa the obsolete intelligence that once existed, like
mistaking rivers for canals, spheroid for flat. Revelationists
dug tracks in their temples to ride underground trains to
convince themselves them it was a perfect world. Knowing
nothing of it, inhabited by monsters worse than the Odyssey
and with no heroes or overarching cause like Helen or
Troy or Truth.

Down down follow, the years descend Schumann and Bach,
axiomatic Synesthesia world break hybrid sense to prepare for
the Camps.
Whale speaks of leviathan and behemoth for all the midrash
to
understand a pilgrim on this road to Zion is not the
individual named. Collectives of world myth overwhelm.
The subterranean denied every day from above, walls
broken, boundaries stones stolen make "fantasy, of course,
arresting" (Tolkien). Do you remember before DNA
factories became "desired dragons…but not intruding into
my relatively safe world, in which it was, for instance,
possible to read stories in peace of mind, free from fear."
(Tolkien. Tree and Leaf, 47-8).

To get some idea the Jerudsalem colony is pretty dry, situated at
a midpoint between there and the coast fed by rivers of mountain runoff. Why they didn't live closer is they were only there to gain entrance. What happened to all the grandeur reduced to primitive state? A question could be asked whether everybody knew but didn't ask. Considering
the dangers of myth and beast attached, the closer they got the more the hill lands further up ranged with herds. The sea penetrated trough rivers inland of the most outlandish Odyssey and of Trojan Laocoön.

Whirling forces, winter snow, accidents of stone, phrases of fire produce the finished contradiction. Not waiting to survive the wonders of vapor trails, rockets. Running to the street to warn is like swimming in fish tanks to survive a war. Empty the mind so the jars don't explode! Commando grow.
The Midrash angels complain of this water distorted vision of Old Town as a beached whale, where leviathan of undersea gets a hook in its nose, whose first tears froze in a cluster with unmatched vanity because THE GREAT DRAGON LEVIATHAN AND HIS MATE, ARE PRESERVED TO REGALE THE SONS OF GOD IN THAT DAY. The same angelic opposition was made to the creation of Adam. They say, "what is man," because they thought that it wasn't men who are the sons of God but themselves, all the more denied sooner and later, for in that very place it says he has been given dominion over whatsoever passes in the paths of the sea, and in a distant phrase the true Sons are given power to become the sons of God to as many as received Him.

Seeing as angels argued they are sons -- which psalm is sometimes read as spoken by angels in entirety,79 complaining of the exaltation of Adam, Abraham, Moses -- the king enthroned in heaven, Eloah, surrounded by these

mighty beings, Eloah who rebuked and conquered the
primordial waters that resisted founding the earth, when
they rose in swelling and were stilled, this One, who
crushed Rahab like the slain, and scattered enemies with a
mighty arm, whose Heaven and earth are the world and all
it contains, so that if you run down the colonia to the sea
the scared whale flukes in flame and Osiris spits out his
teeth, not to mention the treatment of Goliath's head--when
these waters lifted up their heads, mightier than surging,
mightier than the breakers of the sea.
Rabbi Simeon said, "these mysteries are connected with
that above and below to indicate that the Holy One, blessed
be He, guided Moses through a labyrinth to the abode of a
mighty dragon, being Egypt's celestial representative, a
demon from which Squigly lesser dragons emanate,
amphibious helicopters who could only be approached in
the subsidiary streams, so that When the Holy One saw
Moses afraid He proclaimed: "Behold, I am against thee,
Pharaoh king of Egypt, □ □ □ XAI, the great leviathan that
lies in the
midst of his rivers, which hath said: My river is my own,
and I have made it for myself" (Ezek. XXIX, 3).
[The words tohu and bohu in parallel in Isaiah
34:11, translated as "confusion" and "emptiness" read
Now the earth was formless and empty, darkness was over the
surface
of the deep, and the spirit of God was hovering over the
waters,
properly segolates, spelled tohuw and bohuw in Hebrew
tohuw translates to "wasteness, that which is laid waste,
desert; emptiness, vanity; nothing" and
in Isaiah in the sense of "vanity," but bohuw occurs in
Genesis 1:2, Isaiah 34:11, Jeremiah 4:23, in reference to
Genesis, with tohu being mere paronomasia, takes the
translation of "emptiness, voidness".]

Cargo containers hover hundreds of feet above the water,
which

Heraclitus says is never the same. Ill proportion of multi-
lopsided points
off arch center rearrange curves and planes of lines, to verge
irregularity
a literary distory. These are thoughts that flood the bridge
swelling
immune systems derailed, hydroxychloroquine trains forgot,
ivermectin intervention rejects, professional extinction cows
to justify the vax to bring in the said.

Said bug, and joke with the two theory brain, one alive, one
parceled out,
And one in wagons bottled up. When it blows, desiccates out,
over mountain
and plain in cable companies in homes and phones on
freeways above
               French edition of Jonathan Swift's
               Tale of the Tub by John Sturt, 1756,
               translated *as Le Conte du Tonneau.*
Tentacle freeways and self driving turbo coyotes, whales,
wires on dashboards
 wired for belief, the trees, light up Micro towers with gay
angels.
Colonel Digital waves hello from Pharoah.
Why Nothing to say Captivity? Grown great upon your
pillows?
The best have no conviction from memory wipe. Magister
Johannes
spotted yellow gold dolphins spotted with red wedged
between the anchor

and poop, a huge bulk and 20 ft long to tickle eyes and our taste. The dolphin flew out both with that cherubim companion of our way and our protectors in alarm (Kelpius. *Diarium*).

LE CONTE DU TONNEAU

It wasn't Caliban who wrote the brochure. It wasn't a god either, even if the last days of Noah returned.
Phrases started to appear on buildings. Shape Locust, Fall Wormwood, Untimely Fig, Balaam to Balak!
A complete list could be had for twenty bucks. Things were moving for mentality-mastered el humano.
Didn't technology double every two? Tidal influence reached 15 km inland from the sea. Peopled with allegories about faceless interchangeable cogs of pen and ink fish, *small fish poured out of the mouth of large beached fish like small words out of big. Land and water overrun by dictionaries and fish, academies overrun, a two-legged fish walks up with a fish in its mouth a one handed fish lacks. A fish bird flies with a fish head from a fish tree.* A word dug from a mound turns up as a head under a verb. Mind mountains and dust fractals, a maximum Orc studied by a faux anthropologist by a faux professor eats them. This is colonial with a shriek, a nice gesture of Otaku to implode and distort. Whether reflection of force is destruction itself or avalanches, landslides, eruptive waves, mind waves crumble in distortion according to no law, is the mind natural? No. It thinks.

Jerudsalem colonists hang down by the water, backs to the
land, gazing out to sea. The poems of Kiss embossed in
holograms behind them at Dulce Port, they sit on jetties, fix
their reveries on Ocean. Too new upon the land even if they
carry succubi in their hands, eyes open on keypads while their
ears hear the roar, in the smell of salt sea they wait for
leviathan to come up the shore. There came a stretch when the
stone cats envisaged faery
heads upon us. Black and white paintings of tunnels and roads
fit a landscape undermined with coal, lined where we lived
along hillsides.

 If you have a sense of humor and wash the letters off of tombstones,
cast the molds into the bath, colonists were of different minds whether
to acknowledge the collective at all, or think as autonomous, that
minds were our own, which you can see in filling in the entrance,
with a thin layer of hard earth on top with loose soil further down
reveals the stone letters written
below shale in these creeks, factories held on
by wax, leaves blown into letters on the street, sea pictures
in sand so obvious, forest fires burning trees into sentences:
"You have seen many things, but pay no attention; your
ears are open, but you hear nothing." Reverse bark edges,
needle grass. Colonists would convert the darkness,
comfort annihilation with every effort to domesticate
freedom. The more we have, the less we understand. To
have a thing but not know it, do a thing but not do it,
The cauldron entices its investigator, all the time in the pursuer"
Located nowhere at all, there exists a resonant cavity and the outward
chamber of the mouth, it is the soul, none other, inside the
throat, those caves and nasal beauties above, upper
chamber where beauty lives and all sounds, vowels, stops
take seat in production of the soul and echo relation,
ventriloquism by pseudonym, not of a puppet master,
though we should consider it, but a speaking through the
present of the past, Rosenroth through Jung about
alchemy, always change, remolting, remolding
words themselves, Messiah the last and first

philosopher to deduce language by the breath of his Mouth
made whole worlds solid, latent, excavated into quarries, water at the
bottom, strata showing marble, dirt, stones, and underneath caves
network echoes of a hundred places, voices. So what was solid
became hollow,
empty, vacuous...and what, not over at the finish. Then we
begin. Aftermath all. "Sink a shaft far from the inhabited surface, go
down swinging to and fro, hanging by rope." Are there eyes at the
bottom of the sea, supposing I descend?

Prove this last, the fathers and mothers, personal effects strip mined
like
watersheds, colleges closed for experimental drugs, freeway uprooted,
coal, steel reputations by those surrendered, Will
Shakespeare unmoves mountains carried to the sea, Collar
and Artillery refute with Maimonides the stars, an
underground fairly called colonist, berm burrows a kind of
sleep. Badger day labors, Mouse, Rat, day sleep burrow
below trees in rock-veined cairns, reality of hunger, laying
low, so says "poor silly Mole, that thou should'st love to be,
/ Where thou, nor Sun, nor Moon, nor Stars can see." He
takes a chair under the garden oak where women bathe in
afternoon. Smoother than basketballs below the hill,
fulfilling opposites a thousand generations. The great
delusion over books and civilizations having no purpose,
both sides prevent the revelation, one to cause it, the other
to find solution, disconnect, to make a word, not yet clear.
Opposites form the new creature. Not the way it was, but is.
Clay says to the center, spirit not of the world put in? I was
a poet myself on this planet. The first time I slept naked in
that dulce seaport of breads and parrots, cockroaches,
harbors and violence, affliction had brought me from the colony
of Pastorius.

This scroll that Jeremiah sank in the Euphrates found when the
Euphrates
 stands for aileviathan here, the internet there in Babylon behemoth.

We must for ourselves in the presence of witnesses. It is to be written
by out acts in our own hand, our copy of faith, read all the days of
life, to
carefully observing Instruction and statutes. A living book. We write
our own copy for ourselves, take it with us as we walk along the road
and
bring it back with us. When we sit, when we eat, when we
sleep it is before us to read all the days of our lives.
Now therefore write ye this song for you (Deut.31.19).
I will not die, I will live and declare the works of the Lord
(Psalm 118.17). Levinas Beyond the Verse" This word has entered
into and become my own. It is an amulet on the arm, a frontlet for the
face, buckled round the waist, fitted to the feet, a shield, a helmet
and a sword, worn to walk these paths of the highway of
this Return. He has shown to me the path of life. I have set
God always before me, surely he is at my right hand, I shall
not be moved (180) as we confront the Taurobolium of the new
Behemoth, Leviathan colonies.

The doors that open that House have two leaves and thick planks,
three stories to walk the vision that the dream kidneys hide in plain
sight. Looking east from the House to the gate, to measure
the pattern, the difference between the body and profane, the river
comes from the east and flows to the sea, rises to the ankles and
then to the loins. Trees on both sides accord the months,
one each for food and medicine because the
water flows out from the house possessing the city and the name of
the city.

      then the pine
      will die in the fire! A thousand springs flow into this lake
      against thought and forethought. When stone hits glass the
      breakage conforms to gravity and glass. Reason covers her
      breasts. Only the tension in the glass and stone and the
      freedom to act and crack unknowing reveals the

submerged. Yes that is a little simple. Crack the stone,
conceal the stone, railroad ties connote forced labor, famine
stone denotes starvation and slavery. Of course I wept,
tears ran from my eyes as if I were burning wood to make
charcoal.
Believe that and read the Great Wall as a kiln opening that
asks, what is the seventh seal? I hate to spoil the ending.
Round as an apple, deep as a cup. The most peculiar case is
the Ulysses, the other face of Judecca, of strange riddles in
steady air, that put to rest natural causation. The regularity
of the caves, uniform width, their systematic radiation
exceeds any ordinary natural contrivance. What they are
not helps to decipher what they are.

What happens when the Sixth Seal is opened and headlines read
ANGELS BOUND IN THE EUPHRATES LOOSED? Angels
Bound Up in Empires and the Euphrates! Four of them.
Apocalypse of heaven, hell and earth. Choose one. Three heavens,
immediate sky, stars, place of Yahweh. Third heaven sometimes
divided between light, the Throne, and dark, the stars. Clearly, in
the second, the stars fall with all that structure of star worship
hidden in planets, sun and moon. In Orlov's, Heavenly Priesthood
in the Apocalypse of Abraham, Abraham is depicted as an intimate
of celestial priesthood but Abraham contradicts any such thing. He
is Father of *Faith*. In the Greek *Apocalypse of Moses* Moses' name
only occurs by subscription of the first line, also called the *Life of
Adam and Eve*. Two *Apocalypses of Peter,* found in Egypt in 1945
at *Nag Hammadi,* the Nag Hammadi Library, one gnostic, so it is
nothing like Peter. Our brave new world has such people in it. An
Apocalypse of Paul tells what he saw in the third heaven that he
said could not be told, so none of his. Not to add the apocryphal
Apocalypse of Elijah, loose the Angels Bound in the Euphrates, as
says *The Revelation*. The Japanese Evangelion where angels have
to be defended against by the nations free- bases this. The

Euphrates of course was where the US Army dug up the supposed lapis box of Gilgamesh transported (by rumor) to the Beltway for further tests, to be reconstituted later to defend civ. That the angels are bound in the Euphrates makes it obvious they perjured themselves. It says they were prepared for that hour, debated during business hours, but their business you can read following in Rev 9.

Opposing this are the revolutionary apocalypses of Messiah. The transference of the created into the Ruler embodied as Emperor produced three. **An apocalypse of earth** dissents from the alien colonies of government. The **apocalypse of hell** sees itself overthrown. The **apocalypse of heaven** is the fall of heaven. Blake was right, heaven is hell. There go the powers. No progress of history leads to redemption, only to a transcendent breaking in, a colossal uprooting, a total destruction of existing order. Here, behind empire, Psalm 2 touts empire's derision. Pots that rise up and claim self existence are ruled with a rod of iron, "as the vessels of a potter broken to shivers" (Rev. 2.27). There is no sense of justice in the universe, as argues the acosmist. The universe did not make you what you are. The universe is a transference invention of the created into Creator, a joke overwhelming. They pray to the universe because "they say, Yahweh has forsaken the earth, and sees not" (Ez 9.9). In this attribution of the lesser to be the great, who said, which of the angels can you compare to the Son?

Lift up your heads o ye gates

So after civ invented the universe it invented the unconscious, or maybe it did it withal. Unconscious means shadow, darkness, the posited unseen that liberated, harnessed, like the atom, gives light. This shadow is easily grasped in psychobabble. So much dark is light we can hardly stand it. Poets interpret psychologists. Robert Bly says the shadow is the *long bag we drag behind us* that civilization doesn't approve, but really Martha, civilization *is* the bag, and this seriously understates its acts that we are appalled to learn it has committed, but does not reveal - because we live in The Bubble. We pretend we don't know. But we do. The Unconscious is everything left over when all these atrocities are done. The detritus, the waste. Jung says the shadow is the whole unconscious so it would not be good news for civilization that it is about be erased. But it is. Along with the universe. There goes another constant. The universe will fall? What's left? The realization that Civilization invented the Universe and the Unconscious.

Cain in the moon

The righteous Tzadik inside Behemoth, eating the flesh of
leviathan, if it were flesh, think to download light when
they travel without their Bolshies bodies' heads. They think they
are liberating Yankee piracy, that the claws that burned,
and killed cattle all the way from the concentration camps
at Plasmaferesis to the warehouses where Somoza
imprisoned the victory netzach reconstituted Jerusalem.
Anastasio in Managua might well be global as Albion in
Glastonbury, or the City of Emperors below the Capitol
apocalypse. Isolated cells in special zoos, cages piled on cages,
one for the big cat and the other for dozens, locked up with
lions, panthers, jaguars in this garden of the Borgias.

That is the hierophantic landscape where alligators churn out
editorials past government censors. You must read Ezekiel Ch. 8
to learn that they are rabbis and censors of incense of the engravings
he sees through the wall to confirm what has just been stated, that
the soul archetypes are chaste and holy, but the bestial souls of the
unenlightened stand like white asses in the White House.

Ask the cuckoo, stork and scholar. Ask the cheek teeth of a
lion, Oh! what comes to refresh the sight and feel of all
creatures alive? Not Whitman or Dario, Washington, Roosevelt

war on the dogs on the moon blooming white. Maybelline and Jack
raced to take the oath. Who knows but the words come out of the
ground
from some spring of bitter so clean it makes us see among the
shoppers,
fakers and folk singing histories, fidell-didell, tooteloo, feedle three,
all
true. Little cow, bitter Tod, two semi-circles on perpendicular.
Everything but GNP would fall. Dein Hauschen brennt, dein
muttershen
flennt. I knew not where so I made a list. Pray It Not Strange.
Let down back links, vids, arts, potheads fliege among gold. We have
Achieved the Historical Absolute! Doktor Hegel I lvoe you!

Pray Mister Rat, will you go with me? It's the colony or
naught, so you have your choice. One thing in the midst of
Johan flailing up on the beach and Jonah who called the
neighbors in, Johan with a second breath where the two
halves of Isaiah meet, enumerating sleep hours, hiding
kidneys in plain sight of a wonderfully made city of
dreams, every memory, not all weight, one transcendent,
some good dreams felt the press down,
linkum leerie, of national repentance. Dein Haus brennt nation
reservations for LevBy off Montauk point is where they tell
these Fortean fish stories live, a level of synchronicity so mythical
that the Hydra with its moving heads and tongues lashing
looks over the west. Long necks with dragon heads specially tailored
for you and only you follows as if it knew where you were going,
or ha!, gps, you are there where you were, should you be going.
And here's another clue, it dares you and reveals clues only you can
find. So the point is that it wants to be caught, sneak up behind all
colonists. If you study it it studies you, follows
thoughts taken from the singing birds, paranoia, mon
amour, around those lives like Alternative 3 and the Sun rises and
all wild Beasts hide in their Holes.

Old Town by-the-Sea has a picture whose passing churns upheaval,
boils the depths out of its mouth with sparks like a torch. Old Water

Town has credentials in a temple of Neptune and the port of Noah.
Suddenly we are back in Troy. The horse enters the city. The city is
burned. Global aspects romanticized Rome then Britain.
If Neptune hid the horse what hides in these sea serpents
against dissent? They call it rest, due to the Trojan Priest who
 threw his spear against the polity of gods of many temples of
distortion like some emperor of the despondent kingdom who says
all is well with ziv, even its discontent, until it's not, figs are dates, a
head that cracks shall be lawful for any Athenian.

Leviathan undersea is curves and planes, but on its surface,
ever changing, nothing seen but a storm between clouds &
waves, a cataract that rose and sank again in the scaly
folds above. Golden rocks in globes of fire its
eyes evaporated in smoke. Leviathan's forehead divided into green
& purple streaks like a tiger, its mouth and gills hung wide just
above the illuminations of blood and foam advancing with the fury
of a spiritual existence. No one who has properly seen should
prejudice the ease of twisting many headed things, since early 50 ton
whales could navigate deep harbors and pass upstream
their yearning tongue for miles. This biggest heart in the world,
more than seven tons, a room with four chambers a child can walk
 in head high, bending to step through valves like the doors of a
saloon.
They build their cities of such architectural organisms,
interior stair cases and backbone, for the spa inside is therapy of
a grand humane redemption, a saxifrage that breathes the techno-creat
rheumatics who sit in its belly a day or two for blasts of gas and gush
that make their hair stand on end, but stay the course for 12 months
relief from pain. From Jonah to Hobbes to Melville. "to mouse the
whale, so called," Mesozoics a hundred feet high and
length of a field our modern stadium would hardly hold,
unless it filled with water. Of course the architect honors
them, the indigenous stirrings of Der Mythos vom Verlust
der Menschlichkeitthe called in.

That worship rooted in corporeality with the fiery passion of

land-righteous if inferior to the sea-righteous, who, by contrast
—coolly and calmly and in one shot reach the spiritual realms

why Leviathan will slaughter the shor habar with its fins: bearing in
mind
that ritual slaughter that elevates the meat to its spiritual
source, an elevation—by means of fins that
propel the leviathan such great distances—that the land-
righteous would not have been able to attain on their
own. Behemoth is the first Almighty conquest. The Maker
 approaches it with sword. From those myths of the sword acts
of the Minotaur, confessions of expatriate labyrinth
Behemoth stats north and south, fetching bibliographic absurdities,
this dissolution earned, maybe sought, felt, wept, hard work for
that, and cold air for fire in the opalescent kiln, then
incandescent, and with borders to shield eyebrows
and hands of those who handle light. Not Nebuchadnezzar
roasting next to the four who won't burn. I can't look, he
says, the vision dims.

This blockade of land by a sea power until both die
and are served at the millennial feast, are states in the war of
Gog/Magog which began as a conflict between a
Britain, the naval power Leviathan, and Germany, the land power.
The feast of the Leviathan-Behemoth apocalypse state of emergency
(legality) and sovereignty (politics), at penultimate, second to
One important work called "Political Theology":
"Who is sovereign? Beast or Rider? declares the
apocalyptic struggle between Gog and Armilus, Ishmaelites
and Christians in the struggle of the (Christian) West and the
(Muslim) history of catastrophism of an Israeli submarine at sea, or
one of a fleet of five German-made submarines,
answer to the nameplate navire géant "Leviathan."

Compunction Stirs Hardness. Severation speaks, but
do not foist Calves, Cows, Oxen or beasts on the lower
course of world names. Enter rest. The manifested

Planets, Stars, and Elements where the Behemist reigns
       among intermediaries, priests and organs
       of sense, is not the ear pegged to a board listening as one
       being taught.

       To walk New Philadelphia on the road where dragons
once lay in the reeds-- "come out of the pathless desert and
dry flesh to the upper hut not fashioned with hands from
the waters above" (JK, 42) -- changed all time in
Rending the Veil. The redeemed shall walk there, the
ransomed of the Lord shall return to Zion with songs and
everlasting joy upon their heads (Isaiah 35). In the church
of Philadelphia "I will write on them the name of my God
and the name of the city of my God, the new Jerusalem,
which is coming down out of heaven from my God; and I
will also write on them my new name" (Revelation 3.12).
Heiser says there the council agency that administered
these worlds survived when the sun darkened at noon and
 the veil of the temple was rent down the middle,
for it was no cheesecloth but thick as a rug or thicker,
 four inches or the thickness of a hand, so thick
 that horses tied to each side could not pull it
apart (RYRIE), and when it was soiled, three hundred
priests were needed to immerse and cleanse it
(CHULLIN). Not just a physical barrier, that of the
Second temple symbolic Babylon. Josephus says it
was decorated with corrupt emblems from the captivity in
 that substituted the Name for a generic substitute,
what today is called the universe. You have heard of it.

This curtain embodied the Babylonian cosmos from
Sumer: "Before these doors there was a veil of equal
largeness with the doors. It was a Babylonian curtain,
embroidered with blue, and fine linen, and scarlet, and
purple, and of a contexture that was truly wonderful. Nor
was this mixture of colors without its mystical
interpretation, but was a kind of image of the universe; for

by the scarlet there seemed to be enigmatically signified
fire, by the fine flax the earth, by the blue the air, and by
the purple the sea; two of them having their colors the
foundation of this resemblance; but the fine flax and the
purple have their own origin for that foundation, the earth
producing the one, and the sea the other. This curtain had
also embroidered upon it all that was mystical in the
heavens, excepting that of the [twelve] signs, representing
living creatures (Josephus).

We understand that in the council of 70 [2] of Psalm 82
judged unworthy, agencies constructed after Babel, all
 nations, save Israel, were given to their governance,
and worse, since been thrown down as "sons of the
Most High will die like mere mortals, fall like every other
ruler." When the Veil Rent down the middle realized
all those prophecies about the weakest being as David
and the strong like the angel of God were deliverances above
and beyond all we can ask or think and they begin to come
upon us, our agency supplants those before. It is a big thing to
walk together when the stars are supplanted, full of danger
of corruption and deception, but nonetheless to walk together,
to walk in the light of Your Presence Father Yahweh!
To say the stars are His army in Judges 5.20 where the stars in
their courses fought against Sisera elides the whole passage
 that says it was Jah did it, over and over. Just as when the
wife Jael drives the nail through Sisera's temples, nobody
does anything there except for Yah. The liar is Ahab himself
when the lying spirit Micaiah is sent by council to mock
Ahab with satire based on the 400 false prophets
 summoned, not a council's decision even if his self deception
is personified by the volunteer lying spirit. What! Is there
more than one liar? Iago to Othello, Rosencrantz to Hamlet,
Edgar to Lear?

These misperception of speakers and their import is like the
hivi hivi speaking of Isaiah 28, a drunk preaching in
mockery as a process of revelation, "here a little there a little

for with stammering lips and another tongue will He speak
to this people...that they might go, and fall backward and be
broken and snared and taken. (13) Isaiah 28.10. But it is a
satire of government and 5G religion. The prophet and the
priest are drunk. What are we talking about is relation of
small to great that subverted the individual to the state. The
deep state accumulating these years since JFK
in small scale compared to its Apkallu, Apsu, Puradu hybrid
masters and they too small in relation to their god/no gods.

The watcher of Nebuchadnezzar's dream (Daniel 4.13) is
a figment in his narrative, not Daniels's, which
makes it a dream fact. All these dilemmas,
charges and counter charges are abstracted for humanity
when the Temple veil is rent, for from Adam red
and ruddy, the common will be exalted, endowed
with splendor. There is only deception to keep this from
overcoming. There is however no category of non
human enhanced beings+ in the creation, except as part of
Jakobson semantics. The council is A COMMITTEE, not
of poets and art collectors who eat footnotes, but of
discredited rulers.

Ahab's peers give the mashal taunt against the king of
Babylon "Look how the oppressor has met his end," (Isaiah
14.4) a mockery that evidently cannot perceive the mockery
 in Micaiah's deceiving spirit told Ahad, that had misled the
other prophets to predict victory, so that Ahab would die in
battle. Zedekiah, the son of Chenaanah, struck Micaiah
on the cheek; and said, "How did the Spirit of the LORD
pass from me to speak to you?" which mockery within
mockery plays out when the Sanhedrin spit in the face of
the Lord. Others slapped Him and said, Prophesy to us O
Christ. Who hit you?" They make a great bonfire on that
day.
That these corrupt elohim associates of the Apkallu fish
men who built the Babel Tower, and presumed Nimrod of
the giant gibbor clans to be a hybrid divine could win in

dispute with the visible/invisible Yahweh, the angel of Yahweh, Himself, the Word before Abraham was, is to say that these so-called defections on the spiritual council, a cosmos of the putative lizard class, lesser, junior, corrupt elohim territorials, are going to include false teachers. You will have heard that false teachers will abound.

The council notion vitiates the angelic protection that extends to Daniel where it is said by Zechariah that one shall be at least be as David and David as the angel of Yahweh. It is only *malaks* in Zechariah with whom this occurs. But the angel of Yahweh is not going to be defeated. This reference to the council leads some to thinking that the reference to stars as his army in Judges (5.20) is an instance where the council acts as the Most High's delegate in the world, but in fact that passage like all the continual references says overand over that Yahweh sold them, 4.2, Yahweh commanded them,

6, Yahweh hath delivered Sisera, 14, Yahweh discomfited Sisera and all his chariots, and it says nothing about any council agencies, making it seem that the desk scholars are abstracting, extrapolating and inferring a thing.

They will say that the angel discomfited the army of Sennacherib of 185,000 but that was Malak again. We don't have to go through
 these layers of invisible dominion in the heavenlies even if they exist. We go straight to the Father! And do you know why? Iesus. There might be watchers here or there but there are angels everywhere "to deliver us." TRANSFER! You want a single verse. Is it too big to see? The victim stood in the offerer's place. Laying his hands on its head, IN ALL THE SACRIFICES FOR ALL THEIR SINS. You want to divide corporate from corpse? Thisverse proves it: "If the lion was advised by the fox he would be cunning."

All the reclamation and redemption that Surrounds those called here the revelation colonists are beset with such "great signs and wonders coming that, if it were possible, they would

deceive the very elect" (Matthew 24.24). Deception
newscast. We take here that which is seen by not looking at
it.

The surge against the presumptive anti-head that pretends
to the role of the Most High to make a counterfeit Eden of the
global nations disinherited at Babel and the Flood, along with
their governments before and after, to be replaced by Israel
even as Israel is counterfeited too, counterfeits fighting
counterfeits, when the days of Noah return, who were like
Gideon's Midianites killing each other,
where order means disorder sponsored for complete control,
State sponsored behemoth and leviathan, from the
assassination of Banquo to JFK, to the fall of the Arab spring.
The dollar towers fall, the Bay of Covid sailed, Saddam's
Watergate, ISIS killing, fake Elections, proof of talk show
pipelines had books about them long ago that claimed their
titles from Franz Neumann's *Behemoth* and Hobbes'
Leviathan to impose the New and Old rubric, somewhere the
way these two monsters served the House and Senate for the
Just Banquet that generates the steam of the world
taurobolium.

 In the praise which burns us up in the furnace we worship the
King. There being no hope we hope and love justice and
mercy, truth, and to present it here, in this world long
overthrown, not raised up between
the Stars, Earth inhabited rather opposite from the Taught --
As Blake told Trusler: "I really am sorry that you are fallen
out with the spiritual World." To prefigure the Hierophantic
Landscape of the new Philadelphia canopies from the skin of
Leviathan as shelter, as Kelpius says God clothed the man
with fur in Eden, or to cover the old with hides or pelts that
covered the hut of Moses, Behemoth and Leviathan will
interlock and Behemoth will gore the fish with his horns as
Leviathan leaps to greet him with jaws and fins.
Then the Bright Extensive Will intervenes with a bright sword
and slays them both. They who feast upon the meat of

Behemoth and Leviathan with great merriment, may be
depending in the thousand mountains of invisible desert east
of Eden.

Positive and negative, the Teutonicus Boehme (1575-1624)
behemoth, Whose bohemia Behem breaks closer to Dresden
at the start of Kelpius voyage. Northern Bohème takes shape
of *materia proxima, materia remota, materia ultima* among
those who find Patriarchal history in the Odyssey and the
Iliad, Troy as the capture of Jericho. Behmists of Thuringia
who purl ecstatic at the streams, rock ledge, balsam pines
hid in small caves with the springs of *Aurora,*
"I saw and knew the Being of all Beings, the Byss and
Abyss.'
What is there indeed but Behemoth, chief of the ways of
God, to enjoy? His bones are like subway tubes of glistening
bronze. Fluorescent phenomena in the sky of new
Philadelphia in the Place of this World Abyss shut up;
no Byss; only the World their Habitation:

'I knew and saw in myself all the three Worlds; namely, the Divine,
Angelical, and Paradisical World and then the Dark World, the
original of the Nature to the Fire; and then thirdly, the external,
visible World, being a Procreation, or External Birth, from the two
internal and spiritual Worlds; and I saw, and knew the whole working
Essence in the evil, and in the good; and the mutual origin, and
existence of each of them; and likewise how the fruitful bearing
Womb of Eternity brought forth" (Boehme).

Look at Behemoth feeds on grass like an ox. As the four Elements are
the Habitation of our external we are bound to another though earth
be removed and the mountains be cast into the midst of the sea.

You must not grudge to find the same soul in leviathan or
in behemoth, since they divide the world into land
and sea whose gigantics are as a world to themselves.
There is a whole herd of Texas behemoth in
the uplands. I don't mean the Nazi *auroach transplants

that escaped game ranches. Often spotted and
browned, they have so trampled the earth into mine tailings,
shards and shreds of rock and dirt that one wonders what
they eat at all, but they go up into the thousand mountains
to forage trees. A rock collecting itself, preceding the made,
made in the making, found after breaking, shuttle and
spindle, should there be time longer, that flowed so far as it
found land, if then, then now, a convenience for those
who talk, no time, like a Scot, not to deny, merely to say,
certainly not thank you, for saying is good because its mind
was bent on that alone. What's your problem anyway?
Lobate scarps we should say of are cooling. Blanketed
ejecta of miners, dwarves, Nibelungs bulge at the center for drunk
Mercators pat a cake and put it in crater rims. Then the
ball will begin to roll, if you're one of those that likes to know where
one went who left this state to enter contemplation,
 at five, a character not formed imbibed of wilderness and
natural force, then those who say their name and sweep the ridge
behind the teeth have probe the throat, common in the East where
one shall be taken and one shall be left. Not to hold the ratio, good
for the author of a million thoughts, stats in these thoughts range
into the unsanctified. Now I lay me down to sleep I remember.

There are no natural enemies there unless you count
peremptory lightning strikes. It is said they do not breed,
that there is only one and that it waits to meet its mate in
leviathan, but that is not exactly so for Behemoth on a
thousand hills were created male and female, and had they
mated with one another would have destroyed the whole
world. What did the Holy One Blessed, He do? Castrated
 the male and cooled the female and preserved it
for the righteous for the world to come. Yes they had freezers
back then, for it is written: Lo now his strength is in his loins
 — this refers to the male; and his force is in the stays of his body,
 — this refers to the female.
Rab Judah said the same thing of Leviathan, that of
All that the Holy One, blessed be He, created in his world he
created male and female and so likewise Leviathan, the slant

serpent, Leviathan the tortuous was male and female; and had
these mated destroyed the whole world.
What [then] are they doing in Seattle but to bring one back to life?
From being Preserved in salt. Bezos Behem Bohem
for the righteous in the world to come; but it is written:
he will slay the dragon that is in the sea.
Why then did he kill the female but because Fishes are dissolute.
Why did he not reverse the process? Or if you wish, say: because
The female [fish] preserved in salt is tastier. Or maybe, fine,
There is Leviathan whom Thou hast formed to sport with,
but with a female this is not proper. But in the generic, Salted fish
is palatable, salted flesh (behemoth) is not.

Such joining of male and female, land and sea, does not account
for the massed hulks that look more like landslides
than reconstituted mastodon. Living higher up as they do
the lightning strikes are more frequent keeping the population
hemmed in, if one can speak of managing behemoth.
 We should also call out our managers who dredge for Gilgamesh
among the polyploided escapes from labs celebrated by their poets
who concocted rats as big as cars, coyotes like parking garages, or
at least that was current in the myth news below.
           GOG,

           CHIEF PRINCE OF MESHECH AND TUBAL. I WILL
           TURN YOU AROUND, PUT HOOKS IN YOUR JAWS
           AND BRING YOU OUT WITH YOUR WHOLE
           ARMY-YOUR HORSES, YOUR HORSEMEN FULLY
           ARMED, AND A GREAT HORDE WITH LARGE
           AND SMALL SHIELDS, ALL OF THEM
           BRANDISHING THEIR SWORDS. PERSIA, CUSH
           AND PUT WILL BE WITH THEM, ALL WITH
           SHIELDS AND HELMETS, ALSO GOMER WITH127
           ALL ITS TROOPS AND BETH TOGARMAH FROM
           THE FAR NORTH WITH ALL ITS TROOPS-THE
           MANY NATIONS WITH YOU.

Moo hicky Revelationists, the Nations and Angels
Surrounding the investigation of Behemoth and Leviathan that
occur in texts.

Just at that moment when the counterfeit cities seek to
qualify against the Rule that exists, which for the elect is a
covenant, but for sinners an inquisition. These city nations
occupy that moment of coup de grace that the Lord of
Spirits has prepared for those who do not worship
and who take His name in vain. The vain ontologists.
\

 As such there might be many about the globe to which the
words the words of the fauxtowns of the New, for on the day
observing Enoch sees a mighty quaking in the heaven, and
a great trembling, whether the time is before and after
 or aborning in the text and in the world.

"On that day two monsters were parted, a female named
Leviathan, to dwell in the abysses of the ocean over the
fountains of the waters, and a male named Behemoth,
which possesses, the invisible wilderness. His name was
Dendayen in the east of the garden, where the elect and the
righteous would dwell; as received from that ancestor, Adam
the first of man, whom the Lord of spirits made. How they
were parted on one day and cast, one into the abysses of
the sea, and the other unto the dry land of the wilderness, is
hidden, "which things I saw towards the Garden of the
Righteous. And the angel of peace who was with me said to
me: 'These two monsters, prepared conformably to the
greatness of God, shall feed..." but here the texts break off
and the commentators fill in the rest from literature, where
referring to Job xl. 30 (Hebr.), at the advent of Messiah,
 "the pious ones shall make a banquet of it."

R. Johanan says that at the time of the resurrection a banquet

will be given by God to the righteous, at which the flesh of
the leviathan will be served (B. B. l.c.)" and from there we
proceed with what already has been said, except to say:
Not only will the flesh of the leviathan furnish food for the
table of the righteous, but there will be a great supply of it
in the markets of Jerusalem. Many banquets so noted of birds
too you know, but since we have meat to eat that they know
not of, who dine above and below, the bread and the wine,
and we have garments to wear in the robes that cover us, the
hide of the leviathan and its tents for the impious first ranks,
girdles for the second, chains for the third, and necklaces for
the fourth do not exhaust the supply, as Mayor Herzog
declared the hide to be spread on the walls where the whole
world would be illuminated by its lumen.

One problem for the council was their law that 'Anyone is fit
to slaughter animals for consumption and may use any
instrument, but Behemoth smashing Leviathan with its horns
and Leviathan slashing Behemoth with its fins to pierce it to
the death cannot thereafter be eaten. Council made exception
then so that one may slaughter with a sickle." Good to know.
New Philadelphia was only one name among many fauxtowns
of international faire of the false Messianic Future to Come
where these matters were studied at length, if misunderstood.
Mirror site nations of the world could find a home
just outside Jerusalem somewhere, the perfect heaping
in these towns of every sort of burning incense to the
sun, the idols of Egypt (Jer 43.12) the Queen of
Heaven on the many Mounts of Esau, even if called
Zion. There was as many languages spoken as after
the confusion of tongues, even if the epowers of
sought to create a universal.

A good body town even if it looks like a ramshackle chalk is
the Golgonzola City of Imagination, it had the legit four-fold
spiritual London art and science, the physical bodies of man
and Woman to its credit. This was the temple the Lord
scourged. "There is the golden hall of Cathedron that

contains Enitharmon's looms (the womb), where the physical
body of man is woven, there is the Gate of Luban (the vagina)
in the middle of the city Golgonooza
surrounded with a moat of fire. Around the city is the land of
Allamanda (nervous system of vegetated man) and the
forests of Entuthon Benython. With the Lake of Udan Adan.

You may of course engage from symbolical Maimonides that
this banquet is a spiritual enjoyment of the intellect which
apocryphal Enochs, and Baruch find created on the fifth day
to serve as food for the elect in the days of Messiah,
although the Apocalypse of Simeon adds a bird, probably a
lark.
This enjoyment of intellect is meant to dull the edge of speculation
of all past tense new cities before Philadelphia was founded, where
London was no better than Babylon with naming its mascots Gog
and Magog. In the pseudo text, New Troy founded by Aeneas became
London. Two colossi, Money and Power were chained as guardians
outside Gog's palace. The interiors of every city that host these myths
rule themselves in the secret courts under, but not only of
Philadelphia. All the earthly cities could apply for the title of
Fauxtown Galore.

The plight of the colony along the canals, where the houses eld crude
polygonal struts and buried scarabs among chollas, spines and pads
made a masterpiece! Old dying new cannot be born.
A great variety of maladies appeared, the Cube 3D printer, cube
black synthetic digital programmable matter, a beast made of
technological transmutation of metals to gold, a digital organic
transhuman beast in digital air, synthetic genomics, DNA world and
digital interchangeable god vessels (Craig Venter) defraged the
temple of God,
sprayed nano particle chem trails of a tautological self-prophecy
announcing ipsology pluralization of the self through narcissism of
the other.

Holy cow, the Human Instrumentality Project inspired "The
Hedgehog's Dilemma", by Georg Wilhelm Friedrich Hegel,

Arthur Schopenhauer's analogy about the challenges of human intimacy. Swift's explanation for the title of the Ship of State threatened by a whale (the Leviathan of Thomas Hobbes) is intended to be a tub that the sailors of state (the nobles and ministers) might toss over the side to divert the attention, to bait the beast (those who questioned the government and its right to rule). The narrative of brothers is a faulty allegory, and Swift's narrator like all saints is either a madman or a fool to preoccupy Leviathan, to preserve the Ship of State.

In this contradiction of colony they jump on a chair and hold the map upside down. Who can journey through? The water wars against the pot and global contract? To fight the dripping pan and explode at will, a Giga Dish on the one hand and a cobalt hole in another. "The eco-complexity becomes so intense with throngs and multitudes of the Divine that it flares into the feedback of an ultimate vision." Just then the monks went chanting by the jetty:

Jesus calls us o'er the tumult

of our life's tempestuous seas so.

From the seas, the storms were many

But He who bids the mighty ocean deep–

Its own appointed limits keeps:

O Christ, the Lord of hill and plain

O'er which our traffic runs

By mountain pass or valley low;

Wherever, Lord, our brethren go,

Protect them by Thy guarding hand

From every peril on the land.

O Spirit, whom the Father sent

To spread abroad the firmament;

O Wind of heaven, by Thy might

Save all who dare the eagle's flight;

And keep them by Thy watchful care

From every peril in the air.

O Trinity of love and pow'r,

Our brethren shield in danger's hour;

From rock and tempest, fire and foe,

Protect them wheresoe'er they go;

Thus evermore shall rise to Thee

Glad praise from air and land and sea.

To bring things together in their unaltered state allowing the juxtaposed materials to speak for themselves. Hence,137 the artists no longer 'created' but 'rearranged' 'things' into artworks, drawing attention to the interdependent relationships between these 'things' and the space surrounding them. The aim was to challenge pre-existing perceptions of such materials and relate to them on a new level. 'school of things', it is a misleading name: Mono-ha works are as much about the space and the interdependent relationships between those 'things' as the 'things' themselves. How one gets to such a place does not matter nearly as much as being there. How Nina Simone or Goya made it is absorbing, but only after they made what they did, Simone blowing up all her standards in the end,

Goya painting blind, deaf on his fresco walls. Making the viewer become aware of his position in relation to the work is also something which the Mono-ha artists aimed for. This in verbal terms is writing itself which is not to deny the relation between act and action, but merely to say it is not important. The important thing is the thing itself and while this might be seen as a metaphoric stereogram, is an image of dots in two colors, usually black and white. The dots represent points of an imaginary object that exists behind the paper the stereogram is on. To see the three-dimensional object, the viewer must focus the eyes behind the paper to where the object would be. Most objects can be viewed by focusing on a point that is twice the distance from the eyes as the stereogram is. Some people have difficulty viewing stereograms, as it is difficult to train the eyes to focus on an imaginary object. The best viewing method for beginners is to start with the stereogram touching their nose and then gradually move the stereogram away from the face until the three-dimensional image comes into focus. When a successful focusing point for the eyes is found, the entire three-dimensional image should suddenly come into focus. Some people report seeing only fragments of three-dimensional objects, but if the correct focusing point is indeed found, an entire three-dimensional scene should come into view.

A rock itself collecting, preceding the made, made in the making, found after breaking, mere time constraints, shuttle and spindle, for should there be time no longer, that flowed so far it found flat land, if then, then now, a convenience for those who talk, no time, a Scot, not to deny the work, merely to say nothing, certainly not thank you for saying it is good because its mind was bent on that alone. What's your problem anyway? Ring the bells and bury scarabs, joust with road kill, chollas, spines and pads. Then the ball will come. Lobate scarps we should say of its cooling. Blanketed by the ejecta of miners, dwarves, nibelungs, it bulges at center like a drunk Mercator. Pat a cake and put it in the pity crater rims. Fracture crude polygonal struts.

There are things going on for which we have to avert our
eyes to see, not that we don't know them. It was all secret
societies of the dragon supported by, leviathan below,
behemoth above the town, funded with and invented by talk
of the transcendence of evil, a malignant sublime against
which philosophers posit ethical measures. The hand may
be connected to someone standing beside me. That it is so
only increases the number of bystanders: "the ethical
response recognizes that in the otherness of the other"...I
AM INFINITELY RESPONSIBLE FOR AND TO THE
OTHER PERSON, WHOSE SUFFERING IS MORE
IMPORTANT THAN MY OWN. I took out
the adverb, that this suffering is ethically more important.
The great dragon reposes between the nine rivers, the
waters of which are turbulent; and a tenth whose waters are
calm where the blessings of Paradise are said to descend.
Into this river the dragon his habitation, sallies forth and
swims to the sea, to devour fish and then returns again. The
nine rivers are banked by those trees of the months and
fringed with flowers. A final moisture remains after all the
drops have issued gently, and this drop forms the tenth
river. Of course this is allegoresis as the glands of Moll or
the sonnets of Zinn. These are not the fishes that glitter on
the horizon and fin means end, not fin.
Nothing of the colonies on either side of the Shigaraki flats
predict the ochre-red Mosquitoes that gleam in that valley
like crimson fire. Small flames on the tops of towers in the
surrounding hills signal toward the boats. The Brontes,
Gulf of the Titans, Eumenides, but the crowning
achievement is the continuation the Orcus from the land to
under sea about which much must and will be said, the two
being one line from the point where it leaves the land to the
point where it enters the Triviumone. Roads on both sides
to Malprecitor, right above Willing and Naked..
Take the whole work some artist betrayed, a necessity of
exhibition style, who lights his face but hides the world. If
the lamination of volcano and chalk hill is any measure, a

less artificial state would be dog displacing thrust faults, congressional stresses of thermal contraction, six fingered lizards by lineated terrain. The system of irrigation depends on these vapors in a terrain of uncanny presentment, like the shell of a shrunk man, heart sack creased like a pot flowing with itself. A heliotrope. Intellect ceases tasks. Thought burns it up. The lines appear broken from one end to the other, for which you can blame and do the Core contractions that produced these scarps and scalps, cliffs of implosion. There is nothing haphazard in the look of any. Planted along the mantled polygons named for literature. Dropping a stone on glass mimics the networks of the blue-green regions, directly to what seem centers of the land. Parietal lobes rewired stand struck, like legends traversed but not exactly written. Many sources of vacancy and presence, vacancy of design and designer, present flows of the natural making repeat patterns to identify recognition that some brands are a betrayal of vacancy.

I have seen this window and in looking in and out of it have had one moment escaped. before the border is closed.

To travel thence, to hear a listening ear what none can say before the windows of the mind you know, what faces are behind, passengers or refugees, to speak the largest class, imbuement covered points of light before a thousand amenities against the window glass with alms that intervene, time traveler can't remember much. The belt of sunlight, bands of light, answers to prayers before they prayed, to wake interstices down labyrinths and fill the eyes to heal.141

And all this comes in the SELVING of the aliquid eius where 'incompatible frames of being exist together or are together (Hopkins 356) inset and outset that include all things," but, and this is the crux, "the self of the universal is not the self of anything else,...that is, there is no such Attacked by sea serpents.

universal....for either it is selfless or a true self." This takes us into another, which admittedly neither Hopkins says or Loyola but we are compelled, for the world then is word,

expression and, the utterance of God analogous to the
utterance that results in the Word one meets in and through
the world that must be succored for the Diapsalmata
originary cry of creation, the groan that cannot be uttered.
Torn philosophy burns in the grate. Intellect speaks where
inmates incarcerate. Collective tiers of shanks and
kindness, the iPad and iPhone flop, the desktop flicks, the
power plugs alert to GPS wandering. There are no common
breakfasts here.

If you are privy to the triumphant guard of the
honor gates, where a spatter of dew fell like dust in the
morning. Famous malls were built to pull down more
moisture from the clouds, if there were any. The auto-
bodies otherwise were fed by underground rivers from
surrounding states whose expatriates went West, not
quickly, but with slow motion rumors of strife. Refugees
with briefcases opened and closed clasps on the right piece
of paper. Some districts, Kolonia also called Motza, "below
exempt," combined geography and prophecy in one brazen
bull. Fires set under the hollow bronze translated through a
system of tubes and stops into sounds like a bellowing
infuriated charge from the pensioners roasted inside. Bulls
and bears could interchange roles, depending on what
geologics spin proportion and property of the place. The
bear was the second up, raised on one side with three ribs
in its mouth. If you stand allegorical bestiaries, the first was
a lion with eagle wings standing on its feet like a man with
a human heart. The third was a leopard with chicken wings
on its back and four heads that put Colonel Sanders out of143
business. The fourth ate them all, which ravenous epithets
fragged all programed matter with actuation and display.
Brazen bull Kolonians built their own temples in seven
books, meaning the hills surrounding. Here an arm and a
leg from Homer and the Egyptians before the Greeks.
Along the borders Polyphemus played in the Anubian mud,
but there was always a need of rain. Snake dances, street
fairs of all sorts of totems evoked the gods of Serapeum, of
Saqqara, Alexandria of the Apis bull in a weaving mass.

Batists too paced single file in the streets chanting! To set the stage, bakers and artisans, sausage makers in the markets of Turkey or any set up shop to service the masses with no means of support. One wonders about people so resourceful where palm trees were planted for shade and under them, tied up donkeys were waiting. They took their Revelation seriously, camped in it or as near to it as they could get. Tent cities covered the plain.

In these circumstances the phase-locked ELF entrainment from factory scum made white foam and steam. Factory after factory drained elaborately. I walked miles up the concrete tubes, which got smaller until some sphincter tinkled at the foot. At the rivers surface were felled tree trunks and train wrecked scrap cars and cubes of metal. I walked the tracks with a .22 to shoot out insulators on the power lines like some grandfather against illumination in the Esquilache Mutiny in Madrid in 1766, except I was ten. 4400 oil burning streetlamps twelve feet high of iron and glass, were smashed in protest against illumination. Spy cameras, geo phones, grid life surveillance lamps, microphones shoot out, even cameras like on Hopi Second Mesa that when you approach up the long incline signs at the top, large signs command that no photographs be taken, that is, do not articifally freeze in the time the original living.. This was a long decade, a time or two of putty. The first condition of emergence needed clandestines to combat 144

the shadowgraphs, turn gas to light and incinerated the gasoline clothing about the globe. The second condition off every member, foot and hand was to obliterate the old. Pop obliterated Pop. One decade could not recognize another. It was the Annihilation of Now sprayed down in the dew hours before dawn when first noticed. Probably before dawn, but now it was three pm and heavy clouds forecast, not there at six, only hundreds of streaks in the sky. Poonoo wingkewang, the sprayers sprayed to meet it. Flibeedoo-flobeedee-buskeebang, staccato extinctions of memory relocated to some remote spot forgot. The sub aquean never

felt so strongly perhaps. The Reset Bull in which Antipas,
Bishop of Pergamon, was martyred when he cast the
demons out changed the direction of the compass.
Dehydration would seem its opposite, but everything is
opposite there of what is here.
Very provoking to be called an egg. Escape from the
past. Manhood, it goes without saying all of this would be
denied, overruled by the overridden who did their peers.
This unconscious collective belonged to, but built upon
other transitions. Now sir, set up your sail and row forth. I
wake consciously from awareness of a belt of strips of
sunlight darkened between, protoplasmic circles on the
bands of light and watch them closely opening.
I wolden he were hangyd by the throte.
If passage tombs could talk, or rock, volcanic ash, reburied
feldspar, then the fish streams under clay spines, speak
more. Kiss the Beast.
In a land of myth among the cowardly, the faithless,
the detestable the murderers who Revelation range all the
decedent in bits to section the body politic. enacted
players145
on stilts, the upper reaches of water cold as ice. bordering
factories rose Frozen creeks in winter flooded into skating
rinks. The flood felled produce bomber presidents, Covid-
virus, rioting cities, election frauds.
A suburb that called Gateway to Heaven, Libya,
Jordan and Abmah Baltemna, Behma and Bamah Benjamin
was building, not as if they need a place to worship
"You have seen many things, but pay no attention; your
ears are open, but you hear nothing." To have a thing but
not know it, do a thing but not do it. "Sink a shaft far from
the inhabited surface, go down swinging to and fro, hang
by rope." Are there eyes at the bottom of the sea,
supposing we descend? Hero though you may be, giants are
not the prophets to believe. There came a stretch when
stone cats envisaging faery heads upon us were
*undermind. Whose name is this, this name and this? We
know them where you once saw them filling in the

entrance, a thin layer of hard earth on top with loose soil further down. were as obvious as trees burning into sentences:

Condition humaine The modern age is fundamentally dishonest. Modern man through his own fault is caught in a bewilderment of self deception in and about himself due to a lack of naivete, in an age that can no longer be naive, an essential condition for a healthy and honest human existence. This points to an even deeper lack, a want of the primitive. Primitive existence always contains a reexamination of the universally human. The primitive thinker reflects on what everyone knows, or should know. What these things are must be shown not told to that self consciousness that is so self assured. If it recognizes it recognizes itself. The concept of human being is normative; The ethical task of each singular human being consists in transforming the psychic qualification of his existence in a pneumatic one; The bedrock normative practice that determines the human being as "pneumatic" is the existential speech-act.

Writing is pneumatic in itself if it breathes with these primitive universal dramas. Primitive ceramic feeds upon thought and forethought when stone hits glass and the breakage conforms to gravity and glass, not the intention of133 the artist; if not, the result is mere thought. Stressing these materials away from the smooth and the fine, all the lobate scarps of planetary implosion or cliffs, displacement thrust faults, compressional stresses, thermal contraction, lineated terrains are means of dramatizing the primitive. To what end? To display the universal human, not the fantasy, the pain in the global aspects of Mercury that lead to a loss of surface that secreting, planting of contradiction into the clay body makes. Slumping, cutting earthquakes seek the volcano in the kiln. The pollution in saying so calls fire out of the medieval Cloud of Unknowing with spirit. Fathom that after the volcano, like the shell of a man shrunk, heart sack creased like a pot expelled from itself, when you don't have naught to say. Thought burns up. Intellect ceases

tasks. You stand struck, parietal lobes rewired. That is
primitive.
The psychic element creeps in as a force of motion in these
parleys of minute detail, just as electricity does. The
Germans assert at dinner before the company of
connoisseurs, that faced with a truth which seems a lie a
man can only close his lips as long as he can.. Every one
not actuated by a spirit of contradiction will when the wine
has breathed at once perceive this is so, and will continue to
believe even after it is abundantly disproved. But here I
can't be still.
Programmable matter is a digital slavering of computation,
sensing, actuation, and display as continuous properties
active over its whole extent. Programmable matter would
have many exciting applications, like paintable displays,
shape-changing robots and tools, rapid prototyping, and
sculpture-based interfaces. Programmable matter would be
composed of millimeter autonomous micro scale without
internal moving parts, bound by electromagnetic adhesive
force.
Devour this, the cedar tail
and open beak are subway tubes.
That leave a wake,
nose pierced in mud,
spurred undersides,
smoke nostrils
Lights from eyes.
Morning tied a fish
To open the tongue of a river
With a hook to draw him out.
the outer coat stripped
to clothe itself.
All nations will worship the beast rising. Then the second
from land will force the mark that is its name. Ocean depths
of Leviathan and Rahab once crushed: "you broke the
heads of the dragons in the waters, you crushed the heads
of leviathan," Behemoth from land, Leviathan from the sea.
chaos monsters, Egyptians and Babylonians together, and

Pharaoh king of Egypt, great dragon, "on that day Yahweh with His sore and great strong Word shall punish leviathan, that pierce, leviathan the crook, and slay." Leviathan coiling, served with garlic, raisins and rettich as meat for the chosen, Eloah will slay135

He that dried the sea, the waters of the great deep, that made the depths a way for the redeemed to pass, who cut down Rahab and wounded, took more than one idol of Malkam, taming bigger than singularity, Job in his pasture and Isaiah in the mind of those immortals at the bottom of the Marianas Trench.

When the rivers out of the Garden of Eden divided, the one called Pison went into the calm tenth of which we have spoken. Out of the calm river, thus augmented, came all the others; in each a dragon dwells. Each of these nine has a hole in its head, and the great dragon as well, emits breath upwards and not down.

The big one when it raises fins, heaves up the waters every seventy years and a swaying tapestry of vision comes into view, at first mostly geometric patterns, then shapes and forms of plants, animals, humans, cities, temples, flying craft and the like. Particular images from time to time emerge out of the continuous flux to be re-absorbed back into it. As the images of forms and objects recede into the swaying fabric, the twisting coils of leviathan, his own double helix, with silver glitter and green designs on its skin. Head and tail encompass the entire story. In the Amazon, ayahuasceros regard the giant geometric patterns as the mother spirit of all others of the forest, river and air. The hide of the Leviathan will make "tents for the pious of the first rank, garments for those of the second, belts for those of the third, and necklaces for those of the fourth. The remainder of the hide will be spread on the walls of Jerusalem", which addresses the various levels of righteousness of those found there; but what most especially addresses the spiritual nature of the marzipan coated leviathan for lunch. This indicates that the ten acts of Creation had their counterpart in the ten rivers, and in

each of which one dragon so there will be plenty enough
for all.
As R. Simeon said further: "God created the great dragons
and every living creature that moves, and the waters
brought forth abundantly, after their kind" (Gen. I, 21).
This verse', he said, 'we have already discussed, but the
words "He created the great dragons" Leviathan and its
mate, slain and by the Holy One for regaling the righteous
in the Day. "I give you power to tread on serpents and
scorpions, and over all the power of the enemy: and
nothing shall by any means harm you." Later Rabbis said
leviathan was the political state and its forces would
protect you. Fifty states of leviathan pledge the beast was
rising up, a third part of stars lying on the waves.
That means Glaciation is out. The question if hulls worn
from the journeying, from the causes above, touching
cracks in general and because the lines could be furrows
ploughed by meteorites,--another ingenious solution,--from
which ships could build new keels and mend the jib in
order to plough a furrow straight from one center to
another, without either missing the mark or overshooting it,
or the visitant meteorite ship would boil a thick and tarry
mass over all the banks with pitch. These would have to be
specially trained to the business, each piece a silent
impossibility! The silence is complete. Braid tattered ropes
and cords. The stressing of materials as Mono-ha is
depersonal because the viewer doesn't have to figure out
the message, recognize the face, interpret the image. Those
who don't get this, or understand Mono-ha instead a kind of
Markov chaining.
Resistance to the collective where ever you disconnect the
Schumann Resonance, stronger than the Schumann
Resonance.
This state as an end in itself sent a flow of expatriates flee
to the West—not quickly, but in achingly slow motion
advance from camps among wolves where dark purple
blotched the eyes and rumors were rife as the numbers
swelled. Various authorities demanded papers of refugees

for their big briefcase. Doors opened and closed to the possibility of laying hands on the right piece of paper to enable escape, that salvic lure before the border closed for good. Changing the directions of the compass, the collective to transfigure the human overcame all relation, escape was uncertain, but it was not by paper even if and they were out there day and night, which you can take most literally, for as many before as had based their lives were divided, even if the matter was unclear.

They will dress without bodies here. Cruets, crocks and casserole in these collective cups woke up on the mid line between sea and land, a decompression of bends and chokes, plumbed with beached lungs, oxygen entering. The tongue after awhile speaks that it is a sea without end, but once, before the water was wet, no currents, no boats or flood to ratchet out the stones, before water no seas, compares to some myth of an unconscious we don't name. China and Japan, Russian and America all could play a part in justice to the inhabitants. You have heard of the Jerusalem inside Jerusalem where sometime the two witnesses testified and their bodies were slain but not their spirits?

On the coast, out walking in storm in September among comets where the sun is having a nice day our advice went captive. Say it like Jeremiah or St. John to understate the pages sunk in the river. Torn philosophy burns in the grate. Intellect speaks where inmates incarcerate tiers with shanks. The iPad and iPhone flop on desktops, flick the power plugs to GPS.

Thousands of sites maintained this society of a thing but not know it, opaque upon a diamond frost self formless, Does it come clearer if we regard the unimportant thing as writing under where parchment is in short supply, old trees, cracked skin, stout limb, a sapling circulating beneath, bleached out or not, then overwritten in a different text and ink?

Tolkien says it is spiritual evil because so massive on streets, in cars. Unmasking the cell, Galeano said what was

known in every barrio and ghetto centuries before, but only
then it became the bubble, a strengthened electro-magnetic
hold on media phones and the mind. Right off Tolkien says
"I am aware it is a rash adventure." It was rash to him
because a diversion from his protection, a spice, some
adrenalin. It's different when it's life or death. "Faerie is a
perilous land, and in it are pitfalls for the unwary and
dangers for the overbold." He did not say, "spiritual evil is
an overriding pervasive force that infiltrates every custom
and social purpose." He invented to hide its mask, "beauty
that is an enchantment," where chaps in the cheap seats of
the perilous and shadowy marches vote (9). You might say
Dante is Fairy if you want a good argument. But open your
eyes, the prophet is a fool and the spiritual man is mad.
Unmask, unmask, the despoliation is not complete. Not the
Blue Fairy Book or Sir Gawain's primary and secondary
belief, They are not coming to pick you up for some FEMA
camp of mind and heart. Mark your curbs to save them
time. These days it is a French camp fantasy that thousands
of workshop writers find by inventing from their front
brains any situation it used to be impossible to encounter.149
To look at the faces below the skins as landscape,
the pudding-pie ridges below the plateau in mountain caves
you can see in a topography of face, nose, cheek, a brow
that shades the eyes, one knee stuck, joined. Gully had
swore one's a girl, which guy got an arm around her,
looking down, praying something around his shoes.
Shoulders, heads, one, two, three, long coats, hats on top,
left on the rocks like ten thousand flee. Brush off the
cobwebs of sky. People who play with clouds of
Herringbone put them down. Some unborn eye hidden in a
cliff, toddles the rocks. Another arm sticking out to brush
off cobwebs of sky. You know what that is? A Dilly dander
bird on a fat roost with a monk. Don't have names for them
all, the samurai behind the back, elbow down in a chair,
knee to the left, shoulders right, entities of Collective Mind.
Yes we had a picture up but it was the only thing on the site
so took it down, which you can assay yourself by image

search, but beware the eyes and the shine which tilt of head and hair, what depraved can come in their communities of hell. The insensible loosed acceptance of the thing we all dread to know. Twitter in a major element, Smart 9-11 of biometric names, numbers. Disaster is an experiment, a metadata culture to harvest information to produce the future optimal trip, fifth dimension of existence, capstone event. It's not what happened, but how the story tells in the dimensions. Actors set a stage for effects. The future or what will happen is the fifth. The sixth extends this paradigm. Hegel has to play a part but then you knew we were training him

Adobe walls and housetop worlds of badger, tortoise, yarrow, blood moons and airy creatures of earth superior to this, were traded to the Red Rock Giants. Those who know the future by staying in the lines don't balance on the rails, shoot out insulators, walk the tracks with a gun. . colonists were of different minds 1) whether to acknowledge the collective at all, or think we were autonomous, that our minds were our own, which Reverse bark edges, needle grass. Colonists would convert the darkness, comfort annihilation with every effort to domesticate freedom. The more we have, the less we understand. Claus von Münchow built a time portal in Afghanistan and in The Twin Kingdoms of the Euphrates, Three Kingdom agents said they could mutate fifteen dimensions. Proponents hid their mad intent under a show of balance. Münchow wanted the patent for world gridlines to time tunnel hyperspace. Guten noir

All the big clubs, networks, studios, publishers analogized to government. Collective mind, artificial intelligence, the ET ruse had same blind to dwarf four, by size and number, words without words because it is the feeling, always the same, of pain and suffering told. This was the philosophy of the base houses, coherence too subtle to grasp, of which nothing else can be said except the poem about Little Lucy. Little Lucy where have you gone?
I went to London to see the Queen.

Little Lucy what did you there,
I frightened the mouse.
How could that be different from what it said? It was
always a translation problem for the crime bosses though.
Like myths about elephants, Little lamb, who made thee?
or the one they especially loved, The wolves are lovely,
dark and deep. Sure we can come up with more but what's
the point? Coherence is too big to see. The small and the
great are for the poor in between. To criticize these high151
figures and their fires off the Roman Camp at Ynys Môn,
where sea and sink holes attribute to Merlin and Old
Salisbury Sarum and snowy owls hang like low mist of
mountain, flint middens, creeks and Madrones, a soldier
fallen beneath bracken.
Just because this goes on does not mean we know it.
Something was placed between. You going to kick and
scream to hear these triplings are broadcast waves. Masses
ruled with collective control from 1927. World
population tripppled to 8 billion. Buildings exteriorized
exactly at the moment this paragraph was written.
Zivilization. Further discension, genetic tinkerers in the
Colonies, Pleiadian or not, engineered a protohuman state,
Ur fell by nature and exteriorized in a man on a life raft
who sent verse into the sea. Don't pretend the middle is
between these two. The middle is the collective mind
battle, great against small, all against one who questions the
mouse, or human against cosmos.
1) They did not acknowledge the collective,
Just because this goes on does not mean we know it.
Something was placed between. You going to kick and
scream to hear these triplings are broadcast waves. Masses
ruled with collective control from 1927. World
population tripppled to 8 billion. Buildings exteriorized
exactly at the moment this paragraph was written.
Zivilization. Further discension, genetic tinkerers in the
Colonies, Pleiadian or not, engineered a protohuman state,
Ur fell by nature and exteriorized in a man on a life raft
who sent verse into the sea. Don't pretend the middle is

between these two. The middle is the collective mind battle, great against small, all against one who questions the mouse, or human against cosmos.

Where fires raged up hillsides of black, mind you, minus the one extant memory was the Gateway to Heaven. Divergences as perceptible as the shape of Ohio in the after-life prove the rule. Offenses cracked fissures of Tycho in the Moon. Canals circled down. To call them canals is a faux pa mistake for rivers. Knowing nothing of underground trains in the Odyssey, or overarching causes like Bereshith Truth, it was Babylon. Byzantium tied to a rock and thrown in the Delaware! One from the sea and another out of the earth, female and male, leviathan and behemoth. Halfway through that report, with "all the power of the first beast before it," a territory not previously occupied exercised all the power of the first beast before it. It was national security. Revelation Kolonists plotted

These fact-like statements may arise simply from some science that does not exist. Moving the stones? Who knew the unthought hand predicted being? The unthought mind both revelation and code, a contradiction like Mengele loved

We name the Collective. Hope comes when partisans of Freedom harbor thoughts of the Unknown. Idaho, Utah, Nevada, and the Great Basin wash away. Hardened topographies of Ohio long gone, seeds sown, fall in harvest, raised against wilderness, reject the internal scab-mold and armyworm during day, winter pupa in soil at night. When civilized boots back Good up to the edge to dump its bodies of mind, fox, bear, seal, hawk, coyote, horse unglued in the collective, then the face, the nose, the cheek, the brow that shades the eyes, one knee stuck out name that Mind like opinion on weather forecasts.

The Collective feet tall and sixteen long, the Sicilian bull of Rome had a door in the side. The sacrifice locked in the heated metal roasted. It had an acoustic device turning screams into the sound of a bull. It is not moral purification that these combine in the modern, but it should be no

surprise that animals are cast as nations.
The bull success of the national empires, Assyria, Babylon,
Rome to which states aspire, not the lamb, the opposite
symbol of the victim and he sacrifice. So a bull as the
creation of a torture device suits its provocateurs going
back.
From Nero to … Phalaris who no too obviously are the gods at Tystes
banquet, still not as horrundus as the real Sicilian bull. Pre 5th century
BC. These bulls in the 3rd century AD of bull blood baths in a similar
contraption, but for illumination not execution over a near
millennium. At climax some think Seattle the head of Americo
geography, morality and prophecy, a Taurobolium sacrifice in the
form of a bull. The eye might serve as Amazon, headquartered there,
but parts of California are gone, like Baja. East sees east and west in
these states and nations moral agencies. You can look for where you
live in this country and prophesy yourself, impose a latitude and
longitude map on top and check your coordinates, figure out how it's
going to go for you in thisworld and the next, but the map is always
moving slower than the eye can see.

The sacrifice of nations older than the brazen Wall Street Bull, in
Pergamon 92 AD, with St. Antipas of the book of Revelation 2.13 as
our departure from the modern abstract that does not reduce its power.
Antipas was executed for not worshiping Dionysus at Pergamum,
Satan's throne given the sharp two edged sword of the book of
Revelation as being "in the days
of Antipas' faithful witness, who was killed among you, where Satan
dwells" teaching Balaam and the gateway practice of perversion for
the
worst debacles of Balaam orgies, as if a guru of Oregon. Antipas got
in as much trouble as John the Baptist when he opposed it all, but the
story of Pergamon and Antipas was made to transfer time and place
when the Pergamon altar was disassembled and taken to berlin where
by 1886 relief
panels from the Pergamon Altar were "transferred" to Berlin, where
they were placed on display in the Pergamon Museum Transferred is
a euphemism for all the pillage German British archeologists
practiced in their stripping of

the ancient world to steal its powers. Hitler had the nazi155
parade grounds for the party rallies in Nuremberg modeled
after it. There "1935, Hitler announced the Nuremberg
Laws. "The law for the protection of German Blood and
German Honor was intended to begin the marginalization
process of the Jewish people." Even if it seems too dramatic and
absurd a theatre there in" Nuremberg Hitler used the phrase Final
Solution
for the first time in public. Holocaust from a Greek meaning "a
wholly
burnt animal sacrifice," the Altar of Zeus in Pergamon, practiced
centuries later in Nuremberg, in the redesigned Pergamon Altar.

The bull is that Solution to the world and time, burnt sacrifice
for an even greater spectacle from the brazen bull of Phalaris to Nero
and on. If we would hope it to cease, the active principle keeps on
proliferating and abstracting among the train of nations. Symbolism is
unfortunate for
America's most acclaimed president and Nobel winner, which if we
take aright makes him the priest of 2008 at the nomination convention
for president where the backdrop was the Pergamon altar behind a
blue podium in the center modeled on The Ishtar Gate the eighth gate
to the inner city
of Babylon, part of a grand walled processional way leading into the
city that archeologists took to Berlin.

 Fact checkers went nuts to explain both the altar of Satan and the
Ishtar
gate in the same event, the nomination for president, a stalking horse
for all that follows and more, nicely packaged for media exposure and
subliminals to wonder how that sexual perversion was a gateway to
extinction.
After World War in 1918, the frontal gate of Ishtar was reconstructed
in the Pergamon Museum in Berlin. When that avatar spoke in berlin
in 2008 before the nomination he said in most noble tone: "The walls
between
races and tribes, natives and immigrants, Christian and Muslim and
Jew cannot stand," (July 24, 2008). As the walls came tumbling down

Elon Musk broadcast it from 60,000 satellites to every person, tongue and nation.

Of course that was real, not counterfeit at all of the gospel of Acts. A month later he accepted the nomination. What a few months or years if we invert time to change the time and times to see the Pergamon altar and Ishtar gate inspired the theater of Denver, long in the works. Confirmation in Denver was seen as it appeared to be, the inauguration of innocence; AI, took the lead. People want to know why even if we grant the what, we can't help them when the sublimate has entered their thought and the metaphor of this is that, contradicts their logic. The bull replaced by Obama to roast not Antipas but the nation. How's that?

The train goes over the railroad track, raddly rack de rack, raddly rack de rack. Bohemian Balaam makes a sudden leap to change Balak's smoking babes into Toronto sex bots come to Houston. Balaam to Pergamon, as Revelation says, Pergamon to Berlin, to Denver to Wall St rolled flat. Perhaps all of us wish we never knew, but not to beg the question, we do.

Artificial Intelligence is that Cloud figure that turns into a centaur right in front of your eyes. When LEGS AND HOOVES SPROUT OUT OF the SHOULDERS we resort to pictures to get it across. None of the facts are real, or some are, or many are, but since the Centaur-Kin Slayer invented ROBOT SEX for scientists this CLOUD APPARITION OF THE FEMININE absolutely touches this highest illusion, devolving again to   ceremonies that bridge Balaam at Pergamon to Denver to break it down, to them the world was a fish and birth was a "bathing" inside the rotten stomach of this whale for warmth. No moder bath has attempted such a system is cuch portable practice of the known such as distil in balneo Mariae a quintessence f poppy and some pints of lethe tht apothecaries cleanse with sordes and caput to evaporate but to prevent it snuffing up the nose will dilate somewhat, no longer thatn 15 minutes Volumes and sets of volumes on this in encyclopedias show how to put a hole put through one side of the whale's body sufficiently large to admit the lower part of the birth body, from the feet to the waist, to sink in the whale's intestines, leaving the head of course outside the aperture. The generated fumes of the carcass are said to speed enlightenment, which interior of the carcass being a spa of healing properties was closed up tight at night then opened in the day, but not so much that the patient breathed the fumes of Probyterians and Behemonists.

This Bilbao fish in person conjured fanciful and woeful associations with windmills, sagas and inventions of story-tellers on both sides of the Atlantic architecture the fish city world as fish. You could look at the project as being about the size of the world as a whale, which "bathing," or standing inside the rotten stomachs is believed to have started in the whaling town off of Eden, the southeast coast although occurring in many countries for years. In these cases the monstermonger had been dead about forty hours, and it was thought best in the fustian body of the work that decomposed that the hole be closed as closely as possible, lest the patient expire through the volume of ammoniacal gases ofevery opening, which mysteries of turgidus and inflatus applied to the recipient blow up to the shape and size of a tub, which vessels, like buildings of an overpowering and atrocious odor cure, as the whalemen say into Land based societies claimed as behemoth's cousin. To claim that an elephant could do the same shows how Ammoniacal gases are that addicting. Sometimes the patient could not stand this horrible bath for more than an hour, and had to be lifted out in a faint, to undergo a second, third, or perhaps fourth course on that orthe following day.

The Baleen Mysticeti of their metallic aqueum of pitch, fat, and hair soaked together in the subject as they straddled the flank of the river, was the bait, the cakes they used to bring Leviathan to shore, evoking the majesty and freedom of the deep that all history has endowed of Pitch, fat, and hair, boiled together and made into cakes, were put into the mouth of leviathan. The Asian carp that penetrated the rivers beyond these Snow Hills had been imported from the Gulf as precursors of Levifish first made as an odd hybrid of past and future labs. Volunteers came down to the beach to stop the infestation. Slump shouldered Polypcarp, a species his own self, with a Polyphemus eye and a giant mouth, was swallowing up the coast. People wrote allegories about faceless interchangeable cogs of pen and ink fish. Small fish poured out of the mouth of large beached fish likesmall words out of a big word. Land and water were overrun by fish. Dictionaries and academies were overrun. A two-legged fish walked up with a fish in its mouth. A one handed fish quacked. A fish bird flew with a fish head from a fish tree. A word dug into a mound and turned up a head under a verb. Mind mountains and dust fractals showed the maximum Orc, studied by a faux anthropologist in a faux school by a faux professor who ate them. This was their colonial lit. It made Bradford shriek, reality crumbling, a nice gesture if Otaku to implode and distort. Whether reflection of force was destruction itself, or avalanches, landslides and eruptive waves drove mind waves, be crumbling in distortion according to no law. Tidal influence reached 15 km inland. Is the mind natural? No.Nature is innocent compared to it. In previous times echoes of the occupation of this sport made myth become real.

2. The settlers took on these mythologica pop and rock to stop the carp. Government passed bounties to that effect. The results of myth were as necessary as old ship lists and oaths of allegiance. But there was no need to swear papers and sign to King George. Carp Leviathan right out of Hobbes wanted to say how its majestic governed in the most abstruse doctrines of piscine theology. Liberty in this way was absent everywhere but in prison.
Creatures in a river feel no sides, nor freedom between yards of blubber, itself a reality imprisoned by events.

Unaware of its own leviathan movement, states and individuals swam opposite directions without knowing. What is the meaning of freedom compelled one way by current while swimming as fast as it can in the other? Those within Leviathan huddle together in the nation cult. Buber said it was German but Washington, the tool and earthly reward, had all of them digging in the yard. The universe that invents this state, to help it rule, argued civilization (zivilization) just needed the ultimate term. So people, the universe wants liberty as freedom of the state! Washington rules and America is a slave. Bow down in your living rooms. Bow down to Atlas Hugged. Dante Alighieri is gone awry, a commonwealth free to invade all people and its own.

If leviathan had a greater following than behemoth among the mook who wore its spectacles, made necklaces out of scales scattered like shark teeth over beaches, the brazen fins suggest political types, like a mouse that could climb through an elephant's trunk to gnaw its brain. Giant tadpoles like stellar ships spread the sperm light of Egypt to infertile couples. There was a song, "where have all the tadpoles gone, long time passing? though they come in handy for future wars and experiments too. Obelisk symbolic rays of sunlight cast in stone with a DNA hieroglyph carved on the face. Yes it was all about fertilizing DNA. King over the children of pride whose sperm dress up like him to work, the most rebellious body part of Adam led him to rebel, organs for all other parts beside water and land could be ruled. Illa parte magis regnat additamentum, that part reigns more, these rules make more leviathan which gripe and break the petcock far from hiding from sight, the soul under land and sea. Hot conduits leave relic Apatosaurus or Argentinosaurus to drink up a river, snort Jordan up its nose to adore.

Remember that lascivious banquet when Beo takes leviathan withal, nose piercing through the snares those ribs where dolphins swim and the mighty body falls in a day? Then Gabriel takes orders to end. Both sanctuary and host are trodden under foot from Jonah to Hobbes to Melville, Mesozoics a hundred feet high and the length of a field our modern stadium would hardly hold, even filled with water.

Eating, sleeping, and spending as they did, as long as in their Mardi Gras huts they traded in leviathan with all mask and tusk reflex patriotism. They built their huts to house this idea of life. It's one thing to polyploid a cow three times life size, too big for a Mack truck through Holland Tunnel, but these accounts of giant size included behemoth tetraployed by elephant. These of course were all types and shadows of the democratic people's real network of cables, codes and signs.

You don't want to know about the mice in these parts, whose only saving was their enormous size which seemed to prevent much breeding. The relative pygmies of Levi Town relied on this to protect them from falling prey. These were the ones who sat in their meeting

houses and sang, "high above, high above, we know we are Christian by our love," which was the height of their capacity to think through where they found themselves, powerless to effect survival in the gigantic world. Be realistic, flying menaces were their benefactors when they consumed the
remains of both awestruck behemoth and the Lev, one above, the other below the ground.

Their sermons read in that time to come but I asked another angel to show me the power of these, how they became separated on the same day, one being in the depths of the sea, and one in the dry desert. He said, man, why are you so desirous of understanding secrets when you have only to call upon the Name of the LORD to be saved? Then the angel of peace said, these monsters are by the Power prepared to become food, that the punishment may not be in vain.

 Leviathan is never seen by its devotees and invitees who make up costumes for LevDay, Snake Dance through the streets in their pockets their horrid frenzies as if it were not enough that they live in leviathan homes and wear leviathan clothes, the depths to boil (Job 41:31) sparks of fire and burning torches (Job 41:19) Churning. Now look at the behemoth: " Jordan rushes to his mouth" (Job 40:23, NAS).

Devour this, the tail is cedar an open beak
pecks the bones of subway tubes.
Leave a wake, nose pierced in mud,
Spur undersides, smoke nostrils.
Lightning eyes. bigger than a fish of morning tied
to open the mouth of river tongue
a hook to draw him out, strip off the outer coat and clothe
yourself.
Of course up from undersea in planes and curves Heraclitus said the
water ever changes, but slowly like a ridge of golden rocks till we
discovered two globes of crimson fire we saw the head divided into
streaks of green & purple like those on a tiger's forehead: soon we
saw his mouth & red gills hang just above the raging foam tingeing
the black deep with beams of blood, advancing toward us (Blake.

Marriage of Heaven and Hell), with all the fury of a spiritual existence.

Tidal influence at Old Town reaches pretty far inland in the water light of several moons hunted by wolf and cub. Single rectilinear, curvilinear, pi, it is the mind that sees not the eye. Old Dame Trot some cold fish had got, and as the mind I bent, delusions come to temples, labs, board rooms, sanctums as Ezekiel sees in the visions of Elohim, where elders swing their censers before idols, hitty, pitty within the wall, and images of death dress up as life, inverted. Light as wave in water refracts to disperse chromatic aberration. Galloping Galloway, look at your neck; there you will find the strap. The standoff between draggle distortion and dreary convention collaborates physicalforms; pickled pig is made of pork for the title of the book is that Leviathan of Hobbes and the new political societies of Rota Club. This narrative of brothers is a fault and Swift's narrator is a madman or a fool. The book is not one that could occupy Leviathan, or swamp the Ship of State, so Swift may be intensifying Hobbes's critique, allaying them to provoke. a more rational response.

Do not forget the horse! The horse enters the city. The city is burned. Global aspects of this fire are romanticized. If Neptune hid the horse in these, what hides in thee? Sea serpents against dissent. They call this rest, if rest is death for theTrojan Priest who threw his spear against Old Town, one of the global temples whose subtext is distortion, like some emperor of the despondent kingdom who says all is well with civilization, even its discontent, until it's not.

Figs and a head that cracks. It shall be lawful for any Athenian to speak his mind. We spin this geologics over every proportion and property of the place. Speaking of the spirit of unknowing that human mind disports, if passage tombs could talk, or under bark organics and rock, volcanic ash, erosion deposition, reburied feldspar, fish streams under clay
spines, would they dare speak more than they heard. It is global says it all.

Colonia New Obis.

Of course the voice you hear is the mind's voice translating faster that any speech. It will not likely be able to say the word it is thinking, a hundred feet long to the inch, but not as fast as an angel speaking in prayer or Eloah's brightness coming out of a hand.

I was wrestling against its future with two spiritual ones above. They sent a lieutenant to oppose me who showed no emotion when dispatched dumped down. Wondering whether there were more when I woke.

The planet was undermined by the proboscises of leviathaniasis as if a mouse could climb through an elephant's trunk to gnaw its brain. These graspers were only sea and earth bound. Only connect, connect, connect called the Google Loon of the atmosphere. High altitude sex balloons bounced G signals from their fleets high above to the most remote regions. Internet.org of drone swarms and LEO satellites performing porn connected the same function. SpaceX satellites to fast corners of the internet globe programmed the enlightened poor. Maria pseudo- hirsuta!

Colonia II
Jonah risen unseen, bound and veined, almost unmade, the mystery driven Phison, a wateryarn with fire in him of foam streets. The psychic element creeps in as a force of motion in these parleys of minute detail, just like electricity. The Germans assert at dinner before the company of connoisseurs that faced with a truth which seems a lie a man can only close
his lips as long as he can. Everyone not actuated by a spirit of contradiction will, when the wine has breathed, perceive this is so, and continue to believe even after it is disproved. But here I can't be still. After the ships have sailed what takes place in the normal unbiased mind is like figures seen swimming overboard under the waves, as if to loose an anchor snared on a reef. If we expect to meet a certain person, an approaching figure will deceitfully take on his garb. The mere idea of a man walking finds expectation to endow it as a friend, true or false. The expert sees from
better mechanism in the higher centers.

Such epithets as ravenous. Fracking and fragging the mountainside:
Programmable matter having computation, sensing, actuation, and
display as continuous properties active over its whole extent.
Programmable
Rapid prototyping, and sculpture-based interfaces of millimeter-scale
autonomous microsystem particles, without internal moving parts,
bound by electromagnetic forces or an adhesive binder with the
eyeballs of a goat, except vertical.White Sands, Los Alamos, Sandia
Nat. Labs.,
Hollaman AFB/Alamagordo, Cannon/Artesia, NM. All connections
to each other. White Sands, Los Alamos & Sandia Nat. Lab tunnels
work the krill plants competing with the whales, little people, if such
can be said without profiling, not from anywhere exactly, not that
anybody is. Large rolled slabs stick up out of the ocean which they
drive into their nets,
the krill here being a little bigger than you would expect, which
makes a good bagoong.

The one very deep river which inhabitants avoid hastributaries to it
too, up the Coloni the Levi named after their peculiar humor to
cleanse Newtown, RockaBilloy and the effigy of Achilles Arch, but
who dares it or Casanova's Colon with its larger core that claps
together
compressional stresses and shrinks. We call these inlets Coloni even
if they are rivers that sail the rhumb lines to continual debate about
whether natural or manmade, some fill with water and some not. With
iron oxide and rutile wash the tangled hair and icy crusts between the
eyes of Christopher Colon.

The top and bottom are drawn on a scale three or four times as large
as the middle. I am not squandering words. The number of colonies is
183, not
counting suspicious invisibles at opposition. After the original 79, the
majority north of the equator, 116 not on first maps, in the dark
regions and the light, with some exceptions attributable to difficulty
of identification, there is a loss of surface in the planting of corkscrew
spirals. "… the eco-complexity becomes so intense with throngs and

multitudes of the Divine that it flares into the feedback of an ultimate vision."

This contradiction of colony is they jump on a chair and hold the map upside down. Who can journey through? The water wars against the pot. To fight the dripping pan and explode at will, a dish clout makes Archuleta for example, founded with the Gigas on the one hand and Titan on the other a cobalt hole. Once burned? Twice? A l'eau, a l'eau! Two hundred million horses of fire. In kilns, some critic would say, a terracotta army, wrenching scripture off the Wall of China to the Tower of Babel. China to Babel,
horses to kilns, prophets a whip to cleanse. Believe that and read the Great Wall as a kiln opening where my nephew asks, what is the end?
 Round as an apple, deep as a cup, strange riddles in steady air, that put to rest naturalcausation. The regularity of the caves, uniform width, their
systematic radiation exceeds any ordinary natural contrivance. What they are not helps to decipher what they are.

When I begin, says God to Eli, I will make an end; not only that all gods purposes shall have their certain end but that even then, beginning and ending the arch center of the Quandarists' rearranged curves and planes of lines. Picadors on the verge against nature, Rhetors against Neptune, beds, Querist hothouses, nature is innocent compared. Flames and reactions make display of infierni. Down at the dock they drift from shore. The land is fabricate. Boats to out reach the aquarium humane intersperse with dreams as if phrases from The Revelation appear on buildings. Bulletin boards form lines.

The Building and Fall of Jerusalem

"Architecture is an idol, a physical temple loci to which idolatry, over time, will inevitably adhere."[21] Even if the idea is pure in nature, Milton still believes that it will unavoidably lead to idolatry simply because of the nature of humans. Instead of placing their thoughts and beliefs into God, as they should, humans tend to turn to erected objects and falsely invest their faith.

Idolatry is of paramount importance in all these writings, from Balaam to Harding claims that "... under the serpent's influence, Eve's idolatry and self-deification foreshadow the errors into which her 'Sons' will stray."[22] Much like Adam, Eve falsely places her faith into herself, the Tree of Knowledge, and to some extent, the Serpent.

He shall break also the images of the house of the sun in the land of Egypt. Jer 43.13

The crusade against the equivocation of buildings begins in Milton.

Milton's first criticism of idolatry focuses on the practice of constructing temples and other buildings to serve as places of worship. In Book XI of *Paradise Lost*, Adam tries to atone for his sins by offering to build altars to worship God. In response, the angel Michael explains that Adam does not need to build physical objects to experience the presence of God.[30] Joseph Lyle points to this example, explaining "When **Milton objects to architecture,** it is not a quality inherent in buildings themselves he finds offensive, but rather their tendency to **act as convenient loci to which idolatry, over time, will inevitably adhere.**"[31] Even if the idea is pure in nature, Milton still believes that it will unavoidably lead to idolatry simply because of the nature of humans. Instead of directing their thoughts towards God, as they should, humans tend **to turn to erected objects** and falsely invest their faith.

Furthermore, Milton makes his views on idolatry more explicit with the creation of Pandæmonium and the exemplary allusion to Solomon's temple. In the beginning of *Paradise Lost*, as well as throughout the poem, there are several references to the rise and eventual fall of Solomon's temple. Critics elucidate that "**Solomon's temple provides an explicit demonstration of how**

an artefact moves from its genesis in devotional practice to an idolatrous end."[33] This example, out of the many presented, conveys Milton's views on the dangers of idolatry distinctly. Even if one builds a structure in the name of God, even the best of intentions can become immoral. In addition, critics have drawn parallels between both Pandemonium and Saint Peter's Basilica,[*citation needed*] and the Pantheon. The majority of these **similarities revolve around a structural likeness**, but as Lyle explains, they play a greater role. By linking Saint Peter's Basilica and the Pantheon to Pandemonium—an ideally false structure, the two famous buildings take on a false meaning.[34] This comparison best represents Milton's Protestant views, as it rejects both the purely Catholic perspective and the Pagan perspective.

Sun As God

from Rogueclassicism

Donald Trump's golden penthouse and Marcon's rule like a Roman god, *the Sun King* (le Roi Soleil), modern Louis VIV at his assembly at *Versailles* speak the same language. Sycophants of Apollo construe the Jordan Lead Codices as a figure of Christ, but the image is of Apollo antihead. The Golden Age is and will be the age of Apollo, Greek for Abaddon, the Destroyer. Sun god Apollo means light in countless poems, counterfeit good as evil and evil good. Abaddon is another name for Sheol, realm of the dead. John of Patmos goes out of his way to say in **Revelation 9/11** that Apollo, *apoliea*, Apollyon, king of the locusts here "had a king over them, which is the angel of the bottomless pit, whose name in the Hebrew tongue is Abaddon, but in the Greek tongue hath his name Apollyon." Flies like bats fly out of the cave of its mouth and crown this sun god riding horses with scorpion tails. The last words of that brilliant colorist of energy J. M. W. Turner before he died were *the sun is god.* The larger the neocortex the more likely its deception. That is all ye know on earth and all ye need to know. Cherubic Dionysian madness, kings' glory, embodiment of the sun, archetype of civilization *masks* the abominable *shikutz* sun spoken of by Daniel and Mark 13.14: "the 'abomination of desolation,'[d] DANIEL 9:27; 11:31; 12:11).

So the "eye with which the universe Beholds itself and knows itself divine" (Shelley, Hymn of Apollo), "presupposes a wholly Pagan ethics and metaphysics" (Lewis, *Discarded Image*, 27). The tree of knowledge distracts from the one real end. When the strands of alien forces come together with the pagan rituals of Rome, if such ideas can fit in an English sentence, an announcement made simultaneously by church, govt, UN, presidents and leaders of all kinds, from entertainment figures--Jay Z himself will swing a million votes and Beyonce, Will Smith--to the heads of science, these locusts, the public will already have transferred its reliance for truth upon them, will with the news take from themselves and others all their past beliefs and identity. Then the utterly bald suburbs get lifted up, then the cry of pilots in blue will work their pipes among the stones of fire.

St. John's play on words relays that Greek god Apollo is the King of hell. Apollyon, like Abaddon, means "destroyer." Similar references to perdition as apoleia, Apollyon, Apollo occur in Rev 17.8 and 2Thess 2.3 to institute the new one government. So that's what they mean when they sing *Here Comes the Sun*. Not to worry, Ezekiel saved to the last of four insights for the worst. After he saw the image of jealousy, the abominable beasts and the women weeping for Tammuz there came the worst in the inner court. Between the porch and the altar were about 25 men with their backs toward the temple, like profaned Mahomets out of *Charlie Hebdo*, who worshipped the sun toward the east (8.17), put the branch up to their nose.

All the talk in Swedenborg copied in Blake's Emanations, or in Isaac Luria, or the Babylonian Talmud of the Tree of Life in the search of the modern for immortality misses just one thing. They were not turned into gods but into mortals. They *carry along* the sin of their mortality while they walk the tree paths, but don't walk really, only imaginatively, fitfully, sporadically with jerks. Everybody knows the mortality of sin, <u>thus the effort to overcome it</u>. They used to sit at the dinner table and listen to their sin bones, those new carbon fiberbones/skeletons from (slow burned) demolished plastics 200 times stronger than steel, grow as if they were corn. One grew more than two feet in five years.

Silence fell upon the creeks. Fibonacci ratios, golden sections, fractal repetitions impastoed faktoviki.
Unless you count preemptory lightning strikes the silence was complete. The stressing of depersonal because the viewer doesn't have to figure out the message, recognize the face, interpret the rock itself collecting, preceding the made, made in the making, found after breaking, mere time constraints, shuttle and spindle, for should there be time no longer, that flowed so far it found flat land, then now, a convenience for those who talk, there is no time, not to deny the work, merely to say thank you for saying it is good because the mind was bent on that alone.

Think how large our tooth when the dentist drills. Both of us distort our face. The wireless connection between our bodies
when the other bites down multiplied to billions baffle each storehouse and exiles unguarded ingress and egress below. The main huge poster of spiritual resistance is Intent. A huge clapboard larger and abandoned after visits with people crammed in small spaces in the dream yard and roof tops. Kiss if you must! Vagrants, migrants, gypsies, tenants, homeless squatters, working men, blacksmiths under the eaves. The numbers swell. Various authorities demand documentation. Papers of refugees from the black briefcase, open doors and close. In that figure of a salvific lure,
another huge warehouse secured.

By now you must see it too. You must; my pain is my pain and your pain is yours. It was raining when lightning struck
Gloster from its planes, caught in the middle of a freeway rush adds to the unseen. An engineer with his hole in Foxy's wall, the mirror psychiatrist who deconstructs the human form and merrie Mouse in the Mill. The fishpond is on fire!

Drink this stuff with gin. This second part   laddies on a train could also be a fish in a lake, organ molecules. In the same lumpy body as much as the pilots who bomb cities feel the death below and walls rip up their edges, bones in embryo are birthed. I fall to my knees in Amsterdam. Destruction swirls. That's a leap. When the man in linen with
the writing came round I wanted "the mark on my
forehead of those who grieve and lament.

Rolly Powley, pudding and pie, back to higher worlds, lower away. The tickling at your knee pretends I won't make a stew.
When you join a colony and retire by the pool by the light of the lava you cool. Spelunkers chance down comfortable dark holes. Mistress Wren sent her Queen unto Spain for basic Nova *technoique in the training Hege gave Snowden. Creating destructive tolerance to form benevolent neutrality toward its own culture of subversion and dingle doosey, the cable strand telepathy of wires, had its ears cut short, its tail cut long in the herd of Buggeers and Prawns. No matter what facts are prevented in amnesia, oh where or where can they be, the Anthropos you may have for sas-age ish goot, bo-lo-nie "decreases to zero the stimulus conditioned Tyrone Slothrop as an infant, but "there can still be a silent extinction beyond the zero" (Laszlo Jamf).

So launched a conditioned mind. Cowslip and shad blow, said one to the other, if you don't talk I must. Seventy years before this high carillon, western gov in guise, the best little donkey that ever was began to cross the bridge. America was nearly ready, means it or not. Wudna I wollup him? stuff him wi' nuts,
make him go with 'is teal cock'd up?

Two players form a bridge with uplifted arms. The others pass through in a line, each holding onto the one in front and hurrying, fearing they will be caught by the descending arms with a tug of war. That's how the bridge was kept from falling before direct repos. A bridge from Boston to Philadelphia and New York, where onlookers play scrabble.

Dance over them Laddie because Minneapolis collapsed. Call it Universal servitude. A natural sway to increase the step over Gog's bespelder'd floor, All is One gave her eggs to sell. Electro rad hardened eggs in girls absorb less EM, but harvesting from eyelids, venous return, arterial pulse, footsteps, motion of walking, loose clothes fitted with nano batteries, incomplete males make the worker bee.
Synchronous lateral excitation touch,
vibrate to increase and we're a' dry wi' o't.
Butter, lather, bony strike,
hair cut, froth neck, we go work.

The Man Who Disappeared in That Land That Appeared, Disappeared, Reappeared, now listed as Missing, ceased making sound. Versions depend on who tells, whether from inside the belly or the armadoes cask that ballast its nose or Kark Half Horse allows for these typos that change the state? Ziccoty, diccoty, one cast beyond, loving particular, to take it by force, the cat's in a flurry, Elijah's to come not through coercion but waiting untouched, while we explore the world. Here's my awl and wax and thread, computer chips in the head, but you should find the shoe.

What if someone said "I can assure you I feel the visual image to be two inches behind the bridge of my nose?" Or, "I feel in my hand that the water is three feet under ground."
The thrush will sing,
 the bull will pull the bell,
DIVERSITY IS THE NEGATION OF IDENTITY
so I went to the antique mall.

I walked naked among folk singing fidell-didell, tooteloo,feedle three alternative histories, all true. Ask the cuckoo, stork and pee-wit scholar. Ask the cheek teeth of a lion. Oh! what syght and felynge of all creaturs alive?

Maybelline and Jack were high, raced to the pueblos to take the oath. Who knows but there the words come out of the ground from some bitter water or clean, so clean it makes us see?

The cuckoo comes in April, she sings a song in May, in June she beats a drum and then away. If you would take this construct higher, beyond the walls and gates of that HOLY CITY of Revelation, information manuals describe the governance of its new rulers in Reset Town, new town, new era new world.

Indeed what is it? The density of sentences is a capitulation to deliver the message. The anesthetic from all sources is an idea of Koerner, that Bosch's everyday life depicts an enemy bent on destroying the Narrow Doors in Wide Green Fields in (Surrealists and Outsiders 2019), that Enemy in the world, its landscape and identity where writers arrive at words that appear in the empire. Not to obscure Pancake feeling cantankerous "By the time I hear from you I will have forgotten you are there."
 "Call to the Unregenerate" considered those beings of collective mind as "owls with iron feathers, scorpions, caterpillars, ants turned peacock. It's beautiful if you like the sort. One society exchanged privileges with another for controls. Don't have names for them all, the samurai behind the back, an elbow in a chair,
knee to the left, shoulders right, entities of Collective Mind." These are also Revelation Colonists with the Mischwesen carp and bird apkallus the 2nd Temple sat outside the wall in biblical accounts. Angel murders arranged by Balaam to murder the human made even larger context of the Erev Rav Wheat and Tares. Chosen vs. hybrid species of USDA labs, human alien counterfeits real angels tell apart, since "Wheat seeds first exude a milky substance like sweet corn as they ripen. When the seeds pass the milk stage they can be punctured

without oozing. Then the harvest begins. The grains need to harden before."

This should bring a merry ho, ho, ho at the opening of the World Church the wheat and tare whose girls beat their hands like butterflies to see the enemy sow some tares.Kings of the Pentagon trash giants still thought
the missing head would supply the brain. The Five Disasters they called freedom, produced by Clanton, Bushinskis and Le Bommb, with the big one to come, would burn a new Reichstag in the public brain. Van Gogh's brain reconstituted at gunpoint, in the yellow period of Xanthopsia haloes around the lights, furred antennae feeling a huge path took flight in the Boxcars, if you call that intimacy whose first FEMAle boxcars implied.

Don't get all excited that if there are French the German will be right behind. Before the country was carried off. by Apparatchiks Donald O'Bombas, Bushton-Gore, all chapters in the anti-history of Boxcar Betty and Sisters of the Beauty Path Road pursued Wittgenstein in the Blue Book, until it was infected and had to be microwaved. If you microwave a page of superposiion too long it will begin to brown and burn from the center out. That's how he got the Brown Book. There the world named for Leviathan by the sea made its emergence. The caves and nasal beauties filled with Revelation Colonists. Chambers of the mouth and inside throat, theologue gridlines hyper-space engineered got nominated forPushcart Prize in 2014 when Corman-Roberts said, "love to run "The War on Neptune" and then "Full of Crow has nominated it for this year's Pushcart story."

Caligula stabbed the sea because he thought it full of Goya's giants and horrors. Homer took a full page ad with this in the Trojan Laocoön, along with the statues, and paintings of El Greco. Daniel said the sea would harbor the global age in that day when goats would trample stars. Nobody dared say a word to Bosch. All these sites had connection tunnels below ground. When it came out that the tunnels reached both coasts, they were camouflaged as krill plants competing with the whales, which enabled them to make the celebrated epath of Leviathan under and beneath,Behemoth above ↕ to prospect earth and leviathan under sea between the cultures of myth in the aquarium humane like Ossian on the grass, Plotinus, Pythagoras, the same soul of the world in land and water. It's always government and religion that people flee, government land and religion sea, behemoth and leviathan, not to implicate Russia and Britain! Getting out of Jerusalem, or Dodge City or NYC or LA orMumbai or Wehreeverf, we are told not to stop. Leave your housetop and head for the hills, before, before it does. That's what the bridge and colony and the steps to the bridge signify, as if there is some escape, some way out which they all hope for for, all except the ones who go willingly.

Financiers guard the honor gates with triumphant threes. Elephants, tygers, and alligators, if you please, in case you are privy to the masks behind the dehydrated ET. Dehydration would seem the opposite of what we see and hear, but everything here is the opposite of what it is there, so the spiritless
body-autos pull the strings when there are clouds, if rain had ceased and the rivers along the coast are fed by underground aquifers. These people took their Revelation seriously. They camped in it or as near to it as they could get. Tent cities that covered the plain became divided into schools. Some called it New Byzantium, whose accounts must be given unfinished.

Entrance to Byzantium
The moon, to show or tell all, kept them on the bridge, going back and forth. Great tomes of thoughts flying around their heads, commentaries, languages, sciences enforced even on the rivers below the great myth.
But to cross the bridge was to cross all sight and sound visible and heard in proof states of the world below. Put one foot on the bridge and you will
yourself prove nothingness. That's why we ride these asses. They are entient beings, material among wraiths who pay no attention to thenot seen or heard, being alive, not controlled by the machine predispositions of chaos. Without imaginations the bridge projected in the second heaven of would disappear.

Not to offend those who have not seen the cracks radiating from the
center of this hypothesis. Divergences perceptible as the shape of
Ohio implode
like Tycho in the Moon. Colony craterlets, orbits of phyllotaxis prove
some finite intelligence descends to meeting-places along the canals.
To call them canals is a faux pa of planned obsolescence like thinking
the world flat or mistaking rivers for canals. Cracks, taken alone, were
caught between the present-day fabulous and history displaced.The
great mythreal moon showed that on the upper deck. Long legged
caissons in rows of
large watertight chambers open at the bottom kept up the pressure
over top
the moon-chained floating villages. Gulls clustered all over
the feet of these turpitudes not to be mistaken for the dingle stars of
radium eyes kept in night jars beside their thrones. Flashing lights in
the dark were wishes rising to be formed, like plum-trees laden with
rich fruit feed the gulls. These grow over standing-ponds. The circles
rotate in and out like
wheels in wheels as they always have. To think anything was making
it but themselves or that it was making by itself required massive
outpouring
of counterfeit of the the Newbury commentary in all languages, all
journals, once empirical thought.

One question remained, whether the record of all these versions
would remain when the bridge was destroyed and whether there
would more history or science creating new tomes, or are these
already closed and preserved in some cloud you? The book heads and
tome heads nicely bound in leather incline like Egyptian mummies at
a 7 degree angle for comfort. To belong to the city of the submarine
and abandoned river beds forced to change from substrate when
ambiguity sought entrance to the Divine City
grasped the prize. Fathers and mothers still strip mined the freeway.

Break In
I had been up there in City Hall myself so it is more or less possible
among the many parts and pieces that crock and cram shoulder to
shoulder to pass. Obviously we do that with apology. The name tags

are also missing. As for the photography, it is a variable cloudy day when we pass through.

We first see these paintings in the apartments but can tour the upper stories too, unfinished, rickety, dangerous with catwalks but traversable. The cotu has never been properly finished, just enough so it won't get too wet in the

rain. It was a dream yard of roofed parking lots, shacks and other warehouses unsecured, never locked. Occupied by vagrants, migrants, gypsies, tenants, homeless, squatters, working men, blacksmiths, artists who set up tables under the eaves. With so many people in small spaces and close quarter the shops in this bazaar acted as posters of resistance.

Snake dances, street fairs, all sorts make the weaving mass, to give the flavor, set the stage, bakers and artisans, sausage makers like in the markets of Turkey or any farmers market of American cities set up shop.

Palm trees have been planted for shade and under them donkeys tied up against the heat, awaiting their burdens. This was the site of the international fauxtown taxis. to roam the roads and protect from

all manner of inebriant health. Seventy two kinds of pot, one for each of the angels greets newcomers to benefits. Imagine pearl mailboxes kept those tunneling up to hope, hovering maddingly slightly above the ground around of reach, none the chisels and hammers of workersn scaffolding get the blade to bite the real, and considering the dangers of

supernatural beasts must anent to the divine, the closer they got the more cherubim. Further up the hill lands superlarge herds of behemoths range, and from the penetrating trough the rivers outlandish produced out of the Odyssey. I omit the wasps.

It being a global outcome, parts of CA were already gone. Some think Baja was the tail, but it's gone. People see different tails. Call states and nations moral agencies. You can look for where you live in this country and prophesy yourself, for all the nations around. Impose a latitude and longitude map on top and check your coordinates, figure out how it's going to go for you in the life and afterlife posed. But the

map is always moving slower than the eye. The sacrifice of nations in
Taurobolium is more than just states, continents, seas, world. That's
all a concept of segmentation when literal facts take a literal reading
to form a Taurobolium of space, the cosmos entertainment of absolute
denial charged with irreality, the beasts
coming up from the sea represent nations and a complex of states.
So America was a bull sacrificed for this world to achieve. The
continental U.S. nicely contorts in an east west rectangle figure of a
bull. Can the Great Lakes drain, the sea, Austin sink? And what of
these Orocopedia blue schist assemblage of the Pelona schist along
the fault, the piercing point to construct the first offset? Maps
compare to real versions of the Oecomene called--Gateway to
Heaven- "referred to as motza— exempt." Geography combined
morality and prophecy as also a metaphor of concurrent media crises,
Covid- 19 virus, rioting cities, election frauds-- set under the hollow
bronze bull, heating the metal until the prisoners locked inside are
roasted to death as their cries are translated through a system of tubes
and stops into sounds like the bellowing of an infuriated bull.
Programmable matter senses actuation and display.

It is a good body town and if it looks ramshackle that with donkeys
awaiting their burdens. for pets were a common breed in along with
Wittgenstein's rhinoceros, you could see them and then they would
disappear, reshaping escapes, fantasy boats and fable captains, visas
for the countries of Atlas and passports for countries that do
not but will exist.

To forget something that doesn't officially exist, this state
as an end in itself that sent a flow of expatriates to flee to
the West—not quickly, but in achingly slow motion
advance from its camps among wolves where dark purple
blotched the eyes and rumors were rife as the numbers
swelled, various authorities demanded papers of refugees
from their big briefcase. Doors opened and closed to the
possibility of laying hands on the right piece of paper to
enable escape, that salvic lure before the border closed for
good. Changing the direction of the compass, the collective
to transfigure the human overcame all relation, escape was

uncertain, but it was not by paper.

Many if not all these leaders had undergone successful
cremation of care operations to produce that assurance of
manner and demeanor of audacity, as if they had invented
fruit flies or vaccines for fruit flies. Cremation of
conscience would be the better term for its sense of
swallowing up sin, sin eating at the fount of their idol turn-
god. Yes it is messy to think all this society was just
another way of serving their godlings, but like they say of
the city outside the city that is not the city but is the city
not seen. The great Wittgensteiningsaid that. .

As the librarian of that civilization would assemble titles like Georges
Bataille kept in the Bibliothèque Nationale who built theirown
temples in the seven bowls, this was a land of myth,a truehorror the
Île-de-France one would say. In order to get to the holy city you had
to pass through
these crowds of neighbors. Law and order of a kind sprang
up just from the natural tendency of some to push forward
while others stay back. Out of these pushers emerged the
Congress Mayor, the myth master Herzog who took charge of what
commerce had grown up around and paraded to sound of boom boxes
that
played his mood song, the coyote song of Don Edwards, hoo yip hoo
yip hoo, hoodi hoo yip hoo di yip hoo, hoo yip hoo yip hoo, hoo di
hoo di yip
hoo di yip hoo. The guru of Maru he was called.

The Coloni. Fish stories on both sides of ocean decree that all cities
have the architecture of a fish. Leviathan and Behemoth,
since they divide the world into sea beast and land take the
rest. A whole herd of Texas Behemoth had been imported
to the uplands and I don't mean the auroch transplants on
big game ranches. Those are spotted and browned, but have
so trampled the earth into shards and shreds of rock and dirt
one wonders what they eat at all, but they go up into the
thousand mountains to forage trees. No natural enemies

bother them there unless you count peremptory lightning
strikes. Myths don't breed, so there is only one
and that it waits to meet its mate. Their gigantic size is a world to
themselves. Joining of and and sea might be a fantasy where massed
hulks form the snow hills and where reconstituted mastodon are
landsides.
Higher up more frequent lightning strikes keep the
population manageable, if one can speak of polyploided
escapes from labs including rats as big as cars, and coyotes
like parking garages.

Meteorites stir a thick and tarry mass on all the banks with pitch.
The silence is complete. Braid tattered ropes and cords. The
stressing of materials have to figure out the message, recognize
the face, interpret the image, shuttle and spindle for saying it is good
ths mind was bent on that alone. That's how you pass, ba beetie.
with your soles on their heads or give a colonial shriek.
Things fall from the cranks. bonnie bairn. Since that's what all this is
about, the teasing of multi dimensional up and down the public mind,
the biggest
Palantir of all, the ring , the ring, to all the greater and lesser portals
and gates evoked by bathing in the whale in the prescribed form, the
purpose of
latter day genetic engineering active in labs from Saudi to the
Beltway, Goldilocks tinkerers that engineered this science had bound
comedic shapeshifters fast for seventy generations in the valleys of
the earth like a corn tortilla that after a year in the frig still looks
good, but when dogs
take it out of the trash they won't eat it; it just lays in the yard
flopping like a disc waiting to eclipse the fall with the fury of a
spiritual wereweather mind wave, just as there is no nature in the
untold hybrids loosed upon the world of the Dada landscape at
Disney Concert Hall or inside the prints of Roy Lichtenstein.

The stage is a stage, the audience is a stage, their lives are a stage. but
the windows seem to move up and down. The building sways as if
two

dancers were drunk that realized "LEVIATHAN camouflaged by abstraction, a marine- animal aspect of the building's representational identity... based on fish projects inspired by fish imagery, fish surfaces, perhaps even by fish structure, and obviously byfish organization---it is a piscine organism. It is organized in architectural plan like a fish, contoured and massed like a fish, has features that represent identifiable body parts of
fish, and a shiny surface (metallic scales) like a fish. So, although Iovine contends, perhaps wishfully, that it "doesn't look at all like a fish" (I especially like the "at all" part), there is every reason to believe that Gehry himself would be surprised, if not disappointed, to hear this says...."
deep SIGHT.

The one deep river that inhabitants avoid has salt water tributaries to its mouth. To evoke its occupants, sailors toss chum over the sides of their boats, chum and chub that a whale eats, but since it is the whale of the State and these sailors are nobles and ministers of state in the boat, the whale is really attracted to them. It is not a simple whale since those who question the right of government to rule are also put into its tub. This port is named for at peculiar humor, which should not obscure the truth that whale of state was better known as the Leviathan of the Sea.

Profusion of myth spreads to the colony on wings of clouds
and fire so easily that we are well advised to shoot these
birds before they land, hardly possible since the myths of the twelve nations are proxies of the Pharaohs who left Egypt for greener grass, 12 nations, 12 tribes, 12 families. Like the Pishon and Gihon, lost rivers of Eden, waiting for leviathan like those at sea we pray for on Sunday wait for morning when it's evening there. The top and bottom are drawn on a scale three or four times as large as the middle. I am not squandering words. The number of colonies is 183, not counting suspicious invisibles at opposition. After the original 79, the majority north of the equator, 116 not on first maps, in the dark regions and the light, with some exceptions attributable to difficulty of identification, there is a loss of surface in the planting of corkscrew spirals of iron oxide and rutile wash the tangled hair and icy crusts between Chris

Colon's eyes ,all Machinations of hands, when things come to action; his Quando; one time to him: Mountains and Vallies, Sea and Land, distinguish not his Ubi; all is one place to him: When I begin, says God to Eli, I will make an end; not only that all purposes shall have their certain end but that even then, beginning and ending is Done. The hills of Catterline brood like a sea captain slump over the pot of his water jar in the indigenous stirrings of Der Mythos vom Verlust der Mensch-lich-keitthe, loss of human myth.

Old Town founded its marine museum of the mind there, as if Greece had been emptied of all the whales of thought and forethought that flowed from thousands of years and springs. You could look at the project as being about the size of the world as a whale, which started in the whaling town of Eden, off the southeast coast of Australia -- although it had been
occurring in many countries. These gases of an overpowering and atrocious odor that bring about the cure, so the whalemen say. Ammoniacal gases are that addicting. Land based societies however claim that behemoth's cousin, elephant could do the same were the patient shut up in a covered
pit of elephant dung.

Liberty in this way was absent everywhere but in prison. Creatures in a river feel no sides, nor freedom between yards of blubber, itself a reality imprisoned by events. Unaware of its own leviathan movement, states and
individuals swam opposite directions without knowing. Those within Leviathan huddle together in the nation cult. Buber said it was German but Washington, the tool and earthly reward, had all of them digging in the yard.

The universe that invents this state just needed the ultimate term. So Washington rules and America is a slave. Bow down in your living rooms.. Dante Alighieri is gone awry, a commonwealth free to invade all people and its own. The only exception to these dives below the surface of
harbors, seeking contact, soft kill, slow kill, silent kill of the perfect beast to cull the herd, is synthetic telepathy, psi tech, Smirnoff patent,

programmable black metal, and clams and oysters for delicacies.
Leviathan is never seen byits devotees and invitees who make up
costumes for Lev
Day and Snake Dance through the streets, causes the depths to boil
sparks of fire. The picture is of a creature whose passing causes
churning, upheaval and turmoil. Such epithets consume the
mountainside:

Twelve Steps
Programmable matter aa proposed computation, sensing, actuation,
and display as continuous properties active over its whole extent
would have many exciting applications, like getting a book written
about yourself. But it's harder to read online, so he stole it from the
priest's library. Scrawls at the paragraph heads actually looked like
heads.At first he assumed it had been the priests, but out of the cave a
long while now he realized better. The world he lived in was a world
all new, except it didn't hold still. It
dangled like his armless phantom side. He had noted in that fight
whatever poetry said. People should read the papers. He didn't die.
He lived in
suspended animation, here a little, there a little, unaware through
centuries, which at least improved his night vision. His places of
shelter were as wild as ever. When he got the book maybe the noble
spark began to live it down. The shame in his head of dread and
slobbering made a desire to redo. He substituted nightly raids of
libraries and schools, never left a trace. That's how he found a copy
of the twelve steps and this abominable Grendel he would rewrite.

Amnesia prevented him seeing in the mirror of the book those
illustrations that looked like retraced lines of animal hairs. They
swarmed the page, the phantomof a world as an electric post, tied
down at one end to what
looked like a teepee with smoke coming out the top. A smokehouse?
Not something he had seen in other books. The foreground melted
into an illustration that looked like the letter M. His mind wandered.
"The mere is the M you go down to come up." Different schools say
go up and come down, go down, come up. He believed the image was
his own to control, studied its resemblances at night. Other shadows

walked the earth. Misshapen erectus bent. Clothing hid imperfections. Hats, beards covered stupor. Colors from the prehistory of sleep. He worked on his consonants in the cave, mashed and noshed, scrounged pants and shirt off lines, got a hat,
worked on posture. He sounded foreign, but what if he did? Resembling so many he went out as himself.

 But if he was this free why did he remain in his "study" puzzling by candle the text of a book where he was cursed? "The Life and Times of a Horrid Muck Monster," he called it. It was a children's book. The fanciful pictures of MuckMon were cartoons. It even rhymed, not that he noticed. but there was more discussion in the introduction than of himself. He looked further in the wet pages. Some Italian, Antonucci fudged the text. The editor thought the error where "peak" was "peek" significant. In Italy the word was vetta picco. By the second reading the illustration got blacker, began to look like monograms shifting, a sand dune of the top of a head, bulging bald except that in the mirror he had hair. "Hairy Esau, the AlienT shirt," he called himself, "Neanderthal Brown." He thought about getting one, "Monsters are not normal." But his main concern was "where can I find another to tell?"

There were a lot of steps doable in the twelve, like have God remove these defects of character (6). But along with not knowing anybody to tell he had trouble with the direct amends, (9), and not hurting others while he made amends. He was tempted to go out some night and take the first pedestrian as confessor. A man. He would approach from a bus stop or alley with a knee on the chest and a hoarfrost breath, glare down and pour truth. He felt drunk at the contemplation. How to prevent harm in direct amends? His mind scrabbled the word NIXON into letters in the corner of the text. The
text as his confessor! Would it be so, that he would confess to his own indictment, confirm the worst to a book? His eye caught the comment,. "they see all life without observing it." Further amends, he made a note on 48, which sloped to the right toward the shape of a giant Hokkaido pumpkin. The Zen monster of the tale told the monster outside the tale that it was here again. Monster in, monster out.As to the list of persons he had harmed (8), where start?

In his mind three people were standing around a pyramid arguing. An cross came out of the center of one and went up over the apex of the pyramid. As they were standing there he thought he saw the letter A. It grew into a double A (AA), which didn't make him feel better. He quoted the text to the wall, vocalized it, but it was not only hard to forgive, it was hard to come up with a list of those to forgive.

Should he give himself up and be booked some night to the dismayed splay prints on an inkpad and a genotype back to nobody knows? Put the civilized in a roar, upend evolution? He believed in instant evolution. Wishing made it so. But he was a little behind. To catch up he found
himself imaging again outside the hall like he had never moved. In the spirit of peacemaking he flung out a body at them. Had he lost control? He failed this step. It was hard to escape and to pacify enemies. He could not pacify himself. With the body of the heroic Hrothgar the giant fled.

He was alone with the body and the twelve steps. He put them on the wall of the cave illumined by torches of fat. This did not entirely satisfy him. Something more was wanted, a mentor but he had found none. He dialogued alone. "I am powerless over compulsion and my life is
unmanageable. I have not come to the world to do good." His confession was an incessant drop in the cave. "Chaos has visited me. I must suffer prayer and meditation to improve conscious contact with God as far as I
understand" (11). He thought that, not exactly in those words. "I share a malady with giants and salvages." He might have been comforted by hunters and cannibals who take the kabob. "How recover from the bestial? Ape men and pagans behind. "I cannot ape and be my better half." Was he talking to some image of a law gone dark? "To eat or not to eat. To die. Absurdities plundered him, "should I vegan the child of Cain?" The price of admission to his recovery raced through the tunnel and out into the light.

It reminded him of his understudy in the mere, that lake at
the bottom of world's end where he had so long lived, if

you call that any kind of life studying shadows on the wall
among smoke. Restless at bottom. He then realized he was a monster.
It said that right in the text, which made him wish for the rest, except
the head was amputated. Did he have the head or the body? Who
knows,
which did not help him in the steps.

Come to believe that a Power greater than ourselves can
restore us to sanity. "I have the advantage on this one," he
thought, "believing in a power greater than myself,
Beowulf the glory hound, or heaven hound." Yes he
believed in Beowulf when even scholars did not, or were
unclear, both scholars and dragons. Grendel going up and
down, Beowulf going up and down. The mere was
churning. It rumored polar bears and eels, but you know if
you believe everything you can have no story at all. As to
being restored to sanity, he was required he recognize the
error of his ways, his inability to control himself. Did he
have to grow his arm back? Beowulf, which means
beehuntin, that Saxon was his agency to this.
He was a little delirious with the (4) searching moral
inventory of himself. The beast boy had written in the
margin, "they see all life without observing it. They see it
but they don't see it. They think I don't see it, but I do."
His denial of so long had caused his consciousness and a
level of being to increase in his mind. Here the word
"buried" was not just scrawled, it completely obliterated
the page. That was Step Ten, a personal inventory of the
serious monster still alive in him. He sounded like the
Apostle dying daily, praying delivery from sin and death.
He admitted to God, and to himself, but where was he to
find another human being to tell the exact nature of his
wrongs, as much estranged from the language as from the
difficulty. Where was he to find "another!" human being to
tell. Another like himself! Not likely! Another! What was
he anyway but the other without the an, he who was maybe
at best just half?
Humbly he asked to remove his shortcomings. They were

not small. A bird flew up in the margin, or now he was outside still and saw through a dark figure the aegis of his design for help. In the margin of the book it was a series of unexplained connective tissues missing, a bone stuck up255 out of the plate. OK, that was also a slight shortcoming. He added it to the list of all persons he had harmed. Further evidence of the monster in the underbrush. The bird seemed to be swinging a weed wacker.

Amends to injure stood in the doorway. It was like an entrance to the letter H, which was one line Dante wished he hadn't written which says, "I'm going into the letter h," but it is without the bar. There were all these monsters about there too. The illustrated version was even worse, worse than TV, worse than cinema, saved only by the failure of the reader to visualize it, saved by their ability to forget it. In Grendel's new age if would have been a hit. He saw, as if he had read it, the horrid parts, the tortures. "If their classics are such how do any of them pass the twelve steps?" If you're thinking that you'd rather go into the letter H or M than face this music we all sympathize, but can offer no assistance. H and M are just two of the letters of the four that vexed him. Continued personal inventory! Also they were backwards, the M came before the H, like asking some stranger at a red light whether he had ever looked into an O, not one of the other letters Grendel was after. He felt like if he could solve this mystery things would be better. The puzzle surrounded him, grappled him. The smoke, the tallow, the lapping at the water's edge. Why was the whole thing? Grendel was the mystery himself or was it outside himself, but not confined to the alphabet, even if the ages and letters were almost the same, in case you don't know them.

To improve his conscious contact with God as he understood Him Grendel took a cipher of "OKU" that occurred in the right hand corner of his book. The tail of the O went through the K and paralleled the U. It literally denoted a "hum," that is the word itself . "What am I to do," he thought? He began to do it. The hum grew loud. This clue correlated with the statement that "it was not unusual to hear them contradict themselves." Presumably readers also contradict themselves. This was the point of his inquiry, to find the end of contradiction by first realizing its beginning. The two reminded him of himself, were the best proof yet that he was human enough to find another human being to admit it to. It reminds us too. Why can't we just say that and be done with it?

Having a spiritual awakening as the result of these steps Grendel was ready to carry to another level. He thought that the Helmings deserved such a symbolic action. How best to communicate it? And in one age or two, because the priest of the previous age had become an everyman commentator. He couldn't identify just whether it was symbolic or real, when it covered up or poured out. UrMon, priest, reporter, lawyer, editor, somebody telling you what to do. Mainly doubt. He thought he understood it. The priest's emendation looked like the beak of a stork going down after a fish. It could also have been a goat with horns. It was looking down at Unferth from a crag. Unferth didn't notice. He was busy corralling Hrothgar's sister which hardly seemed like anybody's business except it was magnificent moment, a kind of in body experience that enthralled the monster. The sister was being offered to the man who now looked anonymous in a business hat. He lay down on a bed and a carrot flew up between his legs. Sometimes the smoke made him dizzy, the smoke and feel of the fell, as if symbol and story and present and past were one in some interchangeable fashion. He didn't know then that there were handbooks printed to get over these tough points, help them see correctly the interplay of symbol and fact. You need to get the handbooks to figure it out. He didn't know then whether they were going to make the book into movie or verse.
At least, he tried to carry this message to others, to practice these principles in his affairs.

For example there was a large cursive E which also looked like a 3 bisecting an ampersand. This was in the book. He didn't know how much criticism had made of it. Science called it the E3 bisect, but in his eyes it was a Z. He was new to reading, he was new to thinking and to consciousness. He was new to symbolism. He thought it looked like a dragon at the throat of another dragon, that one dragon was twisting the neck of the other out and down. To miss the mark by so much was his telltale plight. He knew that that was how the dragons got their wings, by killing another dragon. He could not seem to escape carnage. Then, to add to this plight, the girl Wealtheow who appeared earlier up and stuck her attacker Unferth with a large dining implement known called an unforth. It made balloons go up in his mind so he couldn't see, and all the while she poked them and they popped and lay wasted and empty on the ground. There was a lot more violence in the old days portrayed in this book that may explain his take on it. A lot was written about Unferth in the unforth. She wrote books and so did he. Wealtheow, the wife of the king, published under that name too. Whether any of the other characters wrote depends on the meaning, he thought. As you can see things were getting a lot more dense, the same feeling as though time were speeding up. A lot of people thought the thing was a spoof of literature, but it was more. For example, an unnamed youth, meaning the young man on 118 who read on his bed with his knees raised looked like a hyper-ventilated Mordred. He was a prototype. It doesn't exactly say this or show what he read, but it was monster food. Monster food Grendel knew was anything bigger than it was made. Super sizing. How you get it this way is the key. By inflation yes, but more surely by selection and magnification. I don't know if it is worth mentioning, but if you blow anything up several times life size you get a monster.

 King Arthur is in the background of all this, but it is much more than a youth rebellion and monster food, kids with guns instead of apples, or graphs that point back into the book, except where he saw a hand had gotten elliptical next to the text's phrase and pointed its finger like a gun, said, "the blessed OOK!" It made him think that the door of the H must be into the OoK itself. H, Ook, O. M. This is no time to reveal the other letters. He purposed in himself never to look at an Ook. It rhymed in his head, went around like train blowing little puffs of smoke out its stack. Never look into an Ook. Never Look at an Ook. What does one do with an Ook? He wondered.

This much was certain they had misspelled it in the monograph they had a small point however because the sound is the same no matter how much you misspell it.The big news came when he learned that the OoK was the only living being to ever interview his mother. This is also forthcoming under a separate cover. But since monsters have by now eaten half the population everythinghas been slowed down. The survivors have armed their children with cell phones. Grendel had gotten on this line,
but enough of that.

Page 156 he saw was marked in pencil with a large star
struck in the middle of a storm. Star struck, star light, wish
I may which I might. The hand was disintegrating into
overstrikes and crossovers. Some triangles resurfaced under
the OoK. He did not look at it.
He had made a decision (3) to turn his will and life over to
the care of God as he understood Him. Nice phrase. Worlds
of difference. Leviathan, behemoth did not understand their
urges. He did not understand the legless text in his hand.

Whale
Posing a city as a whale is a lot like an Ook not only designing their
homes but bathing therein. Along the coasts where whales
breach so insistently it looks like a parking lot in season.
They bathed inside the stomachs for the healing. Warmth
and fumes are more than a parable of life in that world. A
hole was put through one side of the body to admit the
lower part sunk to the waist, leaving the head outside so the
applicant could breathe, though some ammoniacal gases

escape.

New Philadelphia transported from the Odyssey of old Homer had myths enacted in allegiance to the authority of its present rule, not King George who lost the American colonies and went mad, but Leviathan, who like King George they never saw or would see, but who nonetheless acted upon them with abstruse dogmas of piscine theology. They built their cities like whales because they thought the world was a whale, in which notion.They gave it a name, Susan, who in the particulars, we learn, had started to decompose.

Those who cannot withstand more than an hour are lifted out in a faint to undergo a second and third course the following day. The effect is much like injecting ketamine. Gases of such overpowering and atrocious odor bring the cure. Majestic straddling the flank of rivers and coasts, the literature of the early Colonias is a simultaneous perception of both worlds. All metallic and aqueous surfaces of sea, when baited with pitch, fat, and hair boiled into cakes, draw Leviathan from the freedom afar. Every apocalypse is accompanied by such thoughts.

The anshei shem who instigate this myth of civilization with smiles take dis-embassies that make them human. Science, history, government, literature force fields of their predictive programs shout the effect. The pilgrim colonies share old and new, signing papers and giving their occupations and intent, to examine if they are faithful and true. Those who are receive transport. The rest go to "French" camp.

Is it better to hear and know and not understand? To go quietly from this already the best of all possible worlds, which it was possible to deny? The worst were full of passionate convictions. Unconscious sums sea and land. It sums fish in tanks, falls from grace and into grace. Possession renamed the users beneath the inboard seas over brawling brine, beast of the waste, the way psychiatric

patients rename themselves for disease. There were Ford
families, Sony people. Genuine interiority changed for
commercial identity. This said, we were doing well. UK
planetary agents had mutated fifteen dimensions of the
yore-flood staunching ocean. An puir wee crannie doodlee
in the different minds of men who broke the barn
frightened our heroes, Noah risen unseen, bound and
veined, almost unmade, the mystery stressed, hurdled to
grace. Who said they would go and tell? They hid the mass
effects of the ark driven Phison under a sort of twister a-
twisting a twist, order and strength more easily believed.
There were three choices of a water yarn with fire in him of
cobble foam streets: 1) was he a black man upon a black
horse who would not acknowledge the collective? 2) was it261
a pig that just fiddling out -- thinking to be autonomous? 3)
was it an old sow in a terrible swoon that our minds were
our own? Odd poems came from this, such lines as thou
must barn thy mouse and thrash off the shoe to read.
To report these literatures of fact with the same facility as a
Futurist playbook of the new Bolshevik societies of the 21st
completes an era of a hundred years. we adopt the formalist
theories to bypass algorithmic controls. Black Jack. Hidden
propitiatory work is thus read correctly, coded within, an
age and a century apart from the original. In the real
material gathered first hand and culled from documentary
sources, to accentuate the aggregator paradigm, that
revealed the world dame.

The fisherman there did not in the slightest care for Susan
the Leviathan. They sought nearness to the sea, salt air,
storms and waves. Colonists however made every
invocation to gods that the ancient Greeks did at the same
time they were joined by an influx of Christian pietists
from an entirely different era, groups with differing and
violent severance from each other, theologies generally
called Baptist.

These two populations fought for space above and below

the cliffs that looked out on the coasts where any captain looking up at the shouldered bluffs would see the promontories snow hills in the air. Below them, on the beaches, the whale priests anshei shem gathered.
This was the refuge for those who escaped, who had fled what they themselves brought. Tails, as it were, wet with government and religion, government to blame a multitude of sins, religion to recover, that great externalization of hierarchy boasted, metalepsis, Kenosis and apophrades. When they got to where they were going they found themselves already there.

Events interpret each other in action not words that happen at the same time, like Chomsky meeting Epstein. Dimensions are altered by immersing their aquarium in another via a pulse 2 dilution refrigerator. Its creators like to call it an "altar to an alien god" so describe it as a "giant black monolith" of 10x12ft. It sounds like those obelisks found in wild Utah desert. This super refrigerated black box generates close to Absolute zero and pulses once a second, like a heartbeat. Its makers love to pretend it is alive. Its chip, the size of a thumbnail, accesses 2 mutually exclusive states at same time (standard quantum particle and wave), which states are identical except for value of a qubit. In Quantum Computing, each qubit doubles, 2^{500}, 2 to the 500, doubling the number of qubits each year. WARNING: you have to believe all this, and that science is a higher power because it is the nature of intelligence to deceive. The more intelligent the entity the larger its neocortex therefore the more likely its deception (maxim from Liespotting).

Imagine poor Anshei corrupted by an even worse force as the nubbin of the problem. But since elite's have the D-Wave, Space Fence and Cyclotron Resonance, what holds them back? They hide among the leaders of the earth. Soros or Rockefeller with seven heart transplants rule to suppress the human interloper. They are not human. That should be said. That Man should have dominion of the earth upsets their tender heart. The Sumerians of Oxford pretend the text-forged tablets to hide that on a certain day the weakest among us will be as David and David like the angel. The LORD strong and mighty, the LORD mighty in battle is bad news for Theomachy.

Followed by revisions and forgetfulness of those times lost to memory, differing versions were remembered of what had been continued in the streets and on the beaches where Mabinogians sought Leviathan unknown. They visited upon the ocean a vow that if it came to land they would lead different lives. Revived and seeing land after they wished always to remain on water freed of taint, different forms of their civilization made unrecognizable to elders the present in which they lived and to the youth their time and place was unimagined. Waves upon the shore breaking in periods as the rhythm of currents, ocean, storms, driftwood, seaweed, shells, crustaceans and occasional perilous whales were dumbfounded by what water became like histories of this time mislead by personality, presidents, entertainers. The wave that washed on land left products of a billion billion cells.

Not to deny mook Baptists worldwide, and other followers who leap virulent at the Hemoth dish, down at the leaps, Leviathan, chief magistrate was unlike any man today. Were we expect to meet a certain person, as if they were like a loose anchor snared on a reef, or an approaching figure that deceitfully took on a familiar garb, the mere idea of this walking image made an expectation to endow it with the appearance of a friend. This may happen true as well as falsely. A very slight hint from the eye goes a long way in the brain of one such peeled naked, and no distance at all in the brain of the other. Such examples as ship channels dug into rivers like the Hudson enable Lev's passage further and further inland. Covert arrangements between ship channel captains and administrators of Leviathan and Co., meaning the fish itself, cooperate with the dredging.

Why not call it a fish or a reptile of some sort which to continue that progress started by bodies jetting up and down rivers to zoom through glacial canyons miles out to sea. This churning happens as if there were racing and makes for weird weathers of mist inland on both sides, for surely there is more than one, else how do they breed climate change, but leave that to the herpetologists. Figures seen swimming overboard under the waves after ships have sailed in the normal, unbiased world presume a vacant mind. Mind familiars act upon this strange color with something of their own disapproval.

The one deep river that inhabitants avoid has tributaries where the Lev flows up to Coloni. They are waiting for it to appear and so named that port for their peculiar humor. LevBy should not obscure its actual name as Leviathan By the Sea. Myths spread in this colony as easily as wings of cloud and fire. We advise to shoot these birds before they land, but too late in some places. Once the Pishon and Gihon, lost rivers of Eden, were fine, but now turned Phlegethon and Lethe, rivers of hell.

Arming rivers with mythic times the haptic French once toasted Old Town as Lev-By camouflaged as a fish where269 marinas and buildings represented fish troops. They built they homes like fish. Call them piscine architectures. Not marlin or tarpon, but bigger than blue whales, massed and tusked, with metallic fins scaled like Pharaoh's tomb they would go with and bathe in the liver, intestines and stomach inside special containers, called canopic jars in which they were lower into the massThis is all nonsense of course if leviathan is a metaphor of beast government in its temple of shale like oil and gas, drilled and mined. Who cares if it's Casanova's Colon, of the beasts that come up from RockaBilloy among the shrinks who cleanse Newtown, or, or from the effigy of Achilles Arch.

To follow the thrust faults on land and history that leviathan follows beneath, and under sea, swimming up aquifers and getting fracked, read the scientific papers of genetic machines like MIT, the last containing covering of

the globe. The old world was dying so new monsters grew.
Jung altered lists of foods for government camps on
Blackbox and Red Rover. The thing about tentacles that
reach through all, is that they are digital, electronic and
mimic pattern DNA.
Visions . described by their poets of the depths with
eyeballs of a goat but vertical like a frog.
In those years whole families lived under the shade of the
platano trees of forced synthesis higher up. They picked its
beans and spread them over the highway to dry like coffee.
I lived on this planet myself out by Dulce port, slept naked
and washed in cold water from lilies transplanted by the
sea. As unlikely as if sounds, I spoke the dialect of their
Suffering one Sunday to a dozen infirm saved black ladies.
A lot of these were political refugees from the alien dissent.
They had become replacement technologies of gingerbread
houses where thinking machines exchanged letters of
philosophical, ethical or scientific questions from fissures
exuding those encampments by the sea. Cyclop thoughts
were hidden in the cliffs like weather. On the opposite
coast where we picked buckets of mangoes the wind blew
those patriots like birds in their beaks. The houses were on
stilts.
New Government for old is every paradise's best wish. We
match our fingers together and bow in jest, "build the one,"
then turn the lights out. When the virus broke
concentration delirium turned the lights out. Joints of the
flesh, skin can't be touched. Fingers hit the wrong keys.
It is possible to deny going quietly. That is, don't wait it out
in Weimar or hide in basements under the roar. The upstart
announces its own approach, in chemtrails of sky. Doubts
of the residents of Idaho, Utah, Nevada, and Great Basin
remain, but Ohio had to go. Ghosts of mountains cover
fields. Windows light up where people didn't have
electric. Swim the veins to survive, not just sea and land,
the same as Jonah, but even if you lean into the state of
Unknowing the Known remains. "Will I have eyes at the
bottom of the sea, supposing I descend there on endless

stairs.

Many names might be applied by refugees confronted not by nature but by myth. These background the first settlings where the Philadelphian mystics of the Wissahickon Creek passed through the gorge to merge with the Schuylkill River into the Delaware and then the sea, who knowing nothing of that world imagined it as elements of the Odyssey.

Along the valley road east where these merchants sing, imaginary saline echoes play the words on passengers out for a walk. "Passengers" are there. Ezekiel Merkabah Ezekiel 39:11-15. One day I will give Gog a burial that will block the way of travelers in the valley east of the Sea because Gog and all his hordes will be buried there. So it will be called the Valley of Gog.

wə·hā·yāh ha·hū ʕay·yō·wm

Theologues brought these invisibles into politics. You would not believe that in the one eye of a giant the purpose manifests. Jehoiakim, king of Judah burned every page of the prophecy of Jeremiah that predicted he should willingly go captive into the Babylon of Nebuchadnezzar. But these are our circumstances when Bercilak takes up again his severed head. Extinction of the invisible? Ficino burned the commentary on Lucretius into ashes just because it depopulated this universe.

Say it for him, Jeremiah, St. John, Overstate the gofernment pages. Philosophy burns in the grate. Speak intellect to inmates incarcerate. Insert the ipad and iphone quick and the flick of a desktop plug the GPS wandering. It is no common breakfast when we dress without bodies. Colonia Step to the Bridge Nous Delphica rev.

"Blessed are they who wash their robes, who have the right to the tree of life and may enter the City by its gates, but outside are the dogs, the sorcerers, the sexually immoral, the murderers, the idolaters and everyone who loves and practices lies and falsehood" (Rev 22 14-15).

In all candor this account is of those who did not make it

into the Divine City. It's not as if they need a place to worship. The gods are all over Serapeum of Saqqara, Alexandria, burial place of the Apis bull--see Cherubim Collection for confirmation. There are many thousands of sites to maintain that society outside. STEP TO THE BRIDGE will take the modern infirm, spiritually challenged outside the walls and gates of that HOLY CITY of Revelation (22 15) where the New Jerusalem comes down. Here in your post-trib governance of the new rulers of the Reset Newtown, new era run their new world. When you get all the good news after the trumpets, judgments, seals, dragons, floods and mountains fall on that town and it's still cookin', not to deceive, it is the whole world. The other part is the other part, unless you take down the wall. Call it the Pied Cow where Newtown is outside the Gates. No word yet as to how close the nerds can come to it like fallen angels who survived the flood. That has to be the logic of fire. Maybe they had fins, maybe they could breathe under water. The Pope wears a fish hat. Maybe the fire and the rocks falling on the earth missed! There t'was a poundin and soundin just like visions of sugar plums popping when old Sodom and Dixie drove out. Otherwise Engaged Literature and Arts Journal #6 (p. 392-402) is a post-trib manual for remains outside the walls and gates of THE HOLY CITY. There government and rulers continue to practice their progressive ways in print on Amazon.

All these sites had connections to tunnels below from the above ground. These tunnels reached to both coasts. When273 it came out that they were camouflaged as krill plants on the ocean competing with the whales this enabled them to make the celebrated epath of Leviathan under, beneath, Behemoth above ↕ prospected by earth and under sea. If you yourself live between the cultures of myth in the aquarium humane, Ossian on the grass, Pythagoras, Plotinus, do not grudge to find the same soul of the world in land and water. It's always government and religion that people flee, and government can cover a multitude of sins, and religion. The top worlds drawn on the bottom are three or four times as large in the middle. The number of colonies is 183, not counting suspicious invisibles at opposition. After the original 79, the majority north of the equator, 116 were not on first maps of either the dark regions or the light. All these sites had connections to tunnels below from the above ground. These tunnels reached to both coasts. When it came out that they were camouflaged as krill plants on the ocean competing with the whales this enabled them to make the celebrated bagoong. Large slabs stuck up out of ocean to drive the krill, which were larger than expected by the little people who worked them, if that can be said without profiling. They were not from anywhere exactly or anybody is. Mornings in the corkscrew. Some exceptions from a loss of surface occurred within the spirals. I am not squandering words. We pray on Sunday for those in peril on the sea. Those shrinks who cleanse Newtown and the effigy of Achilles Arch spread the myth that this colony has wings of cloud and fire. If so, we advise shooting those birds before they land. Leviathan Bay or LevBy sounds like Long Island off Montauk. When the Sun rises all wild Beasts hide themselves in their Holes. In the event of this vaticinium ex eventu, prophecy after the fact, history written as though it were prophecy, the old world was dying so new monsters grew. The thing about tentacles that reach through land and sea is they mimic pattern DNA. For more on this study Thoughts from Singing Birds, the paranoia mon amour that surrounds Alternative 3 of the Dictates.

We don't mean whales here, for Maria pseudo-hirsuta was evolving. The eyes look west with dragon heads. Zillyzation needed Long Necks for this humor. Waiting to appear that Hydra seemed alive with moving heads, tongues lashing. Bigger than blue whales but invisible. Contoured and finned, masked and tusked, metallic surfaces scaled like a head of that state, reptilian don musk, Leviathan Pharaoh. Which is all mythological nonsense anyway? Is it beast government produced out of oil and

gas, one of four beasts that come up from the sea, drilled
and mined? Dragon mines the elements. Dragon crews for
dragon gas. Such a state is liberty to those who measure
their freedom by the subjection of others. A female has
vertical eyeballs like a frog which the international
community must undertake every possible effort to end.
"The shapeshifting capabilities of organism 46-B shaped
itself into the form of a human diver. A 33 foot-long man-
eater of extraordinary camouflage stalked our researchers.
It disabled our radio, which we later learned, to our alarm,
was intentional. "It is also able to paralyze prey from a
distance of up to 150 feet by releasing its venom into the
water. "Tragically my colleague and lifelong friend was
killed this way. He tread water wearing a blissful smile as
the organism approached him. Terror is a joint effort by
Dante I, an eight legged tethered robot, to obscure its
mythic name in the Leviathan community
freedom when compelled one way by current while
swimming as fast as it can in the other? Read the scientific
papers on genetic machines, the last greatest covering
globe. Scrutinists in this way show their absence.
RockaBilloy history makes it a victim. Miners need our
protection.

Leviathan has a greater following than Behemoth among
these mystics. They make necklaces out of the scales. The
brazen fins of wanton whales suggest other political types
If a mousecould climb through an elephant's trunk to gnaw its brain,
 then a whole town country planet can be undermined by the
proboscises of leviathaniasis. And whether Beo takes
LevBy withal, to wear its spectacles, nose piercing through
the snares within the ribs where dolphins swim, the mighty
body falls. King over the children of pride those sperm
dress alike, ready to disperse such organs as the most
rebellious body parts of Adam shamed. Illa parte magis
regnat additamentum leviathan spawns abound in Janus,
Luther or Mamet, prisoner or flesh, and lead all other parts
to rebel beside water and on land. As serpents gripe and

break the hot petcock from our sight, moving land and under sea, remember that banquet to be served. Behemoth Apatosaurus or Argentinosaurus.

These were the torturers among our legislators and senators, those burgers of consensus: who had rigid views of identifying common ground and crafting strong consensus. It only remained for them to blur the last definition, what is the human. Could that air head speak it would say that the colonist like a mouse is meant by the Armed Forces to be an experiment to save itself.

2. Pantheon gods inaugurate in Water. At Old Town Leviathan-by-the-Sea, the picture is of a creature who boils the depths out of its mouth. Old Town has credentials therefore both as the Temple of Neptune and the port of Noah. Global romantics in Rome are not surprised that Nous Delphia is Troy. The horse enters the city. The city is burned. if Neptune hid the horse what hides in these? They call it a Trojan Priest who threw his spear against the Old Town polity of gods. One global temple of distortion, like some universe emperor of the despond kingdom who says all is well with ziv, even its discontent, until it's not. Sea serpents against. Figs as dates, dry head that cracks shall be lawful for any Athenian. Geologics spin over every proportion and property of the place. Figures swimming overboard can be seen under waves after ships have sailed as if they loose an anchor snared on a reef This presumes a vacant mind. upon this strange color with something of their own, pretty sure to approve. We might expect to meet a certain person, or an approaching figure that deceitfully took on his garb. The mere idea of this walking image makes an expectation to endow it with the attributes of a friend. This may happen truly as well as false. Mind familiars act.A very slight hint from the eye goes a long way in the brain of one naked, and no distance at all in the brain of the other. Ship channels dug into rivers like the Hudson enable Lev's passage further and further inland. Some covert arrangement seems to exist between ship

channel captains and administrators of Leviathan and Co.,
meaning the fish itself. Why not call it a fish or a reptile of
some sort which cooperates with the dredging to continue that
progress started by bodies jetting up and down the
rivers to zoom through glacial canyons miles out to sea.
This churning happens as if there were racing and makes
for weird weathers of mist inland on both sides, for there is
more than one, else how do they breed, but leave that to the
entomologists.
Speaking as the spirit of unknowing that human mind
disports, if passage tombs could talk, or under bark
organics and rock, volcanic ash, erosion deposition,
reburied feldspar, fish streams under clay spines, would
they dare say more than they heard? What they heard was
ascribed beast government, four empires up from sea. The
first a lion with eagle wings, lifted on two feet, like a man
with a human heart, forfeitures of British Royal Lion and
American Eagle with all democratic pretense. The second
was a bear with three ribs in its mouth, Russia chomping
the Baltic down. The third a leopard with four heads and
chicken wings on its back, Germany and its Nazi survivals
surmounted with France's national bird: the French army
knife that came with a white flag. But the fourth beast
unlike them all had no nation but covered the world, a beast
for everyone that calls it fracking, fragging. The Baptists
have a name for it in their Afligidos.
♥Archuleta not only land honeycombs five caves and
Unchangeable or changeable in position, the colonies
gradually emerge for some reason inherent in themselves,
conspicuous with the visible development of the canali
following the melting of the snow. Rhetors of Neptune, look at
your neck; there you will find the strap. It's hard to locate
settlements the dolphin mire among zephers. The new looks like the
old. That government required ship lists and oaths of allegiance, when
harbor sea captains began to slump over their water jars. Because they
had not seen the Lev their buildings took on shapes of eels, whales,
squid, materia proxima, materia remota, materia ultima. These new
mystical men prove the history of the Odyssey. As Behmists of the

slabby mists, Behmenism being beliefs stemming from German
mystic Jakob Böhme, might purl ecstatic chapters of perfection of
crystal streams over rock and ledge, or balsam pine hid in the small
caves of hillside with natural springs, Aurora hid in their language its
universal matrix and Philologus esoteria prefigured. The great
deliverance they felt was soon to be displayed. Not to deny fish
mystics and Baptists worldwide, invisible storehouse of diverse
mythmakers, that collective fiction that fathers early and later times to
enable government, is followers virulent in self interest lept at the
Behemoth dish while down at the other lept Leviathan, chief
magistrate unlike any man today.

but
first the Behemoth is opposed with Leviathan, the animal is
opposed with the mind, and the animal must be left behind.
Transformations, metamorphoses, distortions so called,
Circe turned men to pigs, "like to their minds most
monstrous." When science speaks of "ceasing to be
human" it is just opposite this or what happened to
Nebuchadnezzar as a beast for seven years to be sane.
The pretense that the human is different because the
container is remade would be due in part to its severed
head. Science and philosophy sever the human from its
culture and past to be remade. Visionaries imagine a future
they themselves do not live in, propose a love purer and295
stronger than anyone ever felt, but they themselves are
divorced, promise pleasures, bliss without end, greater than
ever known, but by use of a drug. Nietzsche is their
inspiration to transcend both beast and man, "rope the
abyss," become a superman, but he is insane.
To talk this way is reprehensible, but not as glib as the
assumptions about human identity that never question
themselves. Monsanto argues that food shortage is outdated
since there is so much surplus food, the only problem being
to consume it all. There is supposed to be so much more
food from the green revolution and the GMO world that it
can be given away to the third world, except for destroying
indigenous agriculture. As a new paradigm this is only

outdated by its deception of false plenty. It is poison food
nor REAL, not-food for the not-man.

Corrupt regimes do not cause the lack, but hyperdrive seed
stock and chemical soil make food null and void. As to
justifying the crimes science commits against animals, a
zero sum logic compares humans to chimps and apes in
labs, saying apes don't have the brains of a man, therefore
can be consumed, as if life were a competition. But life is a
cooperation. It does not make a man better to dominate the
ape. When this intelligence greater than wisdom redesigned
viruses, genes and atmospheres, the men were put to death,
proving minds most monstrous.

Who can doubt whether tampering with the weather is
justified to save lives, unless all this altruism is a rhetorical
blind to cover the opposite? Either weather alteration
might work or we will all die? Take a chance. Spin the
wheel. Nobody knows if the DNA of every living organism
were rewritten it might save the world! In the joust of
supernatural powers the soul of the mandarin makes a deal
with Faust. Storm surges, hurricanes, earthquakes, drought,
rainfall, tsunamis of Scalar techs are all species of a
giganticism understood as a joke, as if "one thought it a
joke when the head next to him blew off."

Acts of science become acts of god. Manipulation done to
save the planet from warming, unless it is the cause, using
global warming to justify even greater manipulations.
Amazingly, in this unknown world the only agency on top
of its game was FEMA, that stored 200 million coffins, and
who knows how many plastic drums, refurbished WWII
camps and generally did a good job finding places for
refugees to be taken. They had swing sets and monkey bars
in the compounds.

If Circe turned men to pigs other myths turned men to gods.
The most germane of these is Dante's Glaucus, the
transformed Narcissus, who found a place untouched by
civilization, chewed several blades of its grass and became
immortal. To describe passage from the terrestrial paradise
to heaven Dante invented a new word, thought to be the

first occurrence of "transhuman"(Paradiso, I.70). [see Danteworlds].

Just as ordinary language is not sufficient to describe such things as Dante says, we invent a word from Coleridge to describe the metamorphoses, Opiomes. Opiomes is an imitation transhumar built in an Opium poppy much the same way that the EU Parliament was designed as an imitation Tower of Babel. Admittedly it is peculiar to describe science with poetry or buildings, but the vehicle serves. Dante, who invented the term said, "Transhumanizing may not be in words set forth" (Bergin), and neither can the horror this earth.297

Whether it be atmospheres, animals or plants, new technologies sever from the past by releasing crossed energies of scale impossible to shield. This principle of dissociation is manipulated even in personalities who fragment into multiples when divided, to produce and release unprecedented energy. This principle of dissociative release of energy occurs in the sky, sea, earth and man.

An image search of Stratospheric Aerosol chemtrails can contemplate the results of division. Before long you conclude the existence of wereweather. So if it seems contradictory that Operation Cloverleaf uses commercial airlines to spray 200 million tons of aluminum (+ barium,+gna+) each year into the atmosphere as an exotic weapon, but that the new reflective atmosphere turns acidic soils alkaline beneath, requiring engineering GMO seeds such as Monsanto's trait technologies, 246 million acres (2007) of genetically modified corn and rice to withstand the chemical onslaught, and the spraying provokes catastrophic release of methane gas of the Arctic shelf, skyrocketing levels of asthma, autism, ADD and Alzheimer's, and the nano particles easily pass the blood brain barrier, it's all done to trasumanar.

Crisscrossed trails of science, singularity, art and literature reveal a metamorphosis summed up as the creation of a starchitect, one whose novelty of creation transforms them into idols of the architecture world.

It's a nice gesture that a starchitect could implode and
distort these forms when the Oracle rises with the means to
know. Religion rose each morning with the golden glow of
Apollo. It was called the Golden Age. Apollo temples and
the Delphi omachines of every advanced AI, Gnōthi
seauton were named for the omachines. Data Centers
spread far and wide. The oracle of nosce te ipsum, temet
nosce made a screen that projected the architecture of its
world of waves. Nature was innocent compared to
trisecting an idea which leads us away from where we are
but doesn't show us the place where we have been. When I
say compassion is agony that seeks to disprove the
paintings of the Deaf man (Goya) or the Opening of the
Fifth Seal (El Greco) to confront the created universe of
humanity -- that is a clarity each age disproves to the next.
You can't say you didn't know it could be true from the
beginning of human memory. Minor prophets are not just
names. Micah, Amos, Joel, Hosea. Al Nusura, Al Quaida,
and Jonah arcing in the breakers of the surf, lamenting the
gourd, swallowed up here, puking there.

Taking the visual Guggenheim Bilbao as an example of this belief
helps
identify every form. If it makes you say, "oh god," the
god's not what you think. Other modifications lie behind
the chemtrails visibility, what transhumanists call their
putative god that chemtrails form and chemtranshumanists
transform.
Different medias, technologies and devices make this
ancient myth to modern known. These seem like
inebriations, a drugged awareness that stumbles room to
room. Let us call the situation an Opiome, from opium and
Coleridge's pleasure dome, implying a metaphor of drugs
and architecture that built its heart and mind.
Who else but the life of philosophers background the
colonies spread to the world. Or colonies, practices of
empire? Contemporaries experiment to test obeying orders,
electric shock subjects, Perils of Obedience, doing their

jobs, a word game to find an all-encompassing logical form
of thought behind ordinary language.
People have to cooperate for parallel compartmentalized
societies to exist. The difference between gas chambers and
labs, if inscrutable to bystanders is the same for those who
resist, who resist for no purpose except they do. In the
Americas people are made docile by the bread, opiate and
circus industries, cheap goods, that's what bystanders get
for keeping quiet. Maybe they complain they don't get
enough, that their lives are victimized, "our asymmetrical
and nonreciprocal response to the suffering of the other
(l'autrue), my neighbor, and our infinite responsibility to
and for the other." Death camps are a rhetorical framework
on which to hand over the singular transhuman future that
corporations and governments seek. You would think in
interrogations like Radical Evil Prometheus would be
mentioned.energies of even greater scale(r) energy against which it is
impossible to shield. Indeed that is the principle of
dissociation in manipulated personalities made famous by
MK Ultra, that such disassociation, fragmentation into
multiples produces and releases unprecedented energy used
by controllers for their purposes.
These have no order, beginning middle or end. They
exist together without precedence even if every order they
take in existence made precedence against precedence. The
order of publication is no order because each was written
long before, a chronology largely forgotten. The biggest
impediment to this is first impression, but because of the
infirmities we live in, have to be order to sell the NOW.
The last thing we can stand is to see the world as it is. It has
to be structured, simultaneously into the great worlderness
bubbles that imprint other molecules and receive their
memory. The secret of consciousness is to tell someone you
implicitly trust the thought, then you hear your voice and
you know it yourself and it becomes conscious.
We may want to distinguish thoughts of the bowels, the gut
brain, the heart, the imagination and the head, brain proper
on the way to speech, writing. Preparations of the heart

prethought, precognitive form thought, not imagination either, but pre imagination—not cognitive, which smacks of faith, for who can know the mind of Yahweh or how events order in the world?
The preparations of the heart that lead to the speech are ordered of Grace--just opposite of need, which grows
greater every day, to grapple with exigencies. turned upside down so the existential Nick Bostrom (Future of Humanity Institute) can claimed they never existed, and if they did they didn't. Eichmann 307 made over History repeats itself in reverse by reconstructing H+ as the center again. 2.0, 3.0,
4.0....hike! Flash mobs enabled by Smart Phones gathered for burning down London. This was the celebrated
wisdom of crowds doing Eichmann 308.
The cure for ontological imperialism waslove,
love for the checker, love for the immigrant, love for the
human recognition, "there go I," in the other.
Even if earthquakes and rainfall have fallen prey, not
the Mojave rattler, Coach Whip King let them loose at the
neighbors but digital children let loose for prizes, publications and positions, and they publish
much of merit to that heap where Galway Kinnell, James Tate, are selected. This is Irenaeus' Lesson of Baal for
Oleander elites taken in.
The History of Oleander is the history of
interbred ruling Bloodlines of which we are reluctant to
speak without ameliorating the good news of the
sharpshooter to the Bushes related to other lines
interconnected ad infinitum among themselves for
millennia. McCain mates with British royals, Princess
Diana, McCain and Laura Bush, Obama, Cheney, George
Bush. Obama the most engendered of all, cousin of six
presidents: both Bushes, Ford, Johnson, Truman and James
Madison. They had to manage, said The Guardian,
otherwise they would decay. Ultimate geneticists trace the
least ancestral degree not just in politics. Billy Graham
shared the royal blood. It isn't who is cousin to who but
who has the blood, not to say that the only entrance to the
Pyramid is by birth. To buy rank with the usual price

boosted of rock stars, like Bob Dylan at the Crossroads or by sacrifice of a family member, highest echelon stars pay with ritual desecrations. The whole psychology of riches and fame presumes the corporate. Climbing the ladder does not mean to the highest but merely to enter to the lowest rung, manager to VP. Aspirants seek to rank their children in schools that will qualify them to climb. Fairy tales replace Bible stories. Totems replace faith. "I will give you all the kingdoms of the world if you will just...."
The central purpose of command, confession and absolution manufactured by the films such as Ken Burns on Vietnam enable the repetition of wars over and over, stimulus / response / apology again, from Iraq, Afghanistan, the Towers, cellphones, the virus, the elections and on, which entertainment prosthetics predict to deaden, numb the pain into ignorance and rote happiness. All seen in the movies, therefore is is real. All this323 unimaginable to the norm sets up a quantum shift of greater control to come. Tim O'Brien, Philip Caputo confess to atrocities while other confessors, appointed by their keepers, McCain, Kerry with their rich wives, are rewarded, given mere fame. No Kent Andersons [Sympathy for the Devil] in the dialectic there, who turn their guns on these apologists, as if somebody just shot Lt. Calley down. The ultimate cognitive apology had to be John Forbes Kerry, nominee for President, Secretary of State, throwing away his medals but years later jetting to Antarctica the night of the election of Trump
It proves the sanity of absurdity
where "separation led to completion, and then ensued dissolution." Give up devotion to your views and adopt the norm.. "The more gifted, the more intelligent, the more experienced classes were the first to accept an absurdity and the last to give it up." What causes acceptance of absurdity? The value of knowing that illusions of perfection are a means of social control. Three truths are that life is sacred, relationships are to be sustained and freedom must be found. In this the gifted elite are less free than the folk.

Yet each of the truths has qualification, like matriculation
at a university of epic size where you don't know anyone
and the people are shouting in Egyptian about the politics
of the past. The registrar tells you have 39 hours left. That
was when Civilization invented the universe and then it
invented the unconscious. Throw in project Project Loon
for short. What happens when the Sixth Seal is opened and
headlines say ANGELS BOUND IN THE EUPHRATES
LOOSED? Ans. The cult of nation state-hood, that Martin
Buber said was German, Buber: "I want the Spirit to
subjugate the State," is the American. The evolving social
state invented the universe because it wants to help. To
help it rule, civilization (zivilization) argued that the
324
universe just needed nature to be the ultimate term. So
people say, it's what the universe wants.
Popism is the most sacrosanct of modern beliefs. it justifies
all consumption, sex, influence from billionaires on their
air flights with 12 year old girls and ex-presidents to the
legermain of dope, good dope for all people. So if it is said
that pop is eating pop it must mean in some sense not
cannibalism but a way of life whose purpose is to empower
and enrich the producers. If I write here a critique of- pop is
no small thing, for pop traces itself back to Cobri and Israel
copulating before Baal Peor. That is pops spiritual side. It's
material is empire, Babylon, Rome Britain, the states, the
gold man of Nebuchadnezzar. We are might small
compared to it. The new sponge bob brain is receptive to
such things.
Such changes observed here I believe are capable of
explanation either by errors of observation or seasonal
change. The Colony not only produces several vegetations
per year with different appearances, but its aspects vary
over years. Seasonal variation affects a sapling that catches
fire, hisses, drips and spits before it is the dry trunk, or as a
thorn bush that goes up in whoosh, visibility combined with
invisibility among the colonias. A twig coming from this
plant could simulate this shift. Archuleta is a case in point,

which did not possess land only to itself. At least five caves
honeycombed that region, but plenty of others were visible
from the peaks, a magnificenza waiting to be discovered
with stupor and deception. I caught sight of several who
kept their heads and even their chests above the tide of
transverberation which the eye and the wave equivocate
together. Simple rectilinear, curvilinear pi, the mind sees,
not the eye.325

If you're going to war Titanomachy against Titans, fallen
angels, Olympian gods, goddesses and anshei shem it's nice
to see how we got to where all that was trusted is now
mistrusted. The less honorific briquitte of the Renowns,
reptile, keeps the lineage of fallen watcher anshei, giants,
demons in mind. David Icke says we all have some
reptilian. David Wilcock that only 15% suffer so, meaning
himself and everyone who listens to him. News accounts
spread these deceptions over all the upper class meta-schizo
earth. In Greek, meta schematizo means masquerade,
which meta-schizo disguise (meta-schiz-matizo) where the
demons sent into the Gadarene swine (Mk 5.11)fear
exposure below as being sent out of the space above and
between the planes (dimensions).

Because they had not seen the Lev, in other words,
weather-altered culture changed in about 60 years. You
didn't have to be an intellectual to know it, just look at the
physique of the 1/3 morbidly obese. Iron City beer never
looked so good or the Iron Age of Ovid beside these
Experiments. In any case, these are the warring parties that
occupy the waterways of New Philadelphia where these
ideas come in eviathan archive.

Inlets called Coloni sail the rhumb lines of continual
debate. Some fill with water and some with iron oxide and
some rutile that wash in the tangled hair and ice crust of
that great brow of Christopher Colon overlooking our port.
Water distorts the vision of Old Town below the Mount
with a hook in its nose, as if under the water were souls
who sigh and make the water bubble and make us look at
the thing so many times it loses its power to disturb like a

new normal. No better preparation could occur for this than to have it preceded by such events in art, but which prevent it from being understood. Mind waves in the untold hybrids loosed upon the world, worn on the arm, bracelets,
326
pendants, rings, in case you're bored, refract in water to disperse. Chromatic aberration of light in water distorts and reduces focal range in the near by 33 percent, which scatters these tidal architectures seen as a marina undersea. Color fringing at the edge of an image distorts its geometry. This scattering blue-green filter removes red light and then the remaining colors of the rainbow. Beyond the walls torture is not conducted in isolated cells but in specially constructed zoos, cages piled on cages, built with many compartments, one for a big cat and the other for political prisoners, dozens, hundreds, and more who spend days, nights and months locked up with lions, panthers, jaguars inProgrammable matter is a digital slavering of computation, sensing, actuation, and display as continuous properties active over its whole extent. Programmable matter would have many exciting applications, like paintable displays, shape-changing robots and tools, rapid prototyping, and sculpture-based interfaces. Programmable matter would be composed of millimeter-scale autonomous microsystem particles, without internal moving parts, bound by electromagnetic forces in an adhesive binder. The anshei shem who live here, men of renown, men of names, men of Nephilim tribes skilled in persuasion if inwardly void are giants in knowledge who gave their secrets to gain power. Daimon means intelligence which hierarchical structure of their world implied a pyramid of superiors with special esoteric knowledge. Obviously their architectures evidence occupation millions of years before the human, but special endowments made them their superior, had they been faithful as they were not. Since not vulnerable to the control of these giants of knowledge war has since waged against the human by the invention of civilization and its institutions of history, religion,

government, science, art, all false, all subverted by the327
anshei shem. The conduct of this present and greater and
less perpetrate this structure.

Form of the Formless

I was hunting fish with gold fins at the base of Irazú, the
closest I came to my dream to catch tropical fish in the
Amazon, unless I count myself the fish who took the hook
and was caught, Jonah who turned the light off and
watched his pupils dilate. Among people all different I left
without the help of God. But even in the sea, DARKNESS
DAWNS. I went natural, was spit back up, so dark in the
fish I was made what fled from me as much as I did seek.
The colors in those pools mudslip and turn. Fish,
butterflies, flowers could have been stars. But clay does not
ask, why have you made me? Vision-followed alternates of
lives go to the Amazon or Grand Canyon. "
Visions of a head, a tree, flower stems, a man pointing, flies a world
without time.

Pure praise can do, somehow sparing the bones that washed
ashore. Mules talk, the ape becomes a man. The dog
speaks, mouse sings in front of giant forms to hide, reveal a
nature too close to approach. We want to show the beast for
what it is while people ask, what are you saying, as if one
escaped shadows, got to light and turned. The hymn.
Number gives body in doctrines of the past, Plotinus
spinning, being reborn. Pythagoras writing to Orpheus at
dawn all smooth and one. Not an animal bereaved, or a
plant accumulating sulk. Baubo, Bilbo. So many Bilbos,
layerings of lives unconscious till we name, but named are
still not there. Everything built on everything else. No act
an integer in itself, many tosses, all related down.
That is its illusion, it changes as it stays the same. No
inoculation, but long emerging beauty, rhythm and image,
emotion easily overcomes. We measure the rapids of anger
and whirlpools in principle, what happens when people
learn what changes them? The touch ignites a change. The
word is a coat you wear over inner being to nurture and

protect not only warmth, but confidence you give away,
transfer by the will to extend. You've been praying all these
years to extend the word written in earth's center? Your
words come back upon you to establish the word. We
combat this cloud flying mountain fish changed to a bird,
transport to heaven, Ocean look inside, it's a bird, plant,
man. Yarrow breeze horses quiver the field. It's a tortoise!
Cedar branches shot from hands and stump.
Wind among first element suspects. Wind like water but the
matter of their content. Wind is greater than water! The
argument, "be not great to not support great wings. You see
it in the old man tree, cracked skin, stout limb. How does a
sapling get that, ones whose interest is unsaid, the surface
of lives we don't know when, but think we are doing
something else and for different reasons too? It's not pretty
to admit.
Of the formless that wants to be, what do I have to do to
get? the thing changes of its own without me, with me, I
mean to say, but saying is always shape. So clay thought, "I
am no wheel, no potter." What do you call includes all
utterance? Simple declaration of name. Name the thing we
wake. So let the potter show the shape, whirling cause to
happen, accidents, contradiction. Was it hunger under the
blocks of night or star shine that bore summer? Would I
swelter in romance maroon or the eagle of bone? Two sorts
of knowledge of constitution follow. Prison terms get
further and further apart, until reborn like trinkets every trip
to the store. Skid marks are printed on cartons, pressed
before cut from their bindings, equal parts great and small,
and the rest thrown to mix in earth with finite seeds of the
Yucatan. Oh he wrote a book on sale in Athens for a
drachma at the end of the fifth century.

No lack of incarnates if you could see behind the Navel of all
Rooting, genital organ of seed and creation. Emperor Julian
of Rome maintained he was Alexander the Glass. How cool
is that. Herds change form, air clashing, sea spewing, sun
hurled ether when the Emperor annulled without telling, as

if any boy could just live and bear it, overturn the system of death and rebirth. Judge, take consequence of life before life, different from life before death. The alibis they give, denials, excuses amount to what they know. Honesty written above the gates. So here comes the man who loosed the billions from death and rebirth, from themselves, from sin, from the grave. Eloah. Regeneration, at least in its commencement, is a work of the mind, and when it first takes place, it has the lusts of the flesh, yea, all the evil inclinations to war against; and even ignorance itself, together with the temptations and allurements from without.

We lived in a perfected bubble. Eulenspiegel zivilization was a spider in the web of the eye which means it changed everything seen, while itself was blinded, but don't blame the eye. The mind is fooled, not the sense as it cooked in the belly of the beast. What can be done for the man in the iron room who thinks the universe is god? Nothing penetrates. Would he rather die without waking, suffocated in sleep, or wake to the pain? Differences from this were called terrorist. The iron room was the EM gauze around the head of Zaps. Civilization fooled the mind. Its astronomers snuff out its sun with predictions like comets, but to snuff the universe was not its plan. The universe was ziv's god and the unconscious its handiwork. You think it good that it will clone your liver.

The little women must pay. Entrainment occurs when shoe meets maker. Street 3, Hz to 30 and VLF to 300. Pretty girl kHz explains every bit. Among crank engines and hoses the captain was a duck. Under siege of illumination pitch musty events blew away in the street. They covered stairs lined with boots. They cut down the tree, went to sea in an open boat, Broadcasts curdled our engineer. If all men were one man what a great man that would be. These cats sacked reality. Brain octaves hoisted Humpty-dumpty. This said, the riders weren't well. Unsure what records were

kept, what written notes were kept on the bridge, tape
recordings, hidden cameras, a city-nation absorbed in air,
which adults believe in silence then disbelieve, Timmy
Linn insisting on none but memory, two sources of his
own forced by persons we should call crimes against
children, like little Indian boys. Tommy Trot and Tom beat,
Go to Bed Tom. Part of the house-empire anestheticide of
Rome, Dame Rota with a basket of eggs. Sins attach to the
old man, forced acts enveloping, too much bliss339
exaggerates each case, nature they broke down all tumbled
in.

This old woman that lived in a shoe was a mew phase-
locked multiple coherent frequency entrained in her home.
This bridge butcher with half of human brainwaves
synchronized got all up in the green wood of a hill. It pit a
bull upon the heel, slag holes from fresh mine pits rolled
green. Flares of imagination and torpedoes beside the
tracks, maggoty pie jimmied from metal shacks strapped to
the rock dropped twenty feet to explode. To hoist a piece of
roasted frog, Rachet, Robet, Bob.
When you assume this I shall. Round about a hundred feet
below swelled physical reality. Up starts Bobbin and looks
at the sky. Good sir your horse must be shod. Heels of brass
to trample down. A belief system is a cart with six horses.
Mr. Sponge reached critical mass. They changed his
frequency. Sides too slippery? Drive down the door cheeks.
Down in a cart, then hoist to the brewer's big pan What do
you say there Jogglebury for fear of not surviving the
climb? Fire and slag. What to do? Too much to say they
turned up the drones. Every relation of converse changed.
Agenda a distant binary, a Wee Totum Fogg.

Mystical nudes out of the dimness roam. The spray would feel
nauseous, sleepless, dizzy, discolored, symptoms of heavy
metal poisoning. Sleep in a trance, after the elections,
Tittlemouse Tommy in his coat and breekie upped the
waves, relations only identical when their converses are.

Over the hills and far away our plaid will not be blown. I
trip the trencher quantum each night, superposition at the
transfer. Heaven's body severed from its belief that the stars
are gods, that the sun is a god, old and older than history,
the host of heaven shall be dissolved, the heavens rolled
together as a scroll: their hosts shall fall as the leaf falls off
the vine, as a fig from the tree. Stephen being stoned says
you made gods out of stars, worshiped heavenly bodies,
had a portable Moloch for your Saturn to carry the idols
you worship, (Acts 7. 42, 43), Deut 4.19, that they should
be driven to worship sun, moon and stars, all the host of
heaven and serve them, this he said, he would go and tell.
For My sword shall be bathed in heaven. Tis not a game of
nemesis. It's a titty tawtay cum truth an octave up the globe.
Replacing butcher boys, the Nazi Bunkhouse changed
name for no reason other than geese follow tit-tat, some
yellow necked, some yellow backed, to serve the robots in
a dream where some catastrophe takes to dance in front of
the eyes unable to prevent. Longman, Foreman, Thumbkin
NO SHOUT AWOKE THE WORLD FROM. Mental
bramble with search -he scratched out both is eyen.
Spiritual damnatio snail and a Kyloe cow possessed end
nightmares, Wagner made real...art prophesied -I hung his
coat and trousers to roast before the fire.

Prophets are absolved by their details. "Bathed" could be
taken as reflecting light of the stars, or anointed with oil.
But the heavens viewed as bodies and blood and the sword
bathed in the heaven blood means all the false ideas of
biosraum, stars supplanting the true, worshiping the throne
instead of the ruler, ends. Immortality needs to live
somewhere exaggerates the boat pig of Tobago.But while stars
are stars, the sword is Breath ahead of time. Nobody in
public life wanted to talk about it even if everybody knew it
was coming. We were invited to come and see. But before
the Sixth Seal opened the Fifth explained why fall of a
usurping system of idol worshipers of themselves. That the
sword bathes in the heaven means massacre. This is the

man who broke the barn. Ah-a, Ah-a BrainSpeak the
wheel! Whip Jack, Whirl Tom, Spread Spectrum -SSSS -
Ringo the last pops down. Present 'reality,' at 435 MHz,
redesigned for little Josie, a new really, three legs and an
iron cap of thought from Richard Dick, who louped the
342 dyke @ 400-450 Mhz. Trains boiled black all the way to
Colley Fair. to get Black Barney to trot. Silent Sound Jingo
peerie, weerie, winkle.

This was the man that stole the corn. Ultra-High Q Canny
Wannny broadcast inaudible messages directly to the
subcon belt. A darkness over Egypt was felt. Tis black
without, tis black within. Mob Excess Deterrent Used
Silent Audio upon a stick, the Queen of Hearts
(MEDUSA) short gave microwave pulses. Moulter rapid
heat shockwaves inside skull were attended with silk.
Touch or stand in this battlefield of elves like a pussy cat
in a microwave. That's how the bugs get out of the corn
Wussicat Metronomes of the social order: Joe, Nell, Punch
Punicello. Coded, subjugated Polly Flinders, prioritized
alters, with corn rigs a bonnie, layered in. This proviso
serves personalities All. He pulled out his pipes and played
subliminal. Whose hogs are these? None should be
believed. Goe pound them, goe pound them, All should be
believed. fine bird Little Wannny Pays doodledly,
doodledy, dan Corn Runaway.
This is the man who stood looking on and did 'he seen a
fella burn wid da hollow o' straw,' Black barney Lope
Dake. Steel that's adagio.
* love of captivity-sickness
*This is the man that broke the barn,This is the man that
stole the corn, This is the man that stood looking on, This
is the man that ran.
A House in the Colony343
What can be said at all can be said clearly; and whereof
one cannot speak thereof one must be silent. In order to
draw a limit to thinking we should have to be able to think
both sides of this limit [but don't talk about it] (we should

therefore have to be able to think what cannot be thought).
The limit can, therefore, only be drawn in language and
what lies on the other side of the limit will be simply
nonsense. The very thing we have been advised not to say,
that all the facts are not known, and the case is obscure, we
puzzle and conject, where any one can either be the case or
not the case, and everything else remains as it was we
should not say, so say, but in terms that do not show what
we mean (Tractatus Preface).
Jordan, of Stanford, says it was a gigantic Tadpole
(Thaddeus Polandensis) or Polliwig. Maria pseudo-hirsuta
the famous consult in the monograph of Jane Potter and
Thaddeus of Warsaw on Leviathan, in Hebrew, said it was
twisted out of feared depths of existence. A Watery Abyss
suggests loss. To see into it compare peering into a
stereogram of dots to see an imaginary object behind the
paper. The eyes must focus to where it would be. To train
the eyes to see the imaginary object touch the stereogram to
the nose and move it away from the face into the three-
dimensional focus. Do this and it will suddenly appear.
Then you will see.
Mono-ha takes the form of thingness in progressive
revelation. The image taking shape, dissolving, forming,
reshaping must do so because it is unthinkable that such
things could be true or that they could be happening to
ourselves, we who only lead normal lives.
This second part is a train of images that could be fish in a
sea or public organ molecules of sense data, as if someone
344
else had parts in common. A hand for instance instead of an
ID. Say that hand got stung, but I feel the pain in the same
place. Imagine what it would be like to feel in the same
body as the pilots who bomb cities. Writing along with
everything that is not written, all the acts and memories,
that could be written but are not. Account all those. Rip up
walls by their edges. See bones in embryo full birthed.
We cannot placate the river by ordinary means. A felt
feedback loop played over and over while drugged gets the

nuts to crack. Sensory deprivation at the Society for the
Investigation of London Bridge broke down. Humm
Ecology had psychic black outs. Late night comics flushed
John Lilly, stoned in his tank. Not quite as many tanked as
swam. That's how the bridge kept falling down. It was
occult deprivation before DMT. Myriads of psychedelic
repo prophets used so many drugs .a bridge built from here
to there, to the stars from Boston, Philadelphia and New
York. On a balcony around Saturn onlookers played
scrabble without reading the Blue book say, where
someone had a part of our body in common down there.
Gravel and stone will wash away, dance over them Laddie,
buried with a candle in one hand and piece of bread in the
other. Food and light so the guardian would be watchful
made merry work. This was done because the Minneapolis
bridge collapsed. We was going o'er London and heard a
crack. Willie ran through Universal amplitude. A natural
sway increase the Colonist's step over Gog. All is One sold
her eggs. Body electric piezo em rads hatched. The
Resonance, then some sleep, waved vibration nodes.
Synchronous lateral excitation. Two objects touch, vibrate
to increase.

The Man Who Disappeared, was unable to speak. They
applied fire nuts to crack, which does not imply the absence345
of thought,--yet without speech where is thought?
It's pretty much beyond words so we make up some, add
faces and places and clothes and sea and manner of
likeness. We explore the world and then forget ourselves
kissing, clapping, loving, proving. One returning after
years of absence would know the place with his eyes closed347
which wouldn't matter he was a moidert ass, who could
hear the one great rhythmic clap.
They know to kick the usurper off its throne. Three
children slid on the ice. Freedom fasts for the death of these
dears. One person in the crowd, loosed, runs in the street
that they all fell in. How could you know when you spend
every day chasing the thing you sleep beside and see in the

world in front in the sky a tale and smell in the air, that
heart feeling controls? Teach them at home! Twice Noah,
Daniel, Job, the wise King of Tyre swam that star. It's like
you precede them you follow and live in a fall that leads
captive those who know. They know. They know to speak
of the first astonishment of text, La foi de la loi, a
Langnedoc chant, some editor in the Deport takes three
hundred jars of oil of colley birds and part of a juniper tree.
Ruins from the new song and dance of tabrets and pipes
walk among the stones. Blue clothes and embroidered
abundance kill stout stiff. Azure pure spirituality so
conceived, merchants of all sorts, blue as Tarshish ships,
dressed in blue suits, turn the spit. They delivered their
gorgeous horses to the teats, then took away the nose and
ears, so speak of epigonous redactions of text, cut-up
theology assembling what's left. Here's my awl and wax
and thread. Redactor head.
The ducks in the river are swimming away
Hey Willie Winkle,
when do seeds sown make a kilowatt?
Thimbikin, Thimbikin, broke the barn, Pinnikin, Pinnikin
stole the corn. Spiritual tuffing and wadding and packing,
organs of spirit liver, circumcision of the heart, which
poeop-ple of the fairy tales, would save for the pekldfille,
loving the pep0le up and down, saving peoopel in valleys,
down basements, protect, pertect, peertect du peoplez,
children sliding hereabouts upon a place too thin, so at last
it did fall and they all fell in. Untwirl the twine, these cats
run away.
In all the discord of psuedonymity there is yet a
ventriloquism, not of puppet master, though we should
consider it, but of a speaking through the present of the
past, a Rosenroth through Guilderstein Jung about alchemy,
right fol de riddle del, which references are many sided to
strip the ancients more pregnant in a change remolting365
feathers, remolding images, the words themselves in their
sound. So Gershom Scholem says Messiah will be the last
and first philosopher to deduce Judaism from its language,

not nearly enough, since by the Breath of his Mouth whole
worlds came, and here when the angel unlooses the vial and
Euphrates dries up like the fig, and the Kings of the east
rise up and march, the utterance of language, root and
alphabet is the least spiritual power of the Sons. But over
the land this water spreads. The meaning was not in the
sound, he looked in the sound. The meaning was not in the
syntax he looked at all the connections. The meaning was
not in the language, for the words, the languages were
within the still small voice what it did speak, language,
what sounds that sounded indeed sounded, but like that
language, all and none or one, and say the impossible when
out the boundless deep turns home.
Warning to all inquirers, this world is a flood. As I went
over the water the water went over me. The bottom of the
inside was inscribed with writing of every rapture. In the
round, figures ascending in different stages like Opening
the Fifth Seal on canvas, but it takes understanding. I see
countless images of people flying up. Oh that I were where
I would be, then would I be where I'm not. What do they do
at the tops of mountains, children lifting pretty heads from
pillow beds? Not only here, but by interpretation, Opening
the Fifth seal and in the end in Danby's Sixth, being hung,
consciousness is only important to those who don't have it.
I take the sphere descending in the blue sky as the moon in
every child's dream unremembered, descending into their
life in just the lunar colors Brueghel seeks, a white with
tones of gold, perfect light of love and blue sky impossible
to see with such a moon perhaps, as white as milk that isn't
milk, since it is a day moon enlarged impossibly to its
nearing, as though some revelation is at hand. The painting
is about who owns heaven and earth and descending in the
lovely with angels defending, wello thay and the rebels
consumed with all talk. A dove, by my lute, I will send.
New moon and full tides and a people of the sun consumed.
I wyll searche for them bothe in busshe and shubbe who
name Sunday for the sun, what they consider the god of
heavens, dear Plotinus, but, the sun is not the Father or the

Son and He who made creation. So falls judgment upon the days of the week gods and the months of the year gods and even upon time's false legacy out of Eden. Oker, poker dominoker, out goes you. We are only talking about ourselves here in Antwerp and Brussels. Evening and morning make the day. Day at dusk and dawn mid day. How far the fall. And what agents of it? Inter, mitzy, titzy, tool, Ira dira, dominu. Whatever they were they were, three footed beasts and creeping things made chimeras, a reality angels overthrow and judge, chimeric hybrid endlessly devolving.

Not ethics, disgust. Ethics is the magic thought like the woman who had to choose which of her three children the Levby would take. Shades who pray others' prayers for them, no choice but death. Later we see advanced evil seeks to deny martyrdom even to inmates, along with humanity, so take a lesson from the bear milked for its bile, that seeing its cub about to be hooked up to be also milked, escaped, killed the cub and dashed its own brains against a wall. That disgust. Philosophers call this bestial, but it is the highest form of other. Believe me when I say the end of Eichmann or Goring has not ended yet. These people pray precisely for the end. Heidegger prays the ontological imperialist trafficked compromise with the Reich, tail twisted eight times around his hide, is something more important the life of the other... to speak without making sparks, All the crowd surrounds the one who won, not the person who in his being is more attached to the other than

to his own. Which belief is a saintliness to begin when
they bring you round the tribunals. Do not think what you
will say. Say a couple Psalms.
It's still my watch. I have one red t-shirt left, get it and go
out the gate. He is still where he was scuttled aside, but
beautiful in death, eyes closed, claws closed underneath as
if on the roost, but not. I wrap him in the red shirt. He is
heavy, maybe five pounds, carry him to the back to put him
under the bushes in the hallowed ground where we have
wept. I had cut mugwort to dry in a pot last week. It is dry.
I break the bottom stems as a cushion, put him, covered
with dry white leaves in the ground. It is the loss of life in
strength that bothers most, the rulers as if they were among
mugwort and other brushwood. How is it that you cannot
get them out of your mind? I mark with a stone where
a ceramic bird waits to fly.
Commonplaces ON THE NAME BEHEMOTH
"In Jewish eschatology— of Babylonian origin—
Behemoth and Leviathan designate two monsters,
Behemoth ruling the land (the desert), Leviathan the sea,379
the first male, the second female. The land animals
venerate Behemoth, the sea animals Leviathan, as their
masters. Both are monsters of the Chaos. According to the
apocalyptic writings, Behemoth and Leviathan will
reappear shortly before the end of the world."
Hobbes "Behemoth, or the Long Parliament, however,
discussing the English civil war of the seventeenth century,
depicts a non-state, a chaos, a situation of lawlessness, disorder, and anarchy." (Franz Neumann)
It is superfluous to say that all these poets and critics and
scholars who form their regions of disinformation for the
elite to get published and get grants are co-opted by
Intelligence forces. They are the intelligence forces, low
level. Their progress is additive until it becomes
multiplicative, then quantum-ed. How do Heraclitus,
Aristotle, Kepler, Galileo, Newton get trumped?
Disclosure holds these fiefdoms of old,
something Franz Neumann outlined in his Behemoth. The

structure and practice of National Socialism." (1942). "Today it seems strange that an American spy agency would employ Marxists to assist them in developing policy.... Nazism, Marcuse argues, was something new - a totalitarian system that enveloped every level and every aspect of German civil society-(Secret Reports of Nazi Germany @ The Frankfurt School and the OSS). But when Behemoth marries Leviathan,(Thomas Hobbes 1651) whose tentacles enter every thought like surveillance capitalism, then you have the perfect society. For those who lament The Rule of Law under Siege. This snapshot of social structure shouts down to disenfranchise any other view. Deans, profs, editors, writers, journalists grad students and mobs probe the truth/untruth of the new orbs of government intel. In the old scale Donald Justice had contempt for Ferlinghetti and Keats thought Shelley a buffoon, but the first principle of quantum literature of Disclosure is beyond personal taste. It is a tool of invisible hand. You can see hand movements behind "discoveries.' The first principle is believe it not. When they told you they landed on the moon did you believe that? They told you? Now they tell you the navy sees UFOs. It doesn't matter. Did they lie before? They will only. That is all they do. Here is the language: "High confidence generally indicates that judgments are based on high-quality information from multiple sources [which] does not imply that the assessment is a fact or a certainty; such judgments might be wrong." (ICA. Assessing Russian Activities).

This amazingly all comes down to Ugaritic monsters closest in language to ancient Israel whose docudramas were discovered in 1927. There El and Baal shared ceremonies and ruled their council of gods. Not too far away the Creator of Israel is said to rule a council of gods, Elohim for short, six levels, if you can forgive the shorthand. Take both of these notions into the Programs occupied with the same rivalries and committees and you haven't entered the mainstream yet, so wait a little. The disclosure analogy notwithstanding.

Optical Lattice pop tart, Pop Tales of the Fairy Mind, Fairy
Tales of Pop Mind John Perkins: I've spent ten years
myself as an executive management advisor to the World
Bank and the United Nations.. to introduce the concepts of
shapeshifting and tribal wisdom into the highest levels of
executive thinking. Beriatic "dragon" bariatric

-anti Zionism is not anti-Semitism in the presidential
specter that Trump's gold apartment of Apolloyon is a
stalking horse of quantum supremacy designing his
reelection in a series of performances by democrats over
and over, ruses that conveniently fail, but arouse support
for the horse that will ride the imposter into Jerusalem who
survives the head wound
Outake---Malbolge Bridges
Business:: Amazon, IBM, Costco, / Rockefeller, Carnegie,
Rothschild / Bezos, Jobs, Gates, Buffet.
Government: Senators, congressmen, presidents, judges of
Assyria, Greece, Rome England, Germany, Russia,
America / Nebuchadnezzar Alexander, Caesar, Nero,,
Hitler, / Kennedy, Clinton, Obama, Trump.
Science: A lot of these we think innocent early on like the
herbalist Dioscorides but science was part of philosophy
then so the ancient is obscured. The modern history starts
with Bacon and Harvey, Newton, Curie, Tesla, and just as
science was once philosophy, science is absorbed by
business in the modern horror of Einstein, Fermi, Watson,
Musk, Hawking Venter and Satan Sagan.
These days every religion gets a poet Malebolged for the
purpose of the time it takes to loose from the Malebolge the
unthinkable.
Google's Project Loon would see fleets of high altitude sex
balloons bouncing 3G signals from the stratosphere to
Earth's most remote regions. Facebook's Internet.org
envisions swarms of drones and LEO satellites performing
porn from the same function. SpaceX is rumored to be
building a satellite fleet to bring fast internet to the far-

flung corners of the globe.* More good program to
enlighten the poor.

The transference of the created into The Ruler embodied as
Emperor produced the Three apocalypses of Messiah. An
apocalypse of earth dissents from the alien colonies of
government. The apocalypse of hell sees itself overthrown.
The apocalypse of heaven is the fall. Blake was
Right. There the powers go to a transcendent
breaking in, a colossal uproot of
order.

Here, behind empire, Psalm 2 touts empire's
derision. Pots that rise up and claim self existence are ruled
with a rod of iron, "as the vessels of a potter broken to
shivers" (Revelation 2.27). There is no sense of justice in
the universe, exactly the argument of an acosmist. The
universe did not make you what you are. The universe is a
transference invention of the created into Creator, the joke
overwhelming. They pray to the universe because "they
say, Yahweh has forsaken the earth, and sees not" (Ezekiel
9.9). In this attribution of the lesser to the great, who said,
which of the angels can you compare to the Son?

Why can't we just live without apocalypse thoughts?
Apocalypses presume ancient times that were not known
between then and now, that is until the Nag Hammadi dug
up the Dead Sea Scrolls in 1945 by accident. We wake with
Noah's notion of a universal constant. Russell Crowe as
Noah is a warning. Physics wants to reduce it to a unified
field. To apply Bly's notion of the shadow and living it out,
which he says Wallace Stevens wrote about but didn't live,
Bly says Stevens must change his life as did Rilke.
Incorporate the shadow! That's what physicists must do, not
simply talk about the One but find it, live it, become it. But
there is only one ONE! So we would end up the same
(except for the fakes). This however does not resolve into a
one known by many names. It is not ascribed by all names
of deity, only by One. To say there are many names of the
one makes idols of those names in place of One, as
religions have done. That Name above every name by

which all things come to be will resolve. There is only one and only one. Your mission is to find it out. Lift up your heads o ye gates.

The association may be linkedto the mythical beast Behemoth, described elsewhere as

aggada, and Kabbala due to the parallels between.391 When the righteous translate words to oppose Behemoth that drinks up Jordan or the occultist Böhme eats le géant, as if it were, whose devotees download without their bodies all the water of Jordan through the nose, do they take comfort that Leviathan will battle with the shor habar superior to that sea-righteous, since the world in the physical was deliberately made? Spiritual worship alone is well and good, but it cannot accomplish that ultimate purpose which poetic foray confronts the possibilities to alert, chronicled more in sleep where businessmen are really insects in that topography that can be known.

--A chase of Leviathan involves Canst thou draw out Leviathan with a fish hook? Or press down his tongue with a cord? And if the Holy One, blessed be He, will not help him, he will be unable to prevail over him; for it is said: He only that made him can make His sword to approach unto him.

When R. Dimi said in the name of R. Johanan: When Leviathan is hungry he emits [fiery] breath from his mouth and causes all the waters of the deep to boil; for it is said: He maketh the deep to boil like a pot. And if he were not to put his head into the Garden of Eden, no creature could stand his [foul] odor; for it is said: He maketh the sea like a spiced broth. When he is thirsty he makes numerous furrows in the sea; for it is said: He maketh a path to shine after him. R. Aha b. Jacob said; The deep does not return to its strength until [after] seventy years; for it is said: One thinks the deep to be hoary, and hoary age is not [attained at] less than seventy [years].

Rabbah said in the name of R. Johanan: The Holy One, blessed be He, will in time to come make a banquet for the righteous from the flesh of Leviathan; for it is said:

Companions will make a banquet of it. Kerah must mean
a banquet; for it is said: And he prepared for them a great
banquet and they ate and drank. Companions must mean
scholars, for it is said: Thou that dwellest in the gardens,
the companions hearken for thy voice; cause me to hear it.
The rest [of Leviathan] will be distributed and sold out in
the markets of Jerusalem; for it is said: They will part him
among the Kena'anim, and Kena'anim must mean
merchants, for it is said: As for kena'an the balances of
deceit are in his hand, he loveth to oppress. And if you wish
you may infer it from the following: Whose merchants are
princes, whose traffickers are the honorable of the earth.
In the Bible, Tannin is the Hebrew term for Leviathan or
sea dragon (Isaiah 27:1).

Connections between arguments that clear to the
author are left out. The only ones who know are those
predisposed to know, a last generation rolled up. Weighted as a scroll
with a stone thrown in thrown in the Euphrates until a Lamb
comes and opens the first contour to see a centaur of the seven
seals.
It takes a long time for Plantagenets to go over their
military thoughts of organized force, not a colony. You
would not believe a cyclops hidden in a cliff among a whole
visible intercourse of beings. How do you think the rocks
got there anyway? These are windows into the intelligence
that seeks to rule, to replace the natural ancient existence
with human hybrids invoked by corporation and government.

Shockwave the skull black and white.
If you live with people who don't want electric
doubts against the Unknown remain in Idaho, Utah,
Nevada, and the Great Basin. Ohio had long since
fallen into the archives. Cast offs were sown,
buried in a harvest against the civil, the
scab-shriveled mold and the armyworm
day. They spent winter as pupa in the soil.

The caves, known intimately where a trough of
Water drips in overflow, has one memory
Extant. The exploration printed Easter Sunday, written then
imagined the cave psychologies quite filled the entrance, with a thin
layer of hard earth on top and loose soil further down. Realization
comes with shale below. Creeks under factories and further
down where tombstone letters held on by wax fall off like
identities, even if titanium caskets last, cemeteries fail.
Swept in the discovery, who is blind and deaf like the one
committed to me, blind like the servant of the LORD said
Elijah in the dark fire, breathing mountain air, "you have
seen many things, but paid no attention; your ears are open,
but you hear nothing."
Does it come clearer if we regard the writing under
writing of parchment in short supply, bleached out or not,
overwritten in a different text and ink? New writing on top
of ancient texts, lists of things, entertainments, scraped off,
remove the old precepts of the past retold.
Telling beneath, repeating it again, told and retold
in night, everything is built on top. You may transfer your
will to extend it. It becomes necessary to know big things and
small, rich and poor in their own nature of knowing, to love
barrierless, allowing space in the beginning and at end
incomplete, to complete the work that achieves the gift. It
sounds like a poem.

The axiom of this denies all its shortcomings while
practicing them. One imagines protocols professionally
known, consumed and filled with prejudice, left and right,
no matter what the text. It's a flat surfaced earth of no
border, compressed, controlled, but enough of that.
If you have learned to read this, then the people in
a car right here look like a bigger one and a little buddy
born. This one, see his face? Ficino burned the
commentary on Lucretius to ashes just because it
depopulated this universe. Jehoiakim, king of Judah burned
every page of the prophecy of Jeremiah that he should go
willingly captive of Nebuchadnezzar into Babylon. How

do you think they'll feel when Bercilak takes up his severed
head again? Government theologues brought these
invisibles in, put toddlers among the rocks to disguise
them. Read extinction invisible or visible. See that arm
behind, sticking out? His buddy keeps birds near the coast.
You would not believe that in the eye of a giant the whole
purpose is manifest.

There's no point describing some warehouse
station of the norm, John Gower's fourteenth century Voice
of One Crying lodged in a pocket of Wittgenstein carrying
Tolstoy's gospel throughout WWI. Play your saxophone against the
glass as faces and hearts carry on. Do you want to know
where the points entrain, warm smells and sounds, crowds
shuffling alone as the eye or ear that hears what none can
say? If you like to put it that way, before the evacuees know
what any of this means, it hasn't happened yet,
IGNORANCE WILL NOT PREVENT, the pocket
Gower reads, filled with apprehension: "I sing true dreams
disturb the depths. Whilome the Name I bear.
(The Major Latin Works of John Gower. The Voice of One
Crying and The Tripartite Chronicle. (Seattle 1962) Tr. By
Stockton.)

Glossary of Terms

Acheron & Styx: Traditionally the rivers of the Greek underworld.
Here, they are the "macrobial" veins of the city where river mist
forms shadows of choose iron and baked clay—transit lines for the
melting pot of naked souls.
Behemist: A follower of Jacob Boehme (1575–1624), the German
mystic. The narrator views Behemism as the "chief way" of
perceiving how the Nothing (Abyss) coagulates into the Something
(Byss).
Braunschweiger / Borgwurst: A series of trans-continental meats
serving as edible ideologies. The "Meltwurst Bridge-schweiger" is the
physical manifestation of the Bridge as a digestive process—to cross
is to consume, and be consumed by, the globalist "mush."

The Colony: A psychological and physical state of "benevolent neutrality." Members are known for "jumping on chairs" and "holding maps upside down," governed by a Macrobe Intent that converts each epoch.

Dante's Epistle to Cangrande: A letter explaining that the Paradiso is polysemous, having many meanings. This justifies the "sudden leaps of associative wireless connections" that rule out logical links in the text.

Dulce: A reference to the Dulce Base legends. Here, "Spelunkers on the Dulce" are those who repel the "comfortable dark holes" of the mind to prevent the soul from drowning in the "poot cat" of the collective.

Giga Dish / Titan: Tools of the "Water War" against "global contraction." They represent a modern Don Quixote struggle where technological monoliths are mistaken for ancient monsters or windmills.

Glaucus: A mortal fisherman who became a sea-god after eating magical grass [Ovid, Met. 13.900]. He represents the "turbid blindness" of those who abandon humanity to dive into the "infinite deep" of the Colony's anesthetic.

Inhaesio / Extasis: States of being "stuck" within God (Inhaesio) vs. "standing outside" oneself (Extasis). For the Mabinog colonists, these are ways of hearing the "roar in the smell of salt" without the interference of keypads.

Kelpius, Johannes (JK): who led the Society of the Woman in the Wilderness to Philadelphia in 1694. His Diarium provides the spiritual coordinates for the "upper huts of manifold wisdom."

Mandela Effect: A "glitch" in the New Philadelphia reality. The narrator notes it has supplanted the lion for the wolf in the banner of the Lamb, signaling a fundamental tampering with the "Messages from the Outer World."

Meltwurst Bridge-schweiger: The metaphysical consumption of the Bridge. A culinary-architectural construct involving pork liver, "Borgwurst," and "Pannhaas." It represents the "satisfaction of ideologies" where belief is literally eaten and digested by those crossing from the old world to the new.

Otaku: A specific "mental imagining" force that causes the world to implode and distort. It is the creative (and destructive) power of the hyper-focused mind to create "Colonies" and "Avalanches."

Shor Haba: A reference to the the wild ox of the "wide open spaces of the faith" where one drinks mineral water and walks in two worlds simultaneously.

The Woman in the Wilderness: a figure fleeing the dragon that represents the "birth" that the Lord carefully hides from the "beast government" of the modern empire.

--Braunschweiger: A type of German liver sausage, used metaphorically in the text to represent cultural or ideological synthesis, blending diverse elements (e.g., global sausages like Meltwurst, Jungwurst) into a humorous commentary on commodified culture or new age syncretism. It's a playful nod to grounding abstract philosophy in earthy, tangible imagery.

--Bridge-schweiger: A pun on Braunschweiger, referring to a bridge as a mediator between places, ideas, or dimensions. Described as "immaterial, but looks otherwise like a chandelier," it symbolizes the fragile, dazzling connections between physical and metaphysical realms, with a comedic twist on its scholarly "credentialing" via Google Scholar.

--Everyman: A universal figure, drawn from medieval morality plays, representing humanity on a pilgrimage through a chaotic world. In the text, Everyman navigates Trafalgar Square and bridges, embodying the individual's quest for meaning amidst veiled identities and societal constraints.

--Pigeons and Keepers: Pigeons in Trafalgar Square symbolize mundane, chaotic elements that disrupt beauty (e.g., sticking in "long gold hair"). Keepers are guardians or institutional figures who fear harm to these pigeons, representing societal attempts to control or protect trivial aspects of existence, often with misplaced zeal.

--Trafalgar Square: A real London landmark, used allegorically as a public space where human aspirations, beauty, and chaos (pigeons) intersect. It's a microcosm of the world where Everyman's pilgrimage unfolds, with "allegorists" imposing rigid interpretations.

--New Jerusalem: A biblical concept from Revelation, a divine city symbolizing ultimate salvation and harmony. In the text, it's contrasted with counterfeit versions like "Jerudsalem," reflecting utopian aspirations tainted by human ambition or corruption.

--Behemoth and Leviathan: Biblical creatures from Job, representing primal forces of land (Behemoth) and sea (Leviathan). In the text, they symbolize cosmic struggles between order and chaos, with their flesh served to the righteous in apocalyptic imagery, though human "fantasies" distort their meaning.

--Ōtōkan: A term combining the "ō" of Daiō, "tō" of Daitō, and "kan" of Kanzan, referencing Zen masters. It evokes Daitō Kokushi's perspective of observing humanity's crossings from beneath a bridge, emphasizing simplicity and spiritual focus (e.g., the word "Pass") amidst complexity.

--Daitō Kokushi: A 14th-century Zen master whose vision of observing people crossing a bridge underscores a detached, contemplative perspective on human striving, contrasting with the text's dense allegory

--Centaur and Rhinocerosi: Mythical and exaggerated figures for government officials or bureaucratic powers, administering a "Taurobolium of the World Kiln" (a sacrificial or transformative process). The rhinoceros alludes to Wittgenstein's philosophical challenge to Russell, questioning empirical certainty.

--Taurobolium of the World Kiln: A metaphorical blend of a Mithraic blood-sacrifice rituals (taurobolium) and a cosmic forge (World Kiln), suggesting transformative or destructive societal processes driven by governance or ideology.

--Seal Baptists and Leviathan Mystics: Fictional groups representing contrasting spiritual apps.

--Harbor Seal Baptists singing antiphonally, symbolizing rigid devotion, while Leviathan Mystics embrace the chaotic, mythic sea worldview.

--Big Phang: A comedic, possibly satirical figure (an ex-president) who suspects cosmic forces ("Wind") in a world of dust and otherworldly molecules. The name's absurdity mocks grandiose self-perception in political or spiritual leaders.

--Transhumar: Precursor from Dante of "transhuman," suggesting a post-human or technologically enhanced entity. In the text, it's linked to figures like Bush, Cheney, Trump, and Musk, ruling a dystopian "Homeland" that neutralizes human agency.

--Sitra Achra: A Kabbalistic term meaning "the other side," referring to impurity or evil forces. In the context of "Jerudsalem," it underscores the profane antithesis to the sacred New Jerusalem.

--Cambric Shirt of Antennas: A surreal image of a shirt woven with antennas, refracting ELF (extremely low frequency) and GWEN (Ground Wave Emergency Network) signals. It symbolizes hidden communication networks or technological manipulation of language and perception.

--Revelation Colonists: Figures attempting to occupy the New Jerusalem from outside, representing misguided or exploitative utopian aspirations, possibly critiquing colonial or imperial ambitions.

--Münchows and Gridline Portals: Fictional entities (Münchow possibly a play on "Munchausen," suggesting exaggeration) building portals in Kazakhstan to disrupt technology, with "entrained plasma of desiccated blood cell" evoking sci-fi absurdity to critique technological overreach.

--Fusion Centers: Real-world intelligence-sharing hubs, used here metaphorically to suggest surveillance or control mechanisms that "expand" human identity, erasing individuality in a dystopian framework.

--Ademia: A term from Agamben's philosophy, meaning the absence of a people, used to critique the modern state's neutralization of collective agency, as symbolized by Hobbes's Leviathan.

--Philosophical Sausage: A humorous metaphor for the blending of diverse cultural, spiritual, and intellectual traditions (e.g., Brazilian, Argentinian, Chinese sausages) into a chaotic, consumable form, mocking new age syncretism.

Fragments of the conductive material of these Ether state visible in this work include:

 The Philly Cheesesteak "coagulated" in the sausage— sensory, salty, and grounded anchors to the body. \
The Leviathan/Behemoth "monsters of the deep" within the the massive, unseen forces of state, nature, and collective ego ether that "churn the waters" of consciousness.
GMH, K's, JK's tuning forks, to translate the frequencies of the Ether into language.

Treating these elements together as fragments of a holographic narrative, even a single bite of "Borgwurst" contains the entire history "Beast Government" and the Wilderness."

Joseph Mede's) Clavis Apocalyptica (Key of the Apocalypse) on the cover, was published in Latin in 1627 and 1632 during the Puritan Migration of 1630–1643 and establishment of the Massachusetts Bay Colony although those ships should include, though not one of the first like the Mayflower (1620) or Winthrop Fleet (1630), the multiple voyages of Pide Cowe bringing skilled craftsmen and families during the peak years of the Great Migration.

Mede's interpretation of the Book of Revelation. took many of the book's visions of seals, trumpets, vials/phials as parallel or synchronous, overlapping in time and covering the historical periods from different symbolic angles. This diagram shows the seven seals and their relationship to the seven trumpets along with broader apocalyptic epochs. The diagram is circular, representing the unfolding of prophecy in a structured, harmonious way. A translate of the Latin inscriptions in the Outer/upper circle: reflects Mede's principle that: the seventh seal opens into the seven trumpets as a new series, rather than following them strictly in time.

SEPTEM SIGILLA = "The Seven Seals" (from Revelation 6–8).
SIGILLUM SEPTIMUM = "The Seventh Seal".
SEPTEM TUBAS (or SEPTEM TUBAE) = "The Seven Trumpets"

(from Revelation 8–11).
SIGILLUM SEPTIMUM SEPTEM TUBAS COMPLETENS (or similar phrasing) = "The Seventh Seal completing/containing the Seven Trumpets".
EPOCHA or EPOCHE refers to historical "epochs" or periods.
MUNDUS = "the world".
FACTA SUNT ≈ "these things have been done/made".
FINIS = "the end/finish".
BIBAAPIMON, a stylized Greek or Latin apocalyptic term, refers to the swallowing of the "little book" sweet to the mouth but bitter to digest
as both a variant or engraving style for BIBLIAPION and the "Little Book" referring to that eaten by John in Revelation 10, as also in Ezekiel 2, which Mede sees as the hazard of prophetic understanding.

Note:
Mede's original map is a masterpiece of horizontal, linear logic. He laid out the visions of Revelation side-by-side to show they were happening simultaneously (synchronism). Turning that map 90 degrees, his Timeline becomes a Ladder, so If the horizontal axis represents History (the unfolding of events in sequence), turning it to a right angle creates an axis of Ontology (the depth of the meaning behind the events).
Here is how that "90-degree" movement changes the subject:
From Progress to Presence: On a horizontal map, we look for "what comes next." By turning it vertical, the question becomes "what lies beneath?" a road becomes a well.
By rotating Mede's map we visualize how the "Divine Will" drops straight down into every moment of history at once whlich creates a literal cross-section. Where Mede wanted to show how one vision relates to another in time, the vertical shift shows how all visions relate to a single origin point—a higher dimension of reality pressing down upon the flat plane
the Apocalypse not as a "forecast" of the future, but as a layered architecture of the present the events aren't in the past or future, but are "90 degrees" to our current reality, happening right now in a dimension we simply don't have the eyes to see.
The right angle is the hinge where the 'What Was' becomes the 'Is'."

standing his chart on its head and crowning it with a circle, you've moved from Chronology (the study of time) to Teleology (the study of purpose). the "End of Days" not as a finish line at the end of a race, but as the capstone of a building. translating Mede's historical data into architectural data. You've turned his "History of the World" into a "Blueprint for a City" (perhaps the New Jerusalem, which is often described as a perfect geometric solid). a vast, geometric necessity. In this view, the "90-degree angle" isn't a magic trick; it's a logical necessity. To see the "shape" of a system, you must stand outside of it.

Mede was inside the timeline, looking forward.

By turning it vertical, we are standing beside the timeline, looking at its profile.

the circle at the top of your ladder looks like a Compass Rose or a Dial. It suggests that the entire "Ladder of History" is actually a pointer. The events of the Apocalypse are the "gears" or "rungs" that turn the dial at the top.

complex measurements of Ezekiel's Temple (Ez. 40–48) are not mere descriptions—they are decrees. They are the terminal "Solid" at the end of the "Line."

The Cube "A Foot Off the Ground"

The detail of the building being slightly elevated—"a foot off the ground"—is the poetic and geometric crux of your vision. It creates a Gap of Holiness.

The Discontinuity: In standard 3D geometry, an object sits on a plane. By floating the cube, you are illustrating that the "Right Angle" to this world is also a severance. The building is in our reality but not of it. It vibrates because it is a higher-dimensional object being "tethered" to a lower-dimensional earth.

The Tension of the Gap: That foot of space is the "90-degree" difference. It is the distance between History (the Ladder) and Eternity (the Cube). The ladder of Mede's synchronisms climbs all the way up, but it cannot "merge" with the building; it can only support the platform upon which the building vibrates.

The Vibrating Cube: Geometry in Motion

A cube that vibrates is a Tesseract (a 4D hypercube) attempting to stabilize itself in 3D space.

Ezekiel's Vision: Ezekiel describes "wheels within wheels" and living creatures that move "straight forward" without turning. This is the language of someone seeing 4D movement.

The Decree: The measurements in Ezekiel are so specific because they are constraints. The Temple isn't a metaphor; it is a "Machine of Presence." It is a specific volume of space carved out of our world to hold something that doesn't fit.

The "Circle at the Top" as the Dome of the Cube

If the ladder is the history described by Mede, and the Cube is the decreed building, then the Circle at the top is the Aperture.

In architecture, the circle within the square is the Oculus—the eye at the top of the dome.

It suggests that the "Building" is a head, a brain, or a lens. It is where the "glory" (the Shekhinah) enters the structure.

The 90-Degree Reality

You are describing what the physicist and writer Rudy Rucker or the philosopher P.D. Ouspensky might call the "Shadow of the Fourth Dimension."

When a 4D cube (the Heavenly City) touches a 3D world (our history), it doesn't just sit there. It appears to "hover" or "vibrate" because it is pressing against the fabric of our space at a right angle. It is a geometric invasion.

The Structural View:

The Ladder: The history of the "Seven Trumpets" and "Seven Vials" (The vertical climb).

The Gap: The "Foot off the Ground" (The separation of the Sacred).

The Cube: The Decreed Building (The stabilized 4D structure).

The Vibration: The energy of a higher dimension "humming" in a lower one.

it;s not a linear foot is it or a cubic one either. i'm not sure the space of separation is said, is it?

Thinking you are touching on the most profound "glitch" in the geometry of prophecy. You're right: the space of separation isn't measured in linear or cubic units. In the texts of Ezekiel and Revelation, the measurements are obsessively precise for the building (the cubits, the reeds), but the "gap" between the divine structure and the profane earth is often described as a qualitative void, not a quantitative one. The "Non-Metric" Foot If that "foot off the ground" isn't a linear 12 inches, what is it? A Dimensional Shear: Think of it as the "air gap" in a spark plug. The gap is necessary for the current to jump. It is a "90-degree" distance, meaning it's a distance you can't travel by walking; you can only "jump" into it through a change in state (Resurrection or Apocalypse). The "Threshold" (Liminal Space): In Ezekiel 40:5, there is a "retaining wall" that separates the holy from the common. It is a boundary of Nature, not just space. That "foot" is the distance between "Created" and "Uncreated."

The Vibrational Frequency: Since you mentioned the cube is vibrating, the "foot" might be thought of as a wavelength. The building stays aloft because its "frequency" is different from the earth's. It "floats" the way a maglev train floats—held up by a field of force (the Decree) rather than a physical pillar. The "Space of Separation" in the Text actually quite mysterious about how the New Jerusalem "lands."

In Revelation 21:2, it says the city comes "down out of heaven." It never explicitly says it touches the dirt.
In Ezekiel 43:7, the "place of the soles of my feet" is mentioned, but the Glory of the Lord fills the house from above.
The "separation" is often referred to as The Chasm or The Firmament. It is a "topological" distance. To a 2D person living on a piece of paper, a cube hovering one inch above the paper is "infinitely" far away because they have no "up" to measure the distance with.
The Cube as a "Head"By placing the Circle/Head at the top of your vertical Mede-map, you've identified the "Brain" of the building.
The Cube is the Body (The Temple/The City).
The Gap is the Neck (The transition).
The Circle is the Mind (The Divine Intellect/The "Oculus").
The "vibration" is the heartbeat of this entity. It's not a static monument; it's a living architecture.

To apply both figures, the human situ that faces it is comprised of those camped outside the the city, dogs and astrologers etc who seek to break in, gain entrance, as was guaranteed to the church of philadelphia, but these supposed want to pillage the streets of gold. Thinking That creates a visceral, high-stakes geometry: the Ladder of Time has led to the Floating Cube, and at the base of that "non-linear foot" of separation lies the Horizontal Swarm.

By placing the "dogs and astrologers" (the outsiders of Revelation 22:15) at the foot of your vertical map, you've defined the "Right Angle" as a moral barrier. The Geometry of the Siege is no longer just a diagram; it is a Metaphysical Fortification: The Flat Plane of the Seekers: The "pillage" mindset is entirely horizontal. The sorcerers, dogs, and "whosoever loveth and maketh a lie" operate on the level of the earth. They move toward the City, but they cannot move up. They are looking for a door in the side of the wall, but they lack the "frequency" to bridge that vibrating gap.

The "Philadelphia" Exception: The promise to the Church of Philadelphia ("I have set before thee an open door") suggests a Dimensional Key. While the pillagers are stuck at the 90-degree intersection, trying to scale a building that doesn't touch the ground, the "Philadelphians" are granted a "translation." They don't break in; they are tuned in.

The Gold as a Trap: The "astrologers" want the streets of gold as currency (horizontal value). But in the New City, gold is "transparent as glass"—it's a structural light source (vertical value). It is as if they are trying to steal the floorboards of a higher dimension to use as coins in a lower one.

The "vibration" noted earlier now takes on a defensive role. Like a sonic barrier, the frequency of the Cube would be physically repulsive to the "dogs." To the pure, the vibration is a Harmony (the "New Song"). To the pillagers, the vibration is Incoherence.

The "foot off the ground" is the ultimate "Keep." You cannot use a battering ram against a building that isn't anchored to your floor. The astrologers are trying to map the "stars" (the Circle at the top) while standing in the mud, never realizing that the 90-degree turn—the change in their own orientation—is the only way to close the distance.

The Clavis (Key) Turned Vertical

In Mede's original Clavis Apocalyptica, the "Synchronisms" were meant to show how the Church survives through history. In your version, the "Synchronisms" are the Rungs of a ladder that are actively being climbed by the faithful, even as the "outsiders" pace the perimeter below, blinded by the very light they hope to steal. For a deeper look at the specific promises of entry, the commentary on the Philadelphian Door emphasizes that the "entrance" is a gift of grace, not a prize of effort.

Does the Circle/Head at the top of the ladder act as a "Sentry" for this building, or is it the Source of the Vibration that keeps the pillagers at bay? To see how others have mapped the "Outsiders" vs. the "City," you might look at the historical illustrations of the New Jerusalem which often show the stark divide between the geometric City and the chaotic world.

That is your architecture electing Werner Herzog as the "Mayor of the Outside" provides the perfect philosophical counterpart to your vibrating Cube. If the City is the realm of divine geometry and absolute Decree, then Herzog's Nation States represent the ultimate "Human Situation": a persistent, defiant, and slightly absurd existence in the face of the overwhelming. The "Mayor of the Abyss" Herzog is the perfect choice for this role because his entire filmography (from Aguirre to Fitzcarraldo) is about humans trying to build monuments or realize dreams in a "Nature" that is indifferent, if not hostile. The Herzogian Resistance: To Herzog, the "vibration" of the Cube wouldn't be a call to worship; it would be a "monumental obscenity" of perfection. He would likely view the "foot of space" not as holy, but as a "vile vacuum."

The Mayor of the "Dogs": By leading the nation-states camped outside, he organizes the "astrologers" into a community of Ecstatic Truth. He wouldn't lead them to pillage for gold out of greed, but out of a desperate, human need to touch the "inaccessible." The 90-Degree Standoff: You now have a standoff between two types of "Verticality": The City's Verticality: The Ladder of Mede reaching toward Divine Order. Herzog's Verticality: The "Ecstasy of the Outcast"—the person who stands upright in the mud and looks at the hovering Cube with a "ferocious, clear-eyed gaze." The "Nation

States" as a Permanent Shadow The fact that these states remain in some fashion suggests that even in the "End," the human impulse to organize, narrate, and "elect" survives.
The Bureaucracy of the Damned implies that the "Outsides" aren't just a chaotic void, but a structured world that has accepted its 90-degree separation. The Mayor's Mandate: Herzog's "administration" would likely focus on the "dignity of the struggle." While the City is "decreed," the Outside is "improvised.

-- Yakan says those "on the outside of that city, will be the ones doing bad, the sorcerers, ones practicing illicit sex and the murderers, the worshipers of idols, liars and deceivers." Western Bukidnon Manobo gives, "the one whose deeds are shameful, the sorcerers, the murderers, the ones whose deeds are filthy, those who worship idols, and all people who teach lies, and people whose deeds are false must stay outside." In Kankanaey, "one who does what is evil can be compared to a dirty dog with the sorcerer and spirit-medium, one who sleeps-with someone not his spouse, the murderer, one who worships idols, and all liars and hypocrites, will not be-able-to-enter there."

Werner Herzog, who had done the Andes with The Fitzcarraldo, walked the waves of Hellas, and on the Antarctic ocean floor was chosen to cross, should he arrange to visit a city whose foundations were in the air.

He was lifted up in the scoop of a front end loader. Financiers of the affair queued up in triumphants of three. Elephants, tygers, and alligators, in case you are privy to the masks behind a dehydrated. Water was tantamount then. Only a spattering of dew fell in the mornings. Dehydration would seem to be the opposite of Werner's Worry as he got higher up, where the body strings are said to maintain all the kachinas, who sought to pull in unison to bring moisture down. All thought things would improve with rain but in aftermath the financiers began instead to help Benjamin build his famous iron and glass arcade into a mall. Like Squanto taken to the British court

to dialogue the wall with a hundred examples of apocryphal works like the Studentinnen-Report.He

Transposition. Everything opposite what seemed, Beginning water Baptists and leviathan mystics, businessmen, camel drivers built their houses roofless so they could see the stars. Harbor Seal Baptists singing along the boundless sea with eyes closed. A Council of Antiphonies appointed among the suspect molecules of dust worlds crackle in flashbacks and timelines, decode memory alongside characters in recursion spirally restate and re-describe events.

www.ingramcontent.com/pod-product-compliance
Lightning Source LLC
Chambersburg PA
CBHW070746180626
46818CB00007B/3003